W·CLARK
PUBLISHING
A STATEMENT IN LITERATURE

THE ULTIMATE SACRIFICE II
LOVE IS PAIN

A NOVEL BY

ANTHONY FIELDS

Wahida Clark Presents Publishing, LLC
60 Evergreen Place Suite 904
East Orange, New Jersey 07018
973-678-9982
www.wclarkpublishing.com

ISBN 13-digit 978-0-09759646-1-3
ISBN 10-digit 0975964615

Library of Congress Catalog Number 2011905655
1. Urban, African-American, Washington, DC,
2. Street Lit – Fiction

Cover design and layout by: Oddball Design
Book interior design by: Nuance_Art.*.
Contributing Editors: VIP Editing

Printed in United States
Green & Company Printing. LLC
www.greenandcompany.biz

WAHIDA CLARK PRESENTS

THE ULTIMATE SACRIFICE II

LOVE IS PAIN

A NOVEL BY

ANTHONY FIELDS

ACKNOWLEDGEMENTS

In part one of *Ultimate Sacrifice*, I acknowledged everybody and shouted out all the good men in penitentiaries everywhere. I even shouted out a few people who didn't deserve it. I feel like I said enough in my last acknowledgments to compensate for three books. So therefore, this time I'ma forgo all the shouts and name dropping. I'll just say thanks to everybody who supports Anthony Fields and love my novels. I do it for y'all. I write for the future of my kids and the love of the streets. To all the bookstores, vendors, individual booksellers, and dot-coms—thanks for moving my product. To all the people who respect and recognize a sick pen game—stay tuned for what's coming next. I got a lot more for y'all to check out.

A special thanks goes out to Wahida Clark for believing in my talent. And thanks are in order to the whole WCP staff, especially Nancy Thelot. To all the authors on the WCP roster, let's give 'em something to talk about.

D.C. Stand Up!
One Love,

Buckeyfields

Write to:
Anthony Fields #16945-016
USP CANAAN
P.O. Box 300
Waymart, PA 18472

A NOVEL BY ANTHONY FIELDS

Chapter One
AMEEN

Federal Court House
Beaumont, Texas

"*L*adies and gentlemen of the jury . . ." Rudolph Sabino rose from the defense table and addressed the courtroom. "Everything you just heard from the government is speculation and pure hyperbole. There are many things about this case that we don't know and we won't know. Even once this trial is over. The defendant, Antonio Felder is on trial for his life. It's an important matter to him because if he's found guilty, he can be sentenced to death. So it's your job to hold the government to the highest standard in the land . . . beyond a reasonable doubt. Think about that for a minute, please. Beyond a reasonable doubt. That means that there can be no doubt in your mind that the defendant committed the crime. And ladies and gentlemen, this case screams out reasonable doubt. Why? Three reasons:

"One, there is no physical evidence that links the defendant to this crime. A murder as vicious and as heinous

as this one definitely left physical evidence behind. But none of it connects to the defendant. No hairs, no fibers, no fingerprints, no blood, no bloody clothes, no murder weapon, no motive, nothing.

"Two, the government wants to show you a videotape from the prison's surveillance system. They'll show you the housing unit where the deceased lived, which happened to be the same unit that the defendant lived in. One hundred thirty-nine other inmates also live in that unit. The tape will show you several people coming and going in the unit and that's it. But what it doesn't show is the actual murder scene or the actual murder.

"And lastly . . . and this is important; four other men were taken off the compound and investigated for this murder—"

"Objection, your honor. I think we need to approach," government counsel, Ed Northern said.

"Approach," the judge replied.

Ed Northern's girth around his midsection threatened to pop buttons on his shirt with every step he took. His grey seersucker striped suit had definitely seen better days. Beads of sweat coated his forehead as he leaned on the judge's bench. A scowl crossed his face as his skin took on a pinkish hue that made him resemble Porky Pig. "Your honor, I'd like to renew my objection to the pretrial order to suppress the defendant's signed confession. Mr. Sabino is asserting that the Bureau of Prisons made the mistake of releasing the other men—"

"I don't believe I heard that," Judge Phillip Thomas interjected while adjusting the glasses perched at the end of his nose. "Is that what you are asserting, Mr. Sabino?"

"I never got a chance to, your honor, but yes, that's my assertion to the jury."

"He has that right, Mr. Northern."

"But, your honor," Ed Northern argued, "the truth is probative—"

"Mr. Northern, your objection has been noted and denied. The confession was mishandled by the prison officials, there was no Miranda given, and the statement was not videotaped. So it's now more prejudicial than probative. That was the position of this court before trial and that is the position of this court now. Proceed, Mr. Sabino."

"Reasonable doubt, ladies and gentlemen, reasonable doubt. There were four other men investigated for this crime. Luther Fuller, Vernon Dammons, Harold Howard, and Charles Gooding . . . but the only person on trial here today is Antonio Felder. Why? Listen carefully to everything you hear in this trial, but remember . . . beyond a reasonable doubt. Hold the government to that and then you decide whether or not Antonio Felder is guilty of murder."

Rudy walked back over to the table and sat down beside me. "How'd I do, big guy?"

"The jury looked attentive," I replied, eyeing the twelve people sitting in the jurors' box. They were a tough looking crowd of eight White people, three Hispanics, and one

Black man. I glanced over at the red-faced prosecutor. "What did the judge say to the prosecutor? He looks like he wants to kill me."

"Let's take a twenty minute recess and then we'll reconvene and the government can call its first witness," the judge announced.

"He tried to get the judge to let your confession in, but Judge Thomas wouldn't do it. Ed Northern is angry at us, but fuck him. He'll get over it. Back to what I was saying, I think the jury liked my opening. My argument was short and concise. They looked like they understood everything I said. And that's most important. In order for us to prevail, that jury has to understand what the videotape the government plans to show doesn't show and what it does. You being the only person charged with the murder helps our case."

"Can the prosecutor bring up that other situation that happened in the rec cage? The one the FBI is still investigating?"

"Luther Fuller?" Rudy asked.

I nodded my head.

"You definitely didn't help our case by doing that, but you didn't hurt it, either. And that's because the government can't use unindicted criminal acts against you. The only way they could bring it up is if you were going to testify on your own behalf in this case. Which you're not. So no, the prosecutor's not going to mention what happened to Luther Fuller."

I was relieved. "So you think we can win?"

"I think so. I'm confident that you'll be acquitted. Charles Gooding is the only person other than you that can shed some light on this whole situation, and he wasn't in the room when the murder happened. The tape clearly shows him standing outside the shower area. He can't say who killed Keith Barnett because he didn't see it. There are no eyewitnesses to the murder and that, big guy, is reasonable doubt all day, every day. Besides, I didn't fly 2,000 miles to lose this case."

"I'm sold. You think we can win and that's all I need."

"Let me handle this, big guy. In a few minutes, you'll get to witness your family's hard-earned money in action. When I'm through with them, these rednecks are gonna hate my $1,200 calfskin Bruno Cucinelli shoes."

Rudy leaned forward and scribbled furiously onto his notepad. I sat back and surveyed the courtroom. I felt good. Rudy's arrogance and confidence was contagious. I silently thanked Allah again for giving me the foresight to tell Shawnay to give fifty G's to Rudy before everything went sour with us. Rudolph Sabino was the best criminal defense attorney in D.C. and the whole world knew it. His reputation soared after he got Kareemah "Angel" El-Amin off after she was charged with several counts of murder. That bitch was guilty and the whole city knew it. But Rudy beat that shit for her and I had to hire him.

"Mr. Northern, call your first witness," the judge said as he sat down and shuffled a stack of papers.

"Your honor, I call Dr. Sergi Hamadi to the stand."

THE ULTIMATE SACRIFICE II
LOVE IS PAIN

A Middle Eastern, slightly built man of average height walked up to the witness stand and sat down.

"Please state your name, title, and today's date for me, sir," Ed Northern said.

"My name is Dr. Sergi Hamadi. I am the Chief Medical Examiner for the Golden Triangle of Beaumont, Port Arthur, and Orange, Texas. And today's date is September 16th 2010."

The prosecutor led the medical examiner through the case, some graphs, and a few photos.

"—the left arm was disarticulated here," the ME said, while pointing to a diagram of the human body —" right at the joint between the styloid process of the radius and scaphoid bone. The killer crudely hacked through the carpal bones. He separated the hands where they meet the wrist bones. Here—the hamate bone was completely severed—"

I sat in my seat amazed at how accurately the ME described how Keith's body was chopped up. To hear him put the puzzle together, it was as if he was there that day, too.

"—Doctor," the prosecutor started, "you're saying that in your expert opinion, the decedent died as a result of being dismembered?"

"Not at all. The condition that we received the bodyparts in—after a careful examination—led me to conclude that the body of the deceased was dismembered *after* death."

"So, the decedent was already dead when his body was hacked into pieces?"

"Yes. The actual cause of death was puncture wounds to the chest that severed arteries. Internally, blood poured into the myocardium, the sac that surrounds the heart, compressing it so that it couldn't expand, could not pump. Death was instantaneous. The decedent died of a myocardial tamponade. Those wounds were inflicted by a homemade weapon of some kind."

"Dr. Hamadi, was the decedent stabbed only once?"

"Heavens no, based on what I found, I was able to conclude that the decedent was stabbed at least seven times. Once in both ears, once in both eyes and three times in the chest."

"Thank you, doctor. No further questions."

"Your cross, Mr. Sabino," the judge said.

"Thank you, your honor," Rudy said as he rose, eyes riveted to his notepad. Without looking at the witness, he said, "Doctor Hamadi, you've testified at length about the cause of death in this case, the details of dismemberment, the type of weapon used, and et cetera . . . in your expert opinion can you tell us why this murder happened or better yet, who committed it?"

"Objection, your honor! This witness can't possibly answer that question," the prosecutor exploded.

"Overruled. Answer the question, doctor," the judge responded.

"Uh—no. There is no scientific or medical procedure that can determine why—or who committed—no. The answer is no."

"Thank you, doctor. No further questions."

Chapter Two
AMEEN

The government put a correctional officer (CO) on the stand, who explained to the court how they found the green bag of body parts in the shower room. Then the operations lieutenant, who was on duty that day testified about the executive staff being notified about the murder, the chain of command, and how crime scene investigators worked the murder scene. Captain Garcia testified about locking down the prison and the massive search for weapons and other evidence. He ended his testimony with how I was identified as a person of interest and taken to the Special Housing Unit (SHU). Rudy cross examined the three of them and got the same answer that he got from the medical examiner.

Then the surveillance tape was played for the jury. Lieutenant Darius Neal narrated.

"—right here. This is where inmate Howard exits the shower area and goes to the steps. He grabs something from behind the stairwell and puts it under his arm. We believe this is the green bag that the victim was found in—"

I watched Umar re-enter the shower area. Then twenty minutes lapsed and the tape showed Umar, Boo, and me, leaving the area. One angle showed me walking to my cell with Khadafi's clothes under my arms. They were the bloody khakis that I'd gotten rid of, but nobody knew that but me.

"This is the defendant right here—walking to his cell. He appears to be carrying something. A bundle of clothes it looks like to me. He stayed in his cell for approximately forty minutes and then he hooks back up with Luther Fuller, Dammons, and Howard in Charles Gooding's cell on the bottom tier—"

Thirty minutes later, it was Rudy's turn to cross-examine Lieutenant Neal.

"Lieutenant Neal, does that tape show Antonio Felder killing himself?"

"Antonio Felder is not de—uh . . . no, it doesn't."

"Does the tape show the defendant killing Charles Gooding?"

"Charles Goo—"

"A yes or no answer will suffice, lieutenant."

"No."

"Does by any chance the tape show the defendant killing Luther Fuller?"

"No, it doesn't."

"Harold Howard?"

"No."

"Vernon Dammons?"

"No, it doesn't," Lieutenant Neal stated, visibly vexed. "The tape doesn't show Antonio Felder killing anybody."

"My point exactly. Does that tape show the defendant with any visible weapons?"

"No—but that doesn't mean that he didn't have one. The tape clearly shows the defendant leaving the shower with something under his arms. The weapon could be concealed—"

"Were any weapons found in Antonio Felder's cell?" Rudy asked.

"No."

"Does the tape show the defendant at any time with blood on his person?"

"No."

"And at what moment does the tape show Keith Barnett being murdered?"

"It doesn't."

"No? The tape never shows Keith Barnett again after he went into the shower area, right?"

"Right."

"But the tape does show several people going in and out of the shower area between 10:05 A.M. and 3:40 P.M., correct?"

"Correct."

"So would it be fair to say that any one of those people could have killed Keith Barnett in that room?"

"Well, yeah, but—"

"I have no further questions for this witness."

"Do you know somebody by the name of Eric Greenleaf?" Rudy asked me as soon as we got to the bullpen.

"Yeah, I know him. Why? What's up?"

"He's taking the stand tomorrow. Who is he?"

"A hot rat."

"Besides that, how is he connected to you?"

"He's not. The D.C. homies ran him up in Terre Haute for being a rat. He came to Beaumont and never came to the pound. That's all I know. What is he saying?"

"The government proffers that Eric Greenleaf is going to say that he was in a rec cage in the SHU beside you and you admitted killing Keith Barnett and chopping his body up."

"That nigga lying, Rudy!" I bellowed angrily. "They ain't never rec'd that faggie ass nigga nowhere near me. Fuck I'ma talk to a known rat about my case for?"

"I'll check and see if the prison keeps a log of some kind that records the rec schedule. After Greenleaf, they're putting on Charles Gooding."

"What is his hot ass telling them people?"

"That's the strange part, big guy. They haven't proffered what Gooding is saying. When I asked, they said, 'He made no statements.' From what I understand, the government is compelling him to testify against his will."

"Hold on. If he's on their side, why are they compelling him to testify and how is it against his will? He had to say something to them people. He's the reason all of us got picked up in the first place."

"All I can tell you, Antonio, is this—the government wouldn't come this far and risk blowing their whole case on a technicality. If Gooding made any statements, they would've turned them over by now. We'll see tomorrow. Get you some rest; we've got a long day ahead of us."

I watched Rudy leave. I allowed myself a few moments to breathe in and breathe out. Something Rudy had just said was weighing heavily on my mind . . .

"He made no statements."

After Keith's murder, all of us were rounded up and taken to the SHU. Everybody except Lil Cee . . .

"Didn't they grab Lil Cee, too?" Boo asked.

"Yeah, they grabbed him," I said and dropped down to do my burpees. "From what I heard they grabbed him first."

"Did somebody get word to him to come outside?" Umar inquired.

Khadafi stood up from a set of push-ups and said, "I asked the cop, Baker last night, what range was Charles Gooding on? Baker told me that there ain't no C. Gooding locked up in the SHU. We the only ones on this investigation. Lil Cee's bitch ass is gone."

"Gone where?" Boo asked.

"He ain't on the compound; that we know for sure. He probably over the Medium or the Low. He the reason we all in the SHU. That ain't hard to tell."

"Now, moe. I ain't going for that. Lil Cee been pushing that knife and holding it down since Oak Hill. He ain't

never told on a muthafucka before, why now?" Boo argued.

"If I ever catch his ass, I'll ask him that right before I kill him."

We were all convinced that Lil Cee's absence meant that he was working with them people. At the time, there was no other logical explanation about why he wasn't in the SHU with us.

"He didn't make any statements."

If Lil Cee hadn't made any statements against us, why did they separate him from us? How did they know to grab us? And why were they putting him on the stand if they didn't know what he was going to say? Slowly, I undressed out of my street clothes and put back on my prison khakis. I searched for answers to the questions in my head, but none came. I couldn't figure out for the life of me what was going on.

Chapter Three
AMEEN

"Felder! Felder, drop the knife! Drop it!"

I turned and locked eyes with SHU Lieutenant, Brian Russo. On the other side of the rec cage, he stood visibly flustered clutching a fire extinguisher size canister of pepper spray.

"I'm not going to say it again, Felder! Drop the knife!"

Standing beside Russo was a throng of prison guards, each holding assault rifle styled weapons that fired rubber bullets. All the guns were aimed at me.

"Get medical down here, now!" SIS Lieutenant Neal screamed into his radio before unbuttoning his shirt and taking it off.

The knife slipped from my grasp as I watched Khadafi's chest rise and fall slowly. Lieutenant Neal ripped his shirt into shreds and methodically went about the task of pressing pieces of the shirt into Khadafi's stab wounds. As the door to my rec cage opened and cops rushed in, I was quickly taken down to the ground and Flexi-cuffed. But I

never took my eyes off Khadafi. Why wasn't he dead, yet? A hospital gurney was wheeled into the rec cage and medical staff quickly lifted Khadafi off the ground and onto the gurney. Then he was rushed off the rec yard.

"Get these inmates back to their cells!" Lieutenant Neal bellowed to his staff. The rec yard CO whispered something into the lieutenant's ear. "Everybody except Coleman and Felder. Put Coleman in the day cell on A-Range." Lieutenant Neal walked into the rec cage where I lay on the ground. "I hope you're happy with yourself, Felder. Fuller's not gonna make it. You just caught yourself another body and the death penalty. Congratulations!"

The sound of my food slot opening and slamming down woke me from my sleep. Shaking the memories from my head, I sat up on my bunk. The CO was at my door with breakfast.

"You want coffee, Felder?" the CO asked.

"Yeah," I replied as I jumped off the top bunk. "Give me two cups, Williams."

"You eat a common fare meal, right?"

"Yeah."

"You need hot water? They got oatmeal on your tray."

"Yeah, gimme two cups of water, too." I grabbed the coffee off the slot and then my food tray and sat them on the desk in my cell. Then I went back for the hot water.

"You know you got court this morning again, Felder," Williams said as he closed and locked my food slot.

"I know." I mumbled as I opened the oatmeal packets and poured them into my bowl. I added the hot water and covered the bowl.

After brushing my teeth, I stood and looked in the stainless steel mirror screwed into the wall over my sink. I hadn't aged much in my nearly ten years in prison. My eyes were still a deep shade of hazel. My nose was still a little too large as it spread across my face. My hairline was fading fast, but my waves were still spinning. I kept my shadowed out beard trimmed and lined up right. The only noticeable difference in me was my eyes. They were older, colder, and more distant. The pain, betrayal, neglect, and frustration that lived in my soul was on display. My eyes were an open book. That's why I was a guarded person. If I let people get too close to me, I was afraid that if they read my eyes, my soul would be on full exhibit. My pain would be visible. They'd be able to read all about me. About my love.

Love is always painful, I repeated to myself as I washed my face. As if rising from a baptism, the water on my face revealed a different face. For the briefest of moments, I was transformed. The mask I wore to fool others was off and my true image was unveiled. I was the beast that lived within me. Then the image was gone. My fleeting thoughts drifted for a while, but then settled on the one thing that kept me sane. My daughters, Asia and Kenya. The two people in the world that I loved more than myself. The same two people that I hadn't spoken to in a year and a half. They reminded me so much of their mother; I refused to

call them because of their mother, Shawnay Dickerson. The one that I loved my whole life. My rock. My strength. The woman who had broken my heart into a thousand pieces...

"Felder!" a voice called out from down the tier.

"What's up?" I answered.

"You ready for court?"

"Gimme about twenty minutes and I'll be ready."

"Your honor, my first witness of the day is Eric Greenleaf," the prosecutor said.

As the door to the back cages opened, my heart sank and my blood boiled. I stared into the face of a man that I barely knew and wondered what the government was paying him to lie on me. He looked at me and did the unthinkable. The hot bitch nigga winked at me. *On my dead comrades, if I ever get the chance, nigga, I'ma smash your ass.*"

"Mr. Greenleaf, where were you on August 12, 2008?"

"Incarcerated in Beaumont Pen."

"Do you know the defendant in this case?"

"Yeah. Everybody know him."

"And what does everybody know the defendant as?"

"Ameen. They call him Ameen."

"Did you have the opportunity to rec with Ameen?"

"No. They never rec'd anybody with him. I was in the cage next to him one time, though."

"And what happened that one time you rec'd beside the defendant?"

"He bragged to me about the murder he committed. He said he killed some dude named Keith because he told on one of his men."

"That nigga lying like shit," I whispered to Rudy. "I never rec'd with that nigga."

"I believe you, big guy. Just be cool. I'ma tear him a new asshole in a few minutes. Just so happens that Beaumont does keep a record of their SHU rec schedule and the cage assignments. According to their records, he's never rec'd anywhere near you."

When Rudy finally stood up to cross-examine Eric Greenleaf, it was like a pit bull being sicced on a cat. He mauled him. Then after a brief recess where the judge chewed out the prosecutor, the government called its next witness.

Two minutes after that, the door opened and in walked Lil Cee. I almost didn't recognize him; he'd changed so much since I'd last seen him. Gone was the slender build. In its place was a taller, muscular frame. Lil Cee had grown his hair and now his dreads were almost to the small of his back. Also gone was the baby face and glasses. The low cut beard made Cee look like that beat producer nigga, Swizz Beats.

"Mr. Gooding, were you incarcerated at Beaumont Pen in 2007?"

"Yeah, I was there from 2004 until the day I was kidnapped."

"Mr. Gooding, please refrain from making unsolicited comments and derogatory out—"

"Why? It's the truth, ain't it? That's why I'm here, right? To tell the truth?"

"Yes, but please tailor your answers—"

"All I did was speak the truth," Cee said defiantly.

"Mr. Gooding, do you know anything about a murder taking place in Beaumont in 2007?"

"Yeah, I know about it and I also know who did it."

The prosecutor breathed a sigh of relief and then smiled. "We are going to get to that, Mr. Gooding. Let's back up for a minute. Do you know the defendant in this case?"

"Yes."

"What do you know him as?"

"Antonio Felder and Ameen."

"On July 11th, were you friends with Ameen?"

"I was."

"And did Ameen ask you to stand outside a shower area and keep watch that day?"

"No, he didn't."

"He didn't?" the prosecutor asked incredulously.

"Naw, Umar asked me to look out for the cops that day."

"And Umar is?"

"Harold Howard."

"Is Harold Howard in the courtroom today?"

"He's dead. You know that."

"Mr. Gooding, did you come to know a man named Keith Barnett?"

"Umar told me about him the day he got off the bus, but no, I didn't know him."

"Did there come a time when you had been told that Keith Barnett was dead?"

"Yeah. Moments after we all ended up in my cell."

"We meaning who?"

"Me, Umar, and Boo."

"And how did you come to know that Keith Barnett was dead?"

"Boo told me. Then Umar confirmed it."

"And Boo is?"

"Vernon Dammons."

"Did they tell you who committed the murder?"

"Yeah, they told me."

"And who were you told killed Keith Barnett?"

It was the moment of truth. My heart rate quickened as I looked Lil Cee in the face. Our eyes locked.

"Boo told me that him and Umar killed Keith Barnett. They—"

The courtroom erupted.

"Order!" the judge shouted and banged his gavel.

"—said that Keith had shot Umar's brother on the street. Harold—"

The look on the prosecutor's face was one of constipation. The smug smile was gone.

"—Howard and Vernon Dammons killed Keith."

I was suddenly oblivious to everything going on around me. Lil Cee had lied to the court. Why? I didn't know what to feel as I saw Rudy at the bench talking to the judge.

Relief, happiness, frustration, or anger. Why had Lil Cee lied to protect me? And Khadafi? Not once did he mention Khadafi and he knew that Khadafi killed Keith and chopped him up.

As I moved around in my seat trying to make some sense of Lil Cee, slowly the answers came to me. I stared into Lil Cee's eyes and understood the method to his madness. By putting the murder on the two dead men, that created enough doubt in the minds of the government, who'd never try to prosecute the case again. Lil Cee wanted to protect Khadafi and me from future prosecution. That meant that Lil Cee figured out that Khadafi killed his mother and sister. And he believed that I told him to do it.

A smile crept across my face. I had to respect Lil Cee's gangsta. Now I recognized the look in his eyes. I had totally misread him. What I thought was fear was hunger the whole time. Pure, raw, and naked hunger. Lil Cee hungered for something as old as the existence of the world. He hungered for revenge. He wanted to be able to one day exact that revenge on me. But most of all he wanted Khadafi.

Chapter Four
CHARLES LIL CEE GOODING

Eight days later . . .

"Gooding, you ready to bounce?" the cool black CO asked me through the door.

I looked around the cell that had been my home for the last three years and change. The only thing remaining was my name on the wall. After nine years in prison, I was definitely ready to go. "Yeah, I'm ready."

In the Receiving and Discharge (R&D) of FDC Houston, I was processed out of the federal system.

"Here's your bus ticket, Gooding," my case manager said and handed me an envelope. "The ride to D.C. will take over sixty hours. You'll change buses a few times and endure about twenty-seven stops in various cities and states. You're expected to be at Hope Village Halfway House in Southeast D.C. in seventy-two hours. If for any reason you fail to show up, an arrest warrant will be issued for you immediately. That puts you in violation of the conditions of your release and you come back here. If you

come back here, Gooding, I'ma make your life a living hell. We understand each other?"

"I been wanting to tell you something for a long time, Mr. Gonzales."

"What's that, Gooding?"

"Suck my dick, you racist ass Mexican."

"I'ma remember that when your black ass comes back."

I was driven to a Greyhound bus station in downtown Houston and dropped off. It didn't take long for my bus to come. I found a seat all the way in the back and relaxed. Then I fell asleep.

I woke up in Lake Charles, Louisiana and still a long way from home. I pulled a stack of pictures out of my bag and stared at them. A song playing on the bus radio caught my attention. . .

"—heaven I need a hug/ Is it anybody out there willing to embrace a thug?/ feeling like a change of heart/ And all I really need is a sign or a word from God/ shower down on me, wet me with your love/ I need you to take me and lift me up . . ."

I ain't never really been too religious, but that was exactly what I was feeling at the moment. I needed to be lifted up. I stared at the smiling faces of my mother and my baby sister, Charity and tears welled up in my eyes. All I could do was shift picture after picture and try to remember my family alive. It broke my heart to think about how their lives ended so brutally. What kind of person shoots a three year old in the head? That person had to be part animal,

part wild beast. And that is a beast that I'd have to slay. The next picture I came to was one of the brass head plates engraved with my mother and sister's names on them embedded in the dirt. I looked at their graves and renewed my tears. They weren't supposed to die that day. Not that way. My sister was supposed to grow up and live her life to the fullest, with my mother at her side every step of the way. But that would never be. And it all started with a murder down south . . .

I was eighteen years old when I got arrested in 2001 on a gun charge. I pled guilty to a year and thought that I had gotten over on the system. But life has a way of sitting you down when it felt that you'd been standing too long. A few months after I took the plea, a thirty-three count conspiracy indictment came down on my neighborhood. I was charged with two counts of distributing over fifty grams of cocaine base. I went to court, found out that I had twenty-nine co-defendants, and automatically took a dive. I copped to nine years and kept it pushing. I did a few years in Cumberland FCI, but in 2004, I got shipped to Beaumont Pen.

In Beaumont, the only person that I knew was Boo Dammons. It was Boo who introduced me to Khadafi, Ameen, and Umar. We walked the yard together every day.

Fast forward to July 2007. The word about Keith Barnett coming to Beaumont hit while he was still in the transit center in Oklahoma. He was a rat that told on one of Khadafi's men. Khadafi was amped up about dealing with the rat because he'd promised his man, Mousey he would. Khadafi vowed to kill the dude on sight. I thought he was

just talking until the day Keith arrived in Beaumont. The night before Keith was killed, the four of us; Boo, Khadafi, Umar, and I met up on the yard and talked about everything. After the shit hit the fan, I was snatched up early the next morning, dressed up in transit clothes, and driven to FDC Houston. I thought that my men were already there. When I learned I was the only one there, I asked about it but got no answer. It wasn't until months later that I realized I was a pawn in the game. Lieutenant Neal and Captain Garcia tried to get me to talk, but I never did. They used me to create confusion amongst Khadafi and nem'. For them it worked to a degree. My circle of friends became confused and paranoid. But that didn't make them tell on each other, it solidified their bond. And I ended up paying the ultimate price.

My friends believed that I had betrayed them, so they betrayed me. They wanted blood and mine wasn't readily available. So a decision was made to kill my family. Knowing my circle of friends like I did, the order to move on my family had to have come from Ameen. And the death sentence was carried out by Khadafi. I knew the day that Khadafi was scheduled to go home. My family being killed that same day was all I needed to conclude that Khadafi was their killer.

When I later found out that Boo and Umar were dead, although I was a little messed up about it, I knew what had to be done. Right there in my cell in FCC Houston, the plan formulated in my head. And just as I had planned, Ameen

was acquitted in trial and Khadafi's name had never even been mentioned as the killer.

"I love you, Ma," I said to myself as the bus pulled into the station in Alexandria, Louisiana. "Kiss Charity for me. I love y'all. I'm almost home, Ma. I'ma make sure y'all can rest in peace." Suddenly, a tremendous calm settled over me and I felt better. I kissed the pictures and put them back in my bag. It was time to change buses.

Chapter Five

KHADAFI

Washington, D.C.
October 2010

—talking to? I know everything, slim. You gave me your word that you'd take care of my family. I didn't mean for you to go out there and fuck my woman, slim. You violated the trust and bond that we had. I—"

Ameen reached into his jumper and slowly pulled out a ten- inch shank sharpened to perfection.

"—was my brother's keeper. But my brother didn't keep me. I made the ultimate sacrifice for you and you repaid me by fucking my woman. You stopped writing. You stopped answering your phone. What happened to all the flicks you promised me? Huh?"

"Cuz, I—" I stammered.

"Fuck that shit, slim. Forget I even asked you about that. But answer this for me. Did you ever consider us brothers?"

~ 29 ~

Just as I was about to respond, I felt strong arms reach under my armpits very quickly. The hands attached to those arms locked themselves behind my neck and pressed me up against the fence. Pain set in instantly as I realized I was in a full Nelson headlock.

"Don't do me like this, cuz, we brothers!"

"And just like Cain killed his brother, Abel, I'm about to kill you, brother. Did you really think I was gonna let you get away with everything you did and caused in them streets? Did you really believe that I was that forgiving? If you did, you thought wrong."

I watched in horror as Ameen walked up to the fence and plunged the shank into my stomach. The pain was indescribable.

"This is for Boo—" he said and stabbed me again. "—his daughter and his grandmother."

I felt the cold steel as it entered my chest deeply. I struggled to breathe as I screamed, but my words came out garbled.

"This is for Umar—" Ameen spat as he pushed the knife into me repeatedly, "—and Shawnay."

I felt the blood start to rise in my throat and choke me. My life was slowly leaving my body and there was nothing I could do about it.

"And this is from me!"

"You sure this is the right spot?" TJ asked.

I opened my eyes in an attempt to force my nightmare to fade away. The memories of the day I died for a few minutes in Beaumont, Texas, was my recurring nightmare.

THE ULTIMATE SACRIFICE II
LOVE IS PAIN

But it was a nightmare that had actually happened. I had the scars to prove it. As if my body was reading my mind, a sharp pain raced across my chest and rested in the area of my stomach where the shit bag was attached. I winced as I looked to my left at the man driving the car in which I now sat.

Tyrone "TJ" Carter was one of my childhood friends from down Capers. Since I wasn't operating at a hundred percent physically, I decided that I needed a sidekick. And TJ fit the bill perfectly. A few years younger than me, the dark complexioned, muscular, young nigga with dreads down his back was a lot like me. Vicious, ruthless, and down to bust his gun without provocation. Having him with me comforted me to a degree. I knew that he had just said something to me, but I had been so deep in thought, I never heard him. "What did you say cuz?"

"You sure this the right spot?" TJ repeated.

I looked down at the paper in my hand. On it was the information that my man, Poochie emailed Kemie from Allenwood Penitentiary. It was all the info I needed to make my newest enemy feel my pain.

In the hospital ward at Beaumont after I got stabbed, I ran into an old friend, Alphonso "Poochie" White,' who had broken his leg on the basketball court. He was the one that told me about Tony Coleman.

"—heard you almost died that day, slim."

"They say I did die, cuz. For a minute or so I flat lined. They say that the thing that saved my life was Lieutenant Neal stopping my bleeding and the fact that they already

had a physician and an ambulance on the premises for somebody else. My situation was more serious, so they rushed me up outta here."

"They charged Ameen with hitting you?"

"Not that I know of. They can't press charges without me, and you know I ain't doing that. He should be good on that, but Allah forbids he ever runs across me again on an even playing field."

"I'm hip, slim. You know a rack of niggas fuck with slim, too. When I heard about that shit, I was fucked up about the New York nigga getting with that shit. Twin and Dolla Bill ain't do nothing, huh?"

"Naw, but I ain't trippin' off—hold on, cuz. You just said a New York nigga got with that. What New York nigga?"

"The New York nigga, Tony. The big, strong nigga that grabbed you and pent you to the fence."

"But—Twin said that the dude was a homie. When I first walked in the cage, Twin introduced him to me as a homie that had just got here from Colorado."

"Twin probably ain't know where he was from. Tony been around D.C. niggas so long he sound like us. He from New York, he came to D.C. when all them New York niggas came to D.C. in the 80s. He killed some niggas Uptown on Clifton Street and went down Lorton. So he been around us for twenty years. And he rocks with the homies in every joint."

"Oh yeah? A New York nigga, huh? I need you to do me a favor, cuz."

"What's that?"

I ran the plan down to Poochie. "... info you can on him. That's all I need."

"That's all? You got that."

It took a while for the plan to come together because the D.C. homies got into it with the Texas niggas in Beaumont. Half of the homies went to Allenwood Penitentiary and the other half went to Hazelton USP. But my luck held and Poochie and Tony ended up in Allenwood together. I stared at the email again and read it...

> *Tony got a brother that he communicates with heavy. He lives in New York, in the Bronx. It's a building on Richmond Ave, called Richmond Plaza. Apartment 158. Phone number: 718- 354-7635. No info on the mother. Only the brother. He got one son, but shorty locked up out Maryland. His baby mother is from the city. Her name is Shayla Randall. Address: 5033 Hunt Place NE #3. She works at a restaurant out Maryland called Ms. Debbie's Soul & Seafood Cafe. That's all I could get. Holla back and be careful out there. One love.*
>
> *P*

A big neon sign on the restaurant read Ms. Debbie's Soul & Seafood Cafe. The place was packed with people and looked to be making a lot of money. *I should rob that*

joint. "This gotta be it, cuz. Ain't no other Ms. Debbie's Soul Food Cafe nowhere. I checked."

TJ glanced at the entrance of the restaurant one more time and then opened the driver's side door. "We out here horseplaying. We don't even know if she in there. I'm goin' in. What's her name again?"

"Shayla Randall."

"I'ma see if she in there. I'll be right back."

I reclined my seat and rubbed the plastic colostomy bag that now hung from my side. The constant reminder of the shit bag fueled my desire for destruction and death.

I prayed that Tony's baby mother was in the restaurant. I needed to kill her. I needed to mend my broken heart, and the only way to do that was to kill all those that caused me pain. I fingered the .45 in my lap and thought about life before I got stabbed. I thought about all the capers I went on with my uncle, Marquette. I thought about the nigga, Fat Sean Bundy and the nigga, Poo. I thought about the pretty bitch that Poo fucked with that I killed because she saw my face. I thought about the Escape Records caper and all the niggas we crushed that day. Boo, Marquette, and me. I thought about the nigga, Money and all the shit he put me through after killing my uncle. I thought about the night I raped his mother and father and then burned their house down. The big, brown-skinned dude with the long braids came to mind. The one that tried to take my life, not once but twice. I was positive that he was the one responsible for killing Boo and Umar. My soul ached to kill him, but I still didn't know who he was. It was like chasing waterfalls.

Thinking about the dude with the braids who wanted me dead always led to thoughts about two other men that wanted me dead. Ameen and Tony Coleman. I couldn't kill them because they were both still behind the prison wall, but the people nearest and dearest to them weren't.

TJ climbing back into the car with a bag of food startled me for a second.

"She in there," TJ said and handed me what appeared to be a sandwich and a beverage. "That fat bitch in there looking ugly as shit, slim. She fucked up. An egg with legs, brown skinned, and got the nerve to look like Faggie Love, that be riding around taking the pictures. You know who I'm talking about?"

I laughed as I unwrapped a fish sandwich. "Yeah, I know Love, cuz."

TJ laughed, too. "On my mother, slim, she look like that nigga. The store closes in two hours. You wanna leave and come back? Or you wanna wait for her to get off?"

Biting into my sandwich, I glanced at my watch. It read 8:52 P.M. "I'm tryna crush this bitch and get it over with. I'ma wait right here for her."

Two hours turned into three. It was getting late and I was getting impatient. Shayla Randall turned out to be the manager, and she was the last to leave the restaurant. From my position on the side of the building, I saw the woman that TJ described exiting the door and locking it. *Damn. She does look like Faggie Love.* She reached above her head and pulled down a steel grate. Suddenly, a noise caught my attention on my left side. Quickly glancing to

my left, I noticed a black Lincoln Navigator pull to a stop in front of the restaurant.

Shit. The Navigator window came down and a lone male face could be seen. I saw Shayla turn and signal that she was coming. After the gate was completely covering the restaurant's door and windows, Shayla locked it. From the corner of my eye, I detected movement. It was TJ creeping up on the Navigator.

Bok! Bok! Bok! Bok! Bok!

The dude in the Navigator slumped over and I knew that he was dead. Shayla faced the truck and screamed. I ran out from my position and stopped right in front of her. Her scream died in her throat as she looked at me confused and terrified. I lifted the gun and fired.

Boom! Boom! Boom!

Hollowed out slugs from the four-fifth changed her mind about anything she had ever thought. I stayed and watched her body drop, then I ran to the car.

Inside the car, I quickly detached myself from the murder. I felt a little better, but not quite. I wanted Tony Coleman to hurt. Bad. "Aye, cuz?"

"What's up, slim?" TJ responded without taking his eyes off the road.

"Remember the Spanish bitch you told me you was fucking? The one you met out the Feds?"

"The bitch Tasha that live out Laurel?"

"Yeah. Didn't you say she was from New York?"

"Yeah, she from up top."

"Can you get in touch with her, cuz?" I asked.

THE ULTIMATE SACRIFICE II
LOVE IS PAIN

"I been ducking that crazy ass Spanish bitch, but yeah, I can get in touch with her. Why, what's up?"

"I need her to take me up New York. I'm tryna recreate *A Bronx Tale*."

Every project in ghetto America had a down ass, ride or die chick living in it. In my hood, that distinction belonged to Ronesha "Esha" Lake. She and her mother, Bay One were the thoroughest bitches down Capers. All the real hood niggas loved both of them to death. Esha's house was the hang out spot, the gambling spot, the stash spot, and the fuck spot. I pulled my Caddy behind Esha's Hyundai Sonata and looked up at her house. Most of the lights were out, but I knew firsthand how deceptive that was. Esha's house stayed alive with nocturnal activity. Especially at 4A.M. I decided to sit in the car and wait for the Chevy truck that TJ said he'd be in. Just as I fired up my blunt and took three puffs, the truck pulled onto the block.

The gold Chevy Equinox pulled parallel to my car and TJ hopped out of the driver's seat. Dressed in jeans, a Washington Nationals hoody, and doubled soled Timberland boots, TJ walked around the truck and met a drop dead gorgeous Hispanic woman on the side. They embraced and kissed. TJ's hands traveled down the woman's back and settled on her heart shaped ass that was snuggly encased in a pair of tight jeans. Feeling like a Peeping Tom, I watched TJ caress, then grip the woman's ass.

Finally, she broke the embrace, looked at me and smiled. I smiled back. Then she walked over to the driver's side of the truck and climbed into the Chevy. TJ motioned for me to come on. I locked my car up, got in the backseat of the truck, and lay across the seat. I was high as shit.

The Hispanic woman turned and looked around the driver's seat. "Hey papi, it's nice to meet you. I'm Tasha."

"Khadafi," I said and closed my eyes.

"—I gotta plug Special Ed, I got it made/ If Jeezy's paying Lebron/ I'm paying Dewayne Wade/ three dice cee-lo/ three card molly/ Labor Day parade, rest in peace Bob Marley . . .

Somebody tapped me and my eyes opened immediately. It was TJ leaning over the backseat. "Get up, slim, we here. You want some breakfast?" he asked.

I sat up and looked out the window. We were parked in front of a food spot called Lincoln Chicken. My watch read 7:50 A.M. It was early, but there were people everywhere, moving in every direction. "Yeah, I'm hungry as shit."

"C'mon then, papi. Lincoln's got the best breakfast in the Bronx," Tasha called out then got out the truck.

"We in the Bronx, huh?" I asked, exhilarated to be closer to my prey.

"Si, papi. The neighborhood we in now is called Soundview. I grew up a coupla blocks from here in Bronx Riverdale projects. We on Westchester and Rosedale, right now. Richmond Plaza is about ten minutes from here. What's your chick's name, I might know homegirl?"

~ 38 ~

"Sakina," I lied.

"Don't know her," Tasha said, scratching her head. "Anyhow, welcome to the Boogie Down, pa."

One Richmond Plaza turned out to be a twenty-story, brown brick, high-rise apartment building. I pulled out my phone and called the number I had for Tony's brother.

"Hello?" a male voice answered.

"Yo, is William home, son?" I asked.

"Yeah, son what's poppin'? Who dis?"

I disconnected the call and walked into the building. The elevator smelled like shit, so I held my breath until I got to the fifteenth floor. Reading the numbers on the doors, I followed the numbers until I reached 158. I knocked on the door, then pulled the silenced .9 millimeter out and cuffed it beside my leg. My heartbeat sped up and my adrenaline was now pumping. I knocked again.

The door snatched open and a dude that resembled Tony stood in the doorway with an irate look on his face. Looking me up and down, he said, "Who you, yo? What's poppin'?"

I raised the gun and shot the dude. He fell back into the apartment. I stepped in and stood over him and shot him some more. Then I stepped back and made sure that his door closed. Running down the hallway, I put the gun up and slipped off my Isotoner gloves. There was a stairwell across from the elevator. I shoved the door open and hurtled down fifteen flights of stairs. By the time I reached the bottom floor, I was winded but amped up. I allowed myself a minute to catch my breath and then exited the

building. Tasha's truck was parked down the block. I reached it in seconds.

"What happened, pa? Mami wasn't home?" Tasha inquired as I climbed into the backseat.

"Yeah, that bitch was home. She gotta nigga in there and never told me. I came all this way for nothing."

TJ started laughing. I knew why.

"Damn, pa. I'm sorry. So where y'all wanna go from here?"

"Let's go shopping since we up here. Everything is on me," I told her.

As soon as we got back to D.C. later that day, I picked up my car and drove to the CVS drugstore. I bought a thinking of you card, a pen, and two stamps. At the counter, I opened the card and wrote . . .

You touched me and I touched you back. You should've stayed out of that beef in Texas. Your brother William sends his regards and so does Shayla. We miss you. Hurry home, will ya.

Until we meet again.

K

I sealed the envelope, walked out of the drugstore, and dropped the card in the nearest mailbox. The bags in the backseat of the Caddy made me remember to call Kemie. I dialed the house, but got no answer. I dialed her cell phone and it went straight to voice mail. *Where the fuck she at?*

Chapter Six
KEMIE

*M*y pussy was like a mathematical equation he was trying to solve. Twenty-four licks times three-inches of tongue equaled me with a creamy pie. The Trey Songz CD playing in the bedroom hypnotized me as I grinded myself deeper and deeper onto his tongue. The sixty-nine position was one of my favorite positions and he knew that. His strong arms held me in place as he tasted everything inside me. All I could do was dig my toes into his satin sheets. My face contorted into a grimace as I struggled to concentrate on what I was doing. But when his teeth came down gently on my clit and nibbled it, I let his dick slip from my mouth. I lay down on his leg and softly kissed and licked him. My orgasm was reaching its crescendo and I wanted to scream and let the whole neighborhood know that I was cumming. I needed to get away from him. But the scent of his body, the taste of his skin, it was like the call of the wild. I had to answer it. My hand took on a life of its own as it stroked him, always amazed at his thickness.

My mouth and the pussycat between my legs purred at the same time as I came in gushes. His tongue continued to lick and taste every crease, every inch of my pussy. If tongues were magical elixirs, his was the one that cured all of my body's ills. I wanted to tell him that, but I couldn't. My lips became glued to the side of his dick. Sex between us was animalistic. I was a female wolf howling at the moon. Every time I tried to dislodge my pussy from his grasp, he pulled me back. I tried to tell him that I needed him inside me, but he wouldn't listen. All he wanted to do was eat me until I was completely devoured.

After a few more minutes of trying to wiggle out of his embrace, I gave up. I felt like a UFC fighter inside a caged octagon fighting a championship match. Did my opponent not feel my hand tapping the bed in surrender? The way he was making me feel was starting to border on criminal. It had to be a crime to eat a bitch pussy that good.

When he pulled me down lower and stuck his tongue in my ass, I was done. Every inch of my body shook with incredible orgasms. I rose up and put his and put his dick back in my mouth. I tried to swallow that muthafucka to the nuts, but I couldn't. So I just swallowed what I could and went crazy. In seconds, I felt his lips leave my pussy.

I heard him moan loudly.

"Damn, Kemie!"

Draining him of every drop of his juices was the only thing on my mind as I sucked him. I sucked him just the way he taught me. The familiar twitches told me that he was about to cum. After coating my neck with his seeds, he

probably thought I was finished with his ass. *Not!* I kept sucking and stroking until he was back erect. Then I straddled him. I rubbed my soaking wet pussy all over him until he was as wet as I was. Taking the excess juice from my pussy, I smeared it all over my backdoor. Even inserting a finger to lubricate it fully. Then I grabbed his dick and guided it to where we both wanted it to be. I slid down that pole inch by glorious inch until I was impaled. After a while, I was able to relax enough to move. All pain and discomfort turned to pleasure as I began to bounce up and down like a Cowboy bucking on an angry bull. I reached down, rubbed my clit with one hand, and used the other to hold on. Riding myself into nirvana, it didn't take long for me to climax again. My lover followed suit. Then my reality came crashing down. Gingerly, I got up and walked into the bathroom without saying a word. I hopped in the shower with the intent to wash his scent away from me and his seed from inside me. Guilt washed over me and then my tears formed. They mixed in with the water that rained down all over me. I lathered up and scrubbed my skin raw, then rinsed off. I was physically clean, but I still felt dirty. The sting of my betrayal tugged at my heart. I dressed, grabbed my cell phone, and then my keys off the dresser. Turning around slowly, I looked at the man lying nude on the king-size bed. Sweat glistened off his skin as he smoked a blunt.

"I can't do this no more, Phil. That was the last time." I turned and left the room.

I drove through the streets of D.C. in a daze. My thoughts were on the man that I had just left, and the one that I was now rushing home to. Checking my phone, I saw that Khadafi had called me twice. He was probably back in town and looking for me. I prayed that he wasn't at home waiting for me. I wasn't in the mood to be explaining my absence and why I hadn't answered my phone. With one hand on the steering wheel, I pulled a pack of cigarettes out my purse. I lit one and inhaled the poisons that it held. Instantly, I felt better. Guilty, but calmer. Having Phil walk back into my life after so long was an unexpected twist that had me free falling in a bottomless hole.

Khadafi hadn't been back in Beaumont for two days before I received a call from the prison. Since I was listed as his next of kin, they were required to notify me in case of an emergency.

"Ms. Bryant, we regret to inform you that Luther Fuller was the victim of a serious assault. He's in the emergency room of a local hospital undergoing surgery as we speak and his condition is listed as grave . . . "

I dropped the phone, crying and screaming. I dressed in a frantic pace and was out the door in a flash. Ten minutes later, I was pulling up to Reagan National Airport. American Airlines had an opening on a nonstop flight to Houston and I was on it. Three hours after that, I was running through George Bush International like O. J. Simpson in that old rental car commercial. I rented a car and let the turn-by-turn navigation take me to Beaumont.

THE ULTIMATE SACRIFICE II
LOVE IS PAIN

The prison directed me to the hospital. Seconds later, I was rushing through the double doors of Beaumont General.

"I'm tryna find a prisoner brought in here today," I announced to the first nurse I saw. She directed me to the back of the hospital where a throng of prison officials congregated. I walked up on the crowd, explained my situation, and was introduced to the duty officer, a female. "Is he okay?" I asked, fighting back tears.

"Luther Fuller is still in surgery. We're waiting on the doctors now."

"What happened to him?"

"He was attacked in a rec cage earlier today. We have two inmates locked down under investigation for the assault. Right now, they haven't been charged with anything, but if Luther dies—"

I never heard anything she said after "dies." I was somewhere else. While at Seven Locks Detention Center, Khadafi felt the need to confess his sins to me. He told me about the murder he committed in Beaumont for his friend, Mousey. He told me about his friend, Ameen that stepped up and copped to the murder so that he and his other friends could go home. He admitted killing that lady in Fairfax Village and her three-year-old daughter and why he did it. He told me about his uncle's murder, and all the events that led to Boo and Umar getting killed.

Khadafi cried as he told me that he blamed himself for their deaths. He went on to tell me that he killed Bean and Omar and why he did it. He told me about Marnie and what she told him. Finally, he told me about the woman named

Shawnay and who she was. He said that he felt bad about crossing his friend, Ameen like that.

"—Felder. His nickname is Ameen. We are still trying to figure out—"

An Asian doctor dressed in bloody hospital scrubs interrupted us, "My early prognosis is that he'll live. He was stabbed in the chest, but his heart wasn't punctured. That's the best news. We repaired the damaged muscle and tendons in that area. There was extensive damage done to his peritoneal membrane, so we had to remove it along with about a foot of his large intestine. We had to do a colostomy. He lost a lot of blood, so we had to give him six units—other than that it looked worse than it really was. He'll live—"

I turned and walked to the nearest restroom, dropped to my knees, and did something that I hadn't done in years. I prayed. Six hours after that I was back home in my bed knocked out sleep. I planned to go back to Texas in a few weeks to check on my baby, but in the meantime, I needed to unwind and relax. I ended up going to different clubs in the city and partying with various GoGo bands. One night my cousin Reesie called and told me that Rare Essence was having a reunion party at Club H2O. I knew exactly what a R.E. party would be like and I was pressed to go.

That night at Club H2O, I ran into Phil. Although it had been a little over a year since I'd seen him last, he still looked the same. He was gorgeous. As soon as I looked into his chinky eyes, I melted. His cornrows were gone, replaced by a head full of waves. His dark chocolate skin

~ 46 ~

tone still reminded me of a Hershey Kiss. The Ed Hardy shirt hugged his muscular upper body and his jeans fit him perfectly.

On his feet were a pair of Louis Vuitton loafers. Phil smiled at me without saying a word, and made my pussy wet. Against my better judgment, I programmed his new number in my cell. Two nights later, we hooked up for dinner. Then dinner and a movie. Then that turned into dinner, dessert, and us making a sex movie. It all happened so fast that I never had time to blink twice. That's how I started back fucking Phillip Bowman.

Pulling into my carport, I didn't see Khadafi's car anywhere. *Thank God.* Just as I crossed my doorstep, my phone vibrated. It was Khadafi. "Hello?"

"Man, where the fuck you been? I been calling your ass—"

I listened without responding as Khadafi cussed me out. I didn't have the energy to argue. What I needed was another cigarette. Pulling one from my purse, I lit one and blew smoke O's in the air.

Chapter Seven
KHADAFI

"This is the background I want right here." I handed the tattoo artist a stack of photos. "I want these faces put all over my arm about this big; I wanna whole sleeve done. Take all these flying angels and shit out. I wanna keep the banner that stretches out. Put gone but not forgotten in there. Can you freehand the faces or you want me to come back another day?"

"Dawg, I'ma beast with this shit. All the Mexicans in Cali can't fuck with me. I can have this whole joint done in about four hours. You want names under the faces?"

"Yeah." I wrote down all the names and told the dude where they belonged, with what faces.

The tattoo artist read the paper. "Margaret—she's the female, the only female. Boo, Umar, Marquette, and Damien Lucas. I got you, dawg. C'mon in the back. I'ma have you hooked up and outta here in no time."

Down Capers, I pulled up over Esha's house and saw TJ standing on the front porch. When he saw my truck, he walked down to the curb and met me. "What's up, cuz?"

"Ain't shit, slim. What's up with you?" TJ responded.

"Arm hurting like a muthafucka."

"What's wrong with your arm, slim?"

"Ain't nothing wrong with my arm, it's the tattoos that I just got on there that hurt."

"You got your arm done? Let me see it."

I pulled my shirt off and showed TJ my left arm now covered from shoulder to wrist with tattoos. "That joint like that, ain't it, cuz?"

"Yeah, slim. That joint definitely like that. Is it finished?"

"Yeah."

"Is that right? You missing somebody, ain't you?"

"Missing somebody like who?" I asked.

"Bean. You ain't got Bean on there."

"I'm—hip. I got another joint in mind for Bean. Since cuz was my right hand, I'ma get a whole memorial, face and everything on my right arm," I lied.

"Thats what's up."

"Other than that, what's up?"

"Inflation. My money getting low. I need to get another bankroll," TJ said.

"Let's go get them niggas Lump and Wimp. I heard they sitting on some serious paper."

"Wimp and Lump from Condon Terrace?"

"Yeah."

TJ laughed me out. "Slim, you been locked up too long. Them niggas ain't up there no more. Lil Cinquan came home and said them niggas was rats. He and his little brother Kamal ran them niggas outta the Alley. Ain't nobody seen them niggas since. I got an iron burning in the fire, but it ain't ready yet. I s'pose to hear something later on. If that come through, we gon' be straight." TJ checked his watch. "I'ma bout to roll out. I gotta date lined up."

"With who?"

"My baby, Reesie. You know that's my gangsta bitch."

"I feel you. That gangsta shit run in their family, cuz. Holla back."

I started walking toward Esha's house until my phone vibrated. The number I didn't recognize. "Hello? Who this?"

"Who you want it to be?" a female voice said and laughed.

I recognized the voice instantly. I had been waiting for her call. "Where you at right now? I wanna see you."

As soon as I walked through the door, Marnie attacked me. All five foot four, one hundred-forty pounds of her leapt into my arms and kissed me all over. Dressed in multi colored hospital scrubs and pink Crocs, Marnie reminded me of a thicker version of Jada Pinkett-Smith on her show called *Hawthorne*. It was good to finally see her again and judging by her actions, evidently she felt the same way.

"Why you just calling me?" I asked as soon as she stopped kissing all over my lips and face.

THE ULTIMATE SACRIFICE II
LOVE IS PAIN

"I just got the number," Marnie said as she dropped to her knees, "from Fatima. She just remembered to tell me that you came by the shop and left it. You know I would've been called your ass." Before I could blink, my dick was out and at Marnie's mouth.

"What you doin', girl?"

"Nigga, what the fuck does it look like I'm doing? Getting reacquainted with an old friend. 'Cause I missed him like shit," Marnie said and put me in her mouth.

The hairdo Marnie was rocking was fly; I didn't want to mess it up, but I had to grab her head to slow her down. "Damn, boo, slow down. He ain't going nowhere. You greedy as shit."

Marnie's head was good, but I had an appetite for something else. Besides Kemie, Marnie had the best pussy that I ever had. I pulled her up and kissed her. I reached inside her scrubs and felt her pussy. "Your pussy stay wet."

Marnie tugged her pants down to her ankles. "You ain't know?" She turned her back to me, bent all the way over, and grabbed her ankles. "Do something with it for me."

I loved it when she talked dirty to me. My dick was as hard as her kitchen counter. Rubbing the head of my dick at the opening of Marnie's pussy, I asked, "Who you been fuckin' since I been gone?"

"Nobody."

"Stop lying."

"On my father's grave. The only dick that been in me is made of rubber. So stop rappin' and fuck me."

I grabbed Marnie by her waist and slowly slid my dick into her.

"U-u-g-g-g-h-h sh—shit!" Marnie looked over her shoulder and gave me that Halle Berry in *Monster's Ball* face and I almost came. "Damn. D-a-a-m-m-n, b-b-o-o-y— I—mi-s-s-ed this—di-dick!"

When my knees threatened to buckle, I regained my composure, pulled my dick out of Marnie, and leaned forward. Her pussy was so hot, tight, and good that I had to get eye level with it and make sure that there wasn't a miniature George Foreman Grill inside her. Since I was already face-to-face with her inferno, I put my mouth on her pussy and spit on it to try to put out the flames. After several minutes of that, I put my dick back in her.

"I'm 'bout to cum, boy!" Marnie growled.

"Do it, then," I replied and smacked her ass. "Cum all over this big dick."

I was tired as shit by the time I left Marnie's apartment, but I had one more stop to make and it couldn't wait another minute. Lake Arbor was a gated community in Maryland where mostly rich people lived. I parked my truck on the main street and walked through the gate. It took me about fifteen minutes to get to my destination. The manicured lawn and the exotic whips parked outside were just as I remembered them.

I walked up to the front door and knocked. Nobody answered. With a little more luck I pulled my key ring out my pocket and found my spare keys to the locks on the

door. I tried the keys and click . . . click . . . the door opened. *All praises due to Allah.*

After slipping on my gloves, I walked into my uncle's house and listened for any noises. Then quietly I crept through the whole house to see if anyone was home. No one was. I grabbed one of the dining room chairs and climbed the stairs. I went into the master bedroom, set the chair down in a corner away from the window, and waited.

The silenced Sig Sauer .9 milli was in my lap ready to bark. The voices I heard downstairs belonged to a man and a woman. The woman's voice belonged to Lijah. The voice came closer as I imagined her climbing the stairs. Lijah hit the bedroom light. Then she saw me.

"Khadafi? What the fuck—?"

"Ssshhhhh!" I said and put the silencer to my lips. "Is the dude downstairs the only other person in here?"

Lijah nodded her head.

"Good. Do me a favor and call cuz up here."

"Khadafi, why are you—?"

"Didn't I shush you?"

Lijah nodded again.

"Call the dude up here, Lijah."

"Ronald! C'mere!"

The dude came in the room a minute later. "Who the—"

I stood up and pointed the gun at the dude. "Cuz, go over there by the bed and sit down. Put your head in your lap and don't move. If you try anything, I'ma crush you." I waited until the dude sat on the floor before turning back to

Lijah. "You don't think it's a little disrespectful to have this nigga in my uncle's house? Quette ain't been dead but two years."

"This is my house, too. Quette wasn't the only one payin—" "Shut the fuck up! A lie don't care who tell it, it's just tryna be told. That man bought this house and all this shit in here. Your whore ass got the nerve to have this nigga in his shit."

"What was I supposed to do? Huh? Mourn forever? You want me to dress in black for the rest of my life? Is that what you want? Am I supposed to be dead, too?"

"I don't give a fuck what you do with your life. I was just saying show some fuckin' respect to the dead. But you a whore anyway, so what the fuck. I came for the money, Lijah."

"What money? I don't have no money."

"When my uncle died, he had just made a move with some dudes and he told me what type of money he had put up. So don't bullshit me, Lijah and say you ain't got it. When you bullshit the baker, all you get is a bun. Don't make me look for it. If I gotta do that, I'ma kill you. Simple as that. Where the money at?"

"I-I-I swear I don't hav—"

I walked over to the dude and shot him in the back of the head twice. Lijah grabbed her face and screamed.

"Ssssshhhhh! Don't make me ask you again, Lijah."

"The only thing left—is—it's not that much. I be—en spending—bills—and—and—" Lijah said on the verge of breaking down.

"I don't care what it is. Where is it?" I asked impatiently.

"In—in the safe."

"Get it for me."

Lijah led me to a safe in the closet.

"Open it."

After entering the combination, Lijah pulled the lever and the door opened.

"There—take it. Just leave—"

The safe had stacks of money in it and two stacks of what appeared to be keys.

"Take it," Lijah repeated distraught.

"I can't take it without the other thing," I told her.

"W-w-what other thing?"

I aimed the gun at her head and said, "Your life." I hit Lijah twice in the head and watched her body hit the wall. Five minutes later, I was leaving the house through the back door with a bag full of money and drugs.

I dumped the bag out on my bed and stared at the contents from the safe. There were eight keys and five bundles of money. The money was shrink-wrapped. Popping a bundle, I counted it. Each stack was fifty grand. I didn't give Lijah's death a second thought. *Fuck her*. I been promised myself that I was gonna pay Lijah a visit. I never liked her from the first moment I met her. I knew she was a sneaky bitch. How? Because I had seen ass naked pictures of her when I was in prison. Some niggas had the flicks and passed them around for all to see. I even jerked my dick off to the

pictures a few times, that's how I knew it was her. I never told my uncle because he was sprung off the bitch and I didn't want to hurt him. After he died, the beef with Money took up most of my time and I never got around to Lijah. Then I went back to prison. Well, I'm home now and her time had come to pay the piper.

Chapter Eight
KHADAFI

"*R*emember the iron I told you I had in the fire burning?" TJ asked and pulled off his jacket.

"Yesterday?"

"Yeah. Well, it's a go. I know this dude name—"

I was listening to TJ, but something caught my attention. The baby blue and white button down shirt that he had on opened revealing a T-shirt. There was a picture of Bean and TJ together on the shirt. Bean was standing up and TJ was stooping down. The words over the photo read RIP Bean. An image of Bean rolling around on the ground, bound, and with a bag over his head came to mind. I had to shake it off.

"—Best Time. Mark said that they keep no less than half a mill' in that joint on any given day."

"I'm with you, cuz. You know that. But a job that big, we gon' need another person to pull it off."

"All we need is one good man and I know just the person."

"Who?" I asked.

"Lafayette Dotson," TJ replied and smiled.

"La La?"

TJ reached down on the floor and picked up the bottle of RoseMo that he sat there earlier. He took a big swig, looked at me, and nodded his head.

For every three street hustlers that gained notoriety and money in the life, they kept at least one natural born killer close. My neighborhood bred about four of them kind of killers and Lafayette Dotson was one of them. Everybody who knew him called him 'La La' and to hear him tell it, he gave himself that nickname for a reason . . .

"I call myself that to trick niggas, youngin'," he told me one day. "La La some shit you call a bitch. It sounds feminine, but when niggas play me like a pussy, they the ones who get fucked."

La La was originally from Montana Terrace, but he called Capers his second home. Between the two he was rumored to have killed more muthafuckas than the Swine Flu.

TJ turned the Roadmaster into the parking lot of the Montana Terrace housing project. We spotted a crowd of dudes standing in front of the recreation center. "Slim, I couldn't get in touch with him, he been on some incognito shit lately, but I know he out here somewhere. I'ma holla at them youngins over there."

I watched a brief exchange between TJ and the crowd of youngins. Then suddenly TJ threw his hands up in a sign of surrender. *What the fuck?* I reached under my seat and grabbed my brand new .9 Calico forty-five. I hopped out the car with the Calico visible and walked over to TJ. "Tee, what's up, cuz? We gotta problem out here?"

"Dawgpound," a brown-skinned dude about my height and build dressed in black boots, jeans, and a North Face ski coat, stepped and said, "You must be crazy, coming round here and whipping out like that. You must don't know where y'all at?" Everybody in the crowd whipped out guns.

I smiled my best smile. "I know where I'm at, cuz. I respect y'all gangsta 'round here, but they say I am a little crazy. This hundred round drum on this Calico and me are one person and that makes me a paranoid schizophrenic. That means I gotta hundred different personalities. How many of them do y'all wanna meet?"

Before the dude could say a word, a familiar voice called out, "Redds, put that joint up, youngin', them my peoples right there." Out of the clotheslines across from the rec, stepped La La. He walked over and embraced TJ, then me. To the crowd, he said, "These my peoples from around Capers. Whenever they come through, they family. Y'all got that, right, Malik?"

The dude dressed in all black that spoke up was Malik.

"Yeah, I got that, La La," he answered.

La La walked with us to the car. "I know y'all ain't come all this way just to see how I was doin', so let's ride

down to the Checkers, get something to eat, and we'll talk there."

"When did you get back home, Redds?" LaLa asked.

"A coupla months ago. They sent me back to Beaumont with that little bit ass time they gave me for the hit."

"Oh yeah? What's up with the men down there?"

"They got a rack of anything niggas down there now. Antone went out Atwater, him and Gerald from up 640. LarryMoe, Lil Nut, and Mario and nem' out there, too. Black Rain went down Coleman with Andre Rose, Lil Robert Lane and—"

"I heard that dude Kevin Grey down there, too, huh?"

"Last I heard, he was in the hole down there getting ready to get shipped. Chico out here in the streets somewhere, Goody went to Terre Haute, and Larry Lucas went up Allenwood with Pooohio and nem'."

"That's what's up. The homies holding it down everywhere, I hear. That's what's up. So what's up with y'all? Who I gotta kill?"

"We do our own killing, La, you know that," TJ reminded him. "I got something else lined up and I'm not tryna fuck with just anybody, ya feel me?"

"I feel you, youngin'. Holla at your boy, then."

TJ took the next twenty minutes giving La La the complete run down about the caper.

"That's a whole lot of shit to do the 'Hey baby' shuffle with. I'm in. How can I say no?"

"I knew you'd like it. Okay, look, the joint is closed tomorrow. They don't open up shop on Sundays. So everything is a go for Monday evening. La, you just meet us down Capers over Esha house and we'll roll from there. Be there by six o'clock. Khadafi and me—"

"Khadafi? Who the fuck is that? I thought it was just us three—"

"That's me, cuz," I said, reaching in my bag for some fries. "That Redds shit is over. I'ma grown ass man. I go by Khadafi, now."

La La smiled at me. "Fuck that shit, then, youngin', Khadafi it is. Call yourself whatever you want to. But are you as vicious as that nigga in Libya?"

"Way more vicious, cuz, way more vicious."

Chapter Nine
LIL CEE

*T*he female that worked the morning shift at the halfway house was a bad muthafucka. I stood in the office doorway waiting for her to get off the phone. Her nametag read L. Ransom. She was barely five feet in her black Nike boots. The D.C. Department of Corrections grey uniform shirt she had on was a perfect fit and made her breasts look like ripe honey dew melons. Her uniform pants left nothing to the imagination. Caramel complexioned, long hair, tatted up, and beautiful, girlfriend was a thicker version of Lauren London.

"What can I do for you?" Ms. Ransom asked me as she put the phone down.

You can gimme some of that pussy. "I'm tryna get a day pass, Ms. Ransom."

"Gooding, you just got here. You gotta be here seven days before I can let you go out."

"Look, Ms. Ransom, I'm just tryna go to church. It's my first Sunday on the street in nine years and I'm tryna thank

God for letting me make it home. I know you ain't gon' deny a man a chance to praise the Lord."

Ms. Ransom visibly softened right before my eyes. "You need to take some of these other niggas with you, but okay, I'll let you go to church. Just make sure you get back here before I get off at four o'clock. Or you gon' get me in trouble."

"I got you. Never would I wanna get you messed up for looking out for me." I turned to leave, but heard my name called.

"Gooding! Say a prayer for me, okay? Because sometimes I can get real wicked," Ms. Ransom said and smiled.

I bet you can, Ms. Ransom. I bet you can.

The taxicab dropped me off right in front of Antioch Jericho Baptist Church on 23rd and Parkway. I walked up the steps and entered the church.

"—spirit/ Holy spirit . . . fill my cup/ run it over and let it flow/ One day . . . a long time ago in Jerusalem/ the holy ghost came/ the holy ghost came on a star filled night/ he was speaking in an unknown voice. . ."

I eased into the church and was ushered down the aisle to a seat as the choir sang. People were standing, dancing, shouting, and clapping.

"—Holy spirit . . . fill my cup/ run it over and let it flow/ Spirit . . . Holy spirit . . ."

I played my part and pretended like I was catching the Holy Ghost, although I never believed in any religion. I

swayed, rocked, rejoiced, all the while searching the whole church for the man I had come to see. As the song winded down and the choir filed back to their seats, I spotted the choir director turning around. He was dressed in the same robe that the entire choir had on. He was as dark as night, tall, broad shouldered and completely bald. He looked like Morris Chestnut in the movie *Not Easily Broken*. I stared at the face of the man that had been my best friend for the past twenty years and smiled.

Demetrius Gore moved to Parkland when he was five years old. His family lived in one of the buildings on 21st Street, a block over from me. We met at the playground and formed a bond out of necessity. It was necessary to stick together because the kids our age from Shipley Terrace preyed on us alone. I witnessed a little of the abuse that went on in Dee's house, but he never spoke about it. He held it all in and nobody knew that Dee was a walking time bomb until he turned eleven years old.

Dee went home one evening and killed his mother and his father. Then he left the house, walked three blocks to the church, and attended an evening service. That was where the cops found him. Dee ended up doing two years in a mental hospital out of state then returned to D.C. Rejected by his relatives, I talked my mother into adopting Dee.

One day while we were in my room cleaning up, I asked Dee a few questions.

"You don't have to tell me if you don't want to, but you never talk about it and I'm a little curious."

THE ULTIMATE SACRIFICE II
LOVE IS PAIN

"What's up?"

"Why did you kill her, Dee? I know why you killed your pops, but what did your mother do to you?"

Dee stared into space as if reliving the moment, then his eyes changed completely. They darkened. "I blamed her for letting him abuse us for so many years. She never protected us. She never fought back, never protested, and never sought help. I hated my mother for the coward that she was. A mother's instincts are to protect her children. Every time she cowered in front of him, I hated her. She was never a mother to me and he was never my father. The Bible says, 'Suffer ye the little children, for they shall inherit the earth.' It was time for me to inherit the earth."

I didn't understand what the hell he was saying, but I went on anyway. "And why did you leave home and go to church?"

"I went there to pray."

From that day on, I called Dee, Church. The name stuck and eventually everybody called him that. In 2005 when my mother had my little sister, her boyfriend, my sister's father, beat her up. I was in Beaumont when I heard about it. I called Church and told him to go and check on my mother.

Seven days later, the dude was found in an alley a block away from my mother's house, stabbed to death. The police called it a robbery gone bad, but I suspected different. I received a letter in the mail with no return address:

~ 65 ~

Dear Brother,
Blessed be the God and Father of our
lord Jesus Christ, the father of mercy and
the God of comfort. Who comforts us all in
times of tribulation that we may be able to
comfort those in trouble, with the comfort
with which we ourselves are comforted by
God. For as the sufferings of Christ abound
in us, so our consolation also abounds
through Christ. Amen.

Without a word ever being passed between us, I knew that it was Church who killed my sister's father. The service came to an end thirty minutes later. I waited until the crowds thinned out and then walked up on Church and tapped his shoulder. He turned around and bear hugged me. Church lifted me up off the ground and spun me around. I was embarrassed and felt like a little kid. "Put me down, big boy!" I said while laughing.

"Look at you, baby boy. You all grown up on a brother." Church pulled at my hair. "Dreads, huh?"

"Yeah. This my new look for the 2010. You big as a mutha—"

"Me? Look at you. You left home a little skinny kid and you coming home a big man. When you get out, and why you ain't tell me you was coming? I could've—"

"That's why I ain't tell you. 'Cause I ain't want you to be going out your way doing a rack of sh—stuff for me."

"Baby boy, you my brother from another mother, I gotta look out for you."

"I heard that. On that note, I need to holla at you. But we can't talk in the church. I gotta be back in the halfway house by four. Can you get away from here?"

"Consider my schedule cleared. We can go to my spot, baby boy, and talk. How did you get here?"

"Cab."

"Well, c'mon. My truck parked out back."

"I miss my mother, slim," I told Church as we sat in his living room.

"You, too? Charlene was my mother, too. And little Charity was my sister. I still cry for 'em, baby boy. I was at the hospital when she had Charity. That little girl was my heart. She looked just like you and Charle—"

"I never got the chance to see her in person, but my mother sent me a rack of pictures of her. She was the prettiest. She shouldn't be gone, slim. Neither one of them. That's what I need to talk to you about. I know who did it."

Church leaned up in his seat. His face became that mask of darkness that I'd seen thousands of times as a kid. "Who was it?"

I told Church everything about Keith's murder and what unfolded afterwards. "Until this day, I still don't know why them people did that to me. That left the dudes in my circle to believe that I was a rat. I know how they think. And all of 'em were killers. Two of them went home and got killed

and the other two are responsible for my mother and sister's deaths."

"Are you sure?"

"Positive. Since they couldn't get me, the decision was made to kill my family. Somehow, Ameen ended up taking the beef, so that everybody else could go home. He must've told Khadafi to kill—"

"How you know it was Khadafi that—"

"Khadafi went home May 7th—"

"—same day that Charlene and Charity died."

"Exactly. He must've come straight home and went to my mother's house. It's in his character to do shit like that. He could've waited for another day, but that's not how he operates. He wanted to make a statement. By killing my family the same day that he hit the bricks made that statement."

"How did he know where Charlene lived?" Church asked.

"He got the address from me. I actually believed them dudes were my true friends. Niggas in prison always exchange addresses just in case they get separated. All them dudes had my mother's address and phone number."

"A'ight, now we got all that out the way, what do you wanna do?"

"It's not what I wanna do; it's what I gotta do. You remember when I told you that the nigga Doug beat my mother up? A week later, he was found dead. Even though me and you never discussed it, I know you killed him, Church." When Church neither confirmed nor denied what

I'd just said, I continued. "The Bible scriptures you sent me told the story. I loved you so much at that moment. I knew that my family wasn't out there alone. When they got killed, I knew there was no way you could've seen that coming. I blame myself for their deaths and now I gotta make it right. The dude Ameen is still in prison, hopefully one day I'll be able to get to him and kill him. But right now, I wanna do unto them as they did unto me. Eye for an eye. I'ma kill his family. Then I'm going after Khadafi."

Church leaned back in his seat and digested everything I said.

"I need you with me, slim."

I watched as Church closed his eyes and mumbled to himself. Then aloud, he said, "If any of you lacks wisdom, let him ask God, who gives to all liberally and without reproach, and it will be given to him. But let him ask in faith, with no doubting, for he who doubt is like a wave of the sea driven and tossed by the wind."

"What the hell does that mean?" I asked puzzled.

Church smiled. "That means I'm with you one hundred percent."

Chapter Ten
TYRONE TJ CARTER

"*M*y city ain't the city to whip and don't dump/ my city is the city of Macs, kays and pumps/ candlelit vigils cause niggas get slumped…"

"—it's the District," I rapped along with Young Rome featuring Lil Tay. The young Washingtonians were getting major radio spins. "—when there's drama, we let the fifth kick/ home of the Wizards, the Redskins and Mystics—"

The radio station played the Wale joint *Pretty Girls* and then got on some bullshit with some weak ass Young Money shit. I changed the radio to a CD and then listened as my man Beanie Segal spit that real shit. ". . . nigga, what your life like?/ mines is real/ everything signed and sealed/ So what your life like?"

That's the way I was feeling as I headed to my rendezvous point with Mark. It was definitely a good feeling to be home after doing five years in the belly of the beast. But being broke wasn't no joke, so it's back to the

bricks from which we come. In the last few months, I'd already killed four niggas, a bitch, and robbed damn near a whole complex. Forest Creek was my second home and I repped it to the fullest. I put it on the map and made niggas respect that joint. But when I got locked up, they got a little too brave heart and forgot who was who. With me gone, all the rats and roaches resurfaced, and made it rain money again. The dudes that I gave my loyalty to, the ones that I raised pledged their allegiance to some rat niggas.

Two days after my Kenneth Cole's touched free soil, I traded them in for a pair of black Timbs and two chrome four-fifths. The rat nigga that took over the hood was my first body. I caught him with a bad bitch from the hood named India. Wrong place at the wrong time. I crushed both their asses. Then I smashed all of the dudes that I used to roll with from Forest Creek. One by one.

I pulled in front of Mark's barbershop and blew the horn. He came out and jumped in my car. "What's up, slim?" he asked.

"You. What's up?"

"I'm on my way down there right now. You gotta come through exactly at nine. I'ma be at the door waiting for you. Everything should go the way we planned it. You gon' be ready by nine?"

"We'll be there thirty minutes before nine, trust me."

"A'ight, then. I'm out."

I watched Mark walk down the street and get into a black Benz. Then I picked up my cell and called Khadafi. Then La La.

A NOVEL BY ANTHONY FIELDS

Chapter Eleven
LAFAYETTE LA LA DOTSON

A lot of people don't know but when I was a kid, my nickname was Bubbles. Till this day, I still don't know why my mother called me that shit. That's why as soon as I was old enough to smoke my first cigarette. I changed it. My grandmother named me Lafayette after some freed black slave that helped design Lafayette Square Park across from the White House in the early 20s. I didn't mind my government name too much, but being called a name that Michael Jackson's pet chimpanzee made famous irritated me to no end.

At twelve years old, I left the local rec center, got my first shot of pussy, smoked my first jay of weed, and then smoked my first man. A dude from my hood named Sean Blair ratted on a friend of mine named Stink about a robbery that turned into a homicide. Since Stink was one of the dudes that put on for our hood, I took Sean's betrayal personal. Having watched several people in the hood get

killed, death was nothing new to me. But being the person to cause those deaths were. I decided to kill Sean Blair the same day I stole a gun from my man, Eric Hileigh.

About a week later, I caught Sean Blair hustling in the Bentwood projects. He never paid me any mind as I walked up on him. By the time he realized my intentions, it was too late. I fired my ten shot .25 automatic until it was empty. Every bullet finding an entrance to Sean's body. Before he breathed his last breath, his eyes searched mine for some understanding. I silently mouthed the words "Never tell on your friends." I turned around and ran the short distance back to Montana Avenue. That night I killed Sean, I transformed. I buried Bubbles and became La La.

"I just spoke to Mark a few minutes ago." TJ came around the U-Haul truck and said, breaking my reverie. He looked back and forth from me to Khadafi.

"He inside the spot waiting on us. Everything is just the way he said it would be. They got the new shipment in there. It's eight people in there, including himself. The four in the basement are two niggas and two bitches. The bitches are bagging up the work and one nigga is watching them. The other nigga is counting money on a money machine. Mark and the three other niggas are on the floor above the basement. All them got guns on them. They got handguns on them, but they got bigger shit in the house upstairs. Right now, Mark says all three of the gunners are in the same room gambling. Mark is on his way to the door as we speak. We go in nice and quiet and do what we do. Y'all ready?"

I nodded my head as my adrenaline escalated. I was ready for some action. Whipping out a small glassine bag of raw dope, I lifted it to my nose and took a generous sniff into both nostrils. As the dope drained, I threw back a swig of my orange juice.

"Let's ride," TJ said and walked to the driver's side of the U-haul. I jumped in the passenger seat. In my rearview mirror, I could see Khadafi pulling behind us into the street. I checked and rechecked the clip and the slide action on my AR-15. We pulled up on the side of the spot. Pulling the mask down over my face, I hopped out the truck. A few seconds later, we were in position. TJ knocked lightly on the door. The door opened and a short, stylishly dressed dark-skinned dude, bald with a neatly trimmed moustache opened the door and put one finger to his lips. He pointed to a room down the hall.

"They in there," he whispered.

I followed TJ down the hall. Sure enough, three dudes were in the room gambling. The one with the dice was on his knees. The other two were huddled around him. They never saw us enter the room.

The sound of Khadafi's Calico cocking got everybody's attention.

"Get the fuck on the floor, now! Or I'ma start busting heads in this muthafucka!" TJ said and pointed both of his weapons.

All three of the dudes got down on the floor.

"Put y'all hands on top of y'all head," I added. "Y'all go head, I got these niggas."

Chapter Twelve
KHADAFI

"*G*o head, slim, do your thing," TJ told Mark.

Mark hit the button on the intercom attached to the wall.

"What's up?" a voice called out through the speaker.

"Yusef, it's me, slim. Blackboy just dropped off another bag. He said for you to put it with the other one and call him when you know what it all is," Mark said.

The door that led to the basement clicked. Mark opened the door and went down the stairs first. TJ and I crept down the stairs behind him.

"Where the bag at?" the dude at the machine asked when he saw Mark.

TJ and I stepped out of the darkness. "Everybody be easy," I announced and brought the Calico up. "Don't move for nothing."

"Aye, homie, y'all making a mistake. Mark, you a bitch. I always knew you was—"

Before the dude could finish his sentence, Mark stepped to him and hit him with a lightning fast four piece

~75~

combination that knocked him off his feet. "Get up, you coward ass nigga. I'll beat your ass."

"That's enough, cuz," I said, remembering our timeline. *Where I know this nigga from?* "Everybody get upstairs. Try anything and you die."

Once everybody was upstairs and in the room with La La, face down, I went in search of the guns, while TJ went back to the basement to get the drugs and money together. I found a small cache of assault rifles in one of the rooms. I grabbed the box and ran it out the side door to the U-Haul. It took TJ and me about five additional trips to load all the drugs and money into the truck.

I walked in the room where everybody was, turned to La La and said, "What's up, cuz? Mercy or no mercy?"

The next thing I know the dude Mark pulled out a gun and shoots the dude he knocked out in the basement.

"I ain't letting his bitch ass go. So they all gotta die," Mark said.

"Fuck it. No mercy it is, then," La La said and started shooting.

I joined in. When the gunshots stopped everybody on the floor was dead. "La, you and Tee give me them guns y'all just used. They too hot to hold, I'ma take 'em down the wharf and toss 'em."

TJ and La La both looked at me like I was crazy, but eventually they handed over their guns. On the way out the door, I turned to Mark and said, "Cuz, you ride with me. Leave your car here and send somebody back for it later.

That way, won't nobody see you and think you fleeing the scene."

"You right," Mark responded. "Let's bounce."

About a block past the wharf where all the fisherman hocked their wares, was a marina and harbor. I parked the Caddy, grabbed the bag with all the hot guns, and got out the car. Mark was on my heels. We walked through boat ways and cuts until we reached the water. Pulling the nine millimeter from my waist, I added it to the guns I'd gotten from TJ and La La, then tossed the guns into the Potomac. Mark followed my lead and tossed his gun. "Aye cuz, didn't you used to box professionally?"

"Yeah, I was a world champion," Mark gloated.

"Too sharp Mark Johnson, right?"

"First African-American to win a belt in the flyweight division."

I reached in my back and pulled out my other nine milli'. Fear registered on Mark's face. "Too bad you weren't the first African-American to tell on a muthafucka and you definitely won't be the last. You world class rat," I emptied the gun in his ass and ran back to my car.

"Where Mark at?" TJ asked as soon as I jumped out the car down Capers.

"You know how I feel about them rats, cuz," I replied.

"He was a rat?" Both TJ and La La said at the same time.

"Yeah, that nigga was a rat. He looked familiar when we walked through the door, but it didn't come to me until we were in the basement. When he hit that dude with that

four piece. I recognized him then. His cousin, Lee Lee got killed back in the day and he told on the dudes that they charged with the murder. One of 'em is my man."

"Who he tell on?" TJ asked.

"Sop Sop from up the Gardens and my man, Lil Ed Huff. He got them dudes life in prison. When Kendall from Fifth and 0 went home, Lil Ed sent him to Mark's barbershop to get an affidavit and that hot bitch wouldn't help slim. He wanted to be hot forever."

"Where you leave him at?" La La asked.

"Down the wharf with the fish."

"Man, fuck that nigga," TJ said. "Let's break this shit down and bounce so we can get rid of this U-Haul truck before a muthafucka tell on us."

One by one, we hopped in the back of the truck and broke bread.

My share of the lick came out to thirty-four pounds of lime green skunk, six keys of cocaine, one hundred-thirteen thousand dollars, two AK's, a pistol grip eight shot pump, and ammo for everything. My car was loaded up with enough shit to get me a million years in jail, but I didn't give a fuck as I drove to my house in Tacoma Park. I left all that shit in the car after I pulled into the carport. My house was quiet as hell and I tried to remember if I had seen Kemie's truck outside or not. I couldn't remember. I pulled my gun and walked up the stairs like I always did. The bed in our room was just like we left it and Kemie was nowhere to be found. Checking my cell phone to see if I

had any missed calls, I wondered where the hell Kemie was. *This bitch gon' make me kill her ass.*

I called her cell phone twice but got sent straight to voice mail. Not knowing what else to do I called her cousin.

"Hello?"

"Reesie, where Kemie at?"

"I don't know, Redds. It ain't my turn to watch her."

"You gotta smart ass mouth, cuz," I said, trying to keep my cool. But I wasn't in the mood for Reesie's shit. "You telling me you haven't spoken to Kemie at all today?"

"About an hour ago, yeah. But she didn't say where she was."

"Listen, if you talk to her, tell her to call me, a'ight?"

"A'ight, I will."

"And Reesie?"

"What?"

"Call me Khadafi, a'ight? Redds ain't my name no more."

"Yeah, a'ight, Redds, bye." Click.

The next time I looked at my watch it was after twelve. I was starting to get worried. I called Kemie's phone and again I got no answer. All I could do was call Reesie back.

"What, Red—Khadafi?" Reesie shouted into the phone.

"Did you talk to Kemie?" I asked her.

"Yes, I did."

Instantly I got heated. "Oh yeah? Did you tell her what I said?"

"Yeah, I told her and she said okay."

"That's all she said?"

"That's it."

"What number did she call you from?" I inquired.

"Ain't no number come up on the caller ID. It was marked private.'"

That's when I knew that Reesie was lying to protect Kemie. "You telling me that she called you from a private number, but can't call me?"

"Look, ain't no sense in you calling me, interrogating me like you the police. I don't have nothing to do with you and Kemie's shit. I don't know where she is and why you can't reach her. When she's ready to talk to you, she will. Until then, PLEASE DON'T CALL MY FUCKIN' PHONE NO MORE! BYE!" Click.

That bitch hung up on me and I was livid. If she weren't fucking with my man TJ, I'd kill her ass. Frustrated, I threw my phone across the room. *I can't believe this bitch, Kemie playing with me like this.*

I thought about all her sudden unexplained absences and closed my eyes. As the headache started in my eyes and spread across my temples, a harsh reality set in. *That bitch cheating on me.*

Chapter Thirteen
KEMIE

I know what I said the last time I was with this nigga, but hey, a little bit of guilt is nothing compared to the way he makes me feel. I bit down into the pillow and wanted to cry. His dick, long and thick was in me to the hilt, in and out like a drill diggin' for oil. Sometimes it felt like he was purposely trying to bust out of me on the other end. I whimpered and wrapped my feet and ankles around his in an attempt to stay connected to him. Phil loved fucking me in my ass and I always let him. Why? Because I loved every minute of it. I needed every minute of it. I wished it could last forever. It was the swivel of his hips, the motion of his ocean, the places he reached, and the things he said as he reached them. In anticipation of the moment, I made sure I sucked his dick twice and drained him. I wanted him to last in this ass. He never disappointed. His stamina under pressure was another reason he had my ass turned out. I needed multiple orgasms and I just wasn't getting that at home. Khadafi was so caught up in the streets again that we

barely made love. And when we did, his staying power was zero. I gotta take some of the blame, though. I can't lie. That nasty ass shit bag that he got on fucks my head up. Just the thought of it some days made me wanna hurl.

So instead of being sick to my stomach, I always end up back on my stomach in my comfort zone. My new comfort zone. With Phil. It's almost kinetic, like we're connected by some kind of cosmic force. I got my days though, when I'm trying to be strong and resist that force. I go through my 'I'm mad at him' phases because of the way he dumped me the last time we were together. But like I said, I always end up coming back to him. Like this time right here. I was at home chilling when he called. I started not to take the call, but curiosity got the best of me.

"Kemie, what's up with you, boo?" he said when I answered.

"Ain't shit, Phil, what's up with you? Your baby mother let you get on the phone again, I see," I responded and laughed.

"Ha ha ha. You got jokes, huh? On some real shit, I need to holla at you about something important."

"A'ight, holla."

"No bullshit, Kem, I need to see you."

"Yeah, right, nigga. What you gotta holla at me about that you can't say it over the phone?"

"You know I don't like talking on these phones. Plus, I got something that I wanna give you."

"I bet you do, Phil. I know exactly what you wanna give me."

"You on that bullshit again. I promise I won't touch you."

"Nigga, you always say that and then I end up with a sore ass, a stretched out pussy, and mouthful of dick. No thank you."

"Kem, on some real live stuff, this is important. I need to see you and it won't take but a few minutes."

I gave in and went to see what he wanted. After all he said it would only be for a few minutes. I could see him and then get back home to cook something for Khadafi. That was four hours ago and I'm still here. Now look at me. Ass up, face down. Again. I heard my phone on the floor belting out a ringtone that I recognized instantly. Reesie was calling me again. "Hold on for a minute, baby," I said to Phil, reached down, and picked up my phone. "What Reesie?" Phil started humping me again.

"Fuck you mean, 'what Reesie?' Like I'm bugging you. You and your man starting to blow me. You need to call your man and tell him something so he can stop blowing up my phone."

"W-w-what he say?"

"The same thing he said the last time he called. Do I know where you at and all that shit. He wants you to call him. I fucked up by telling him I talked to you. He asked me where you called me from."

"W-h-what you t-t-te-tell him?"

"Bitch—I know—your nasty ass ain't— Here I am tryna cover for you, and you somewhere with that nigga getting fucked. Then you got the nerve to be talking to me

while you're doing it. Moaning and shit. When you finish fucking, call your man. Bitch. You know that nigga gon' fuck your silly ass up. Stupid ass hooker. Bye!"

Phil had his hand under me rubbing my clit, licking on my neck, and playing with one of my nipples all at the same time. When the phone slipped from my grasp, I didn't even know it. I was in another part of the world . . .

As soon as I walked into my front door and smelled weed, I knew it was about to be some shit. I know how crazy that nigga gets when he smokes too much weed. And the way the house smelled he must've smoked a whole quarter pound or something. Reesie's words on the phone came back to me: "You know that nigga gon' fuck your silly ass up. Stupid ass hooker!"

All I could do was shake my head. *Reesie was right. I am a stupid hooker.* I kicked off my shoes and walked into the kitchen to get something to eat. Ain't no sense in facing a major crisis on an empty stomach. I put two hot pockets in the microwave and waited. I needed a cigarette, but that would only fuel the fire that I knew was kindling upstairs. He hated it when I smoked. The microwave beeped. I grabbed the hot pockets and a soda out the fridge and walked upstairs.

Khadafi was laid out across the bed smoking a blunt and watching a movie. He looked in my direction as I entered the room and the first thing I noticed was his bloodshot eyes and the gun laying next to him. *Shit. Here*

we go again. "Hey boo," I said halfheartedly as I sat my food and soda down on the table next to our bed.

"What you eating?" Khadafi asked me calmly.

He was too calm and it scared the shit out of me. "Hot pockets."

"That nigga ain't feed you after he fucked you?"

"Khadafi, don't start that bullshit. Ain't nobody been nowhere fuckin'. You the only one fuckin' me, so ask yourself did you feed me," I said sarcastically.

Khadafi stood up and put his blunt out in the ashtray. "You think I'm pumpkin pie, huh, cuz? I'ma damn fool nigga, huh?"

I sat on the bed eating my hot pocket and ignored him. That was the wrong thing to do.

"Bitch, where the fuck you been at, then?" he asked and walked around the bed to my side.

"My aunt Joyce had to go to the hospital—"

Smack! "Bitch, stop lying! Why you ain't call me and tell me that, then?"

I held the side of my face and cried. I was mad as shit. "I didn't know that I had to check in and report—"

Smack! Smack! Smack!

Khadafi smacked the shit outta me two more times and then smacked my food and soda across the room. Pizza sauce and soda covered the wall by the door. All I could do was lay on the bed and cover my face. And my tears. Trying to fight back would only egg him on.

"I should break your muthafuckin' neck, bitch! You gon' sit here in my muthafuckin' house and talk that slick

shit to me? Bitch, is you crazy? You prance your stinking ass in here at one o'clock in the morning and talk shit like you got it like that! You wasn't at no muthafuckin' hospital—'cause if you was Reesie nosy ass would've said that when I talked to her earlier.

"Stupid bitch! You called her twice from somewhere, but you forgot to call me—that gave you up right there. With your dumb ass. You don't even know how to cheat right. Yeah, bitch—that's right—you cheating. I can respect that. But what I can't respect is you coming in this muthafucka eating my favorite hot pockets. I ain't gon' take no dick for you, so you can fuck anybody you want. But you can't eat my *fuckin' hot pockets*!"

Tears dropped from my eyes as I watched Khadafi walk into the bathroom. I could still hear him cussing me out under his breath.

"Stupid ass bitch got me fucked up. Like I'm a pussy or something . . . one o'clock in the morning . . . gon' pop that slick shit at me . . . bitch got me fucked up."

Khadafi came out of the bathroom a few minutes later with his hand behind his back. I knew that he had a spare gun that he kept in the bathroom. I became very afraid. The jig was up. He was finally going to kill me. "Khadafi don't start playing with them guns, boy! I just told you where I was. The hospital makes you turn your phones off. Call and ask my mother. I swear to God, boo! On Marquette grave! I wasn't fuckin' nobody!" I started backing up across the bed. "You remember what happened last time we went through this shit! The people next door gon' call the police!"

With a deranged look on his face, Khadafi said, "Bitch, fuck you and fuck them. You know what you are? You some—" Khadafi's hand came from behind his back in a flash. "—shit."

I felt the warm liquid hit my face and body before I smelled it. It ran down my face, chest, and hands and I was hurt, mortified. In all my life, I had never felt so humiliated. I looked at Khadafi with murder and hate in my eyes. He stood in front of me with the empty shit bag in his hand and laughed. I wanted to kill him.

Chapter Fourteen
DETECTIVE MAURICE TOLLIVER

"*T*his ain't no crime scene, Mo, it's a fuckin' slaughterhouse," Detective Rosario Jefferson whispered in my ear.

"I've seen pigs treated better than this in death," I responded, but kept writing notes on my notepad. Having been at the house on Canal Street for several hours, I was tired, cranky, and in desperate need of a shower. The hunger pangs that I felt before I arrived had all but vanished. There was no way that I could imagine a lamb chop, steak, or burger while I stood over seven bodies. The bodies of seven people that had been massacred. It was a scene straight out of your favorite mafia movie. One of the victims had been shot so many times that his head was nearly severed from his neck.

A crime scene tech walked past us snapping photos. "Somebody was really pissed off to do this," he said in between snaps. I had seen a lot of death in my day as a

D.C. police officer. In order to wake up every day and do this job day in and day out, you must understand that all major metropolises and urban city are synonymous with crime, AIDS, and death. But the seven murders at Canal Street were by far the worst examples of wholesale slaughter that I had witnessed in my twenty-one years on the force. The identities of the dead were unknown, but their profiles were the same. All seven people, two women and five men were young and black. My trained eye scanned the room and counted over seventy-five different shell casings lying like witnesses to the crime, waiting to tell their story. I silently prayed that one of the people responsible for this crime had forgotten to wear latex gloves as he or she loaded ammunition into the several different guns and rifles used. I prayed for a fingerprint, a partial print, anything.

I walked slowly around all the bodies again, examining them for the fiftieth or sixtieth time and wondered to myself what they had done to deserve such a vicious death. Maybe a lot, maybe nothing at all. The initial guess was robbery gone bad. But there were no signs of forced entry. With all the evidence I was able to gather, it was still almost nothing. And learning something fast was the key to solving crimes like this in the first forty-eight hours.

The people from the medical examiner's office had put the time of death for all the victims at between 9:20P.M. and 10 o'clock. How they determined the actual time of death always amazed me, especially since they were right ninety-nine percent of the time. I stood over one of the female

victims and something caught my eye. Something that hadn't jumped out at me before. I got down on one knee and moved within inches of the dead woman. Her body was turned sideways and her face was covered in blood. The blood had run down her neck—but enough of her neck was exposed. Even though the room was well lit, I pulled a miniature flashlight attached to my keychain out and shined its fluorescent light on the woman's neck. Dark green ink became visible. The woman had a tattoo across her neck. Enough of the tattoo was shown to make out exactly what it said: M.O.N.A.E. (money over niggaz all day every day). It was a tattoo that I'd seen, photographed, and recorded on an arrest sheet twice. All I could do was shake my head. The woman on the floor was Adrienne Graves. I had arrested her twice for drug distribution. She was thirty-five years old, the mother of three children, and now very, very dead. Standing up, I fished my cell phone out and dialed a number. I knew exactly who to call for information. I had just caught my first break in the case.

I pulled into the parking lot of Anthony Bowen Elementary School and went all the way to the back of the school. I parked and waited for my contact to arrive. It was pitch black outside at 2A.M., so I knew that the man I awaited had no fear of being seen with the police. I smiled to myself as I thought about Robert "Boo" Haygood. In the daylight hours, Boo was as thuggish as they came. He had people terrified of him on his block at third and L Street Southwest. But I knew that was all a façade. The real Boo

Haygood was a confidential informant for the First District Police Department and had been for years.

And although I loved him for the wealth of information he provided in the open, deep inside I loathed everything about him. That was the dichotomy in me. I'm a cop who needs rats but hate them. Every time I saw Boo Haygood, it brought on thoughts of another notorious rat who faked everybody out. This rat was responsible for the bad fates that had befallen all of my childhood friends. Boo Haygood reminded me of Rayful Edmonds.

Growing up in the Trinidad section of Northeast, D.C., our neighborhood was one unit and we loved each other. Me, Roy, and Cliff Cobb, Michael Jackson, Blind Deon, Brandon, and Gary Terrell, Columbus "Lil Nut" Daniels, Jim Jim, Bay, Jawbreaker, Marcus Haynes and Adolph. We were family. Rayful came from Orleans Place, but he became linked to us as he became the biggest drug dealer D.C. had ever seen. His extravagant lifestyle led to the Fed's indicting him and instead of manning up and staying true to the codes of the street, he turned rat. He told on everybody. With the heat crawling down my neck, I made the smartest move of my life; I ran for cover in the D.C. Police Academy. Working to become a cop and a whole lot of prayer saved me from the long arms of the Fed's, but none of my friends were as lucky as me.

And even now, twenty-one years later, as my men all still rot away in their graves or federal penitentiaries around the country, I still blame and feel bitter toward Rayful Edmonds and all the rats just like him.

My reverie was broken by a light knock on my passenger side window. Rolling the window down, I saw that it was Boo, so I unlocked my door. Seconds later, Boo Haygood slid into my passenger seat.

"Tolliver, dawg, what the fuck? I was in—"

"Shut the fuck up, Boo and let me talk. I talk, then you talk. I talk, then you talk. Got that?"

"I got—" Boo started, visibly vexed.

"Let's make sure you got it. Repeat what I just said."

"Go head with that bitch shit, Tolliver —" "Repeat it!" I hissed emphatically.

Boo Haygood took a deep breath, leaned back in his seat and said, "You talk, then I talk."

Now that our roles had been re-established, I proceeded. "Good. Have you heard about the Canal Street house murders?"

"C'mon, dawg, who hasn't? Canal Street is only like two blocks from here. Of course we heard about it."

"What do you know about it?"

"About the murders? Nothing. Niggas been whispering and shit, but nobody knows what happened. But I do know whose house it was."

"You mean the person that owns the house?" I asked.

"Naw, not like that. At least I don't think he own it like that, but I know who controls the activity that went on in the house," Boo explained and smiled like the cat that ate the canary.

"Tell me what you know and leave nothing out?

"Mind if I light one up?"

Boo extracted a pack of Newport's from his coat pocket.

"Naw, go ahead, but talk as you smoke." I cracked the passenger side window a little.

Once he had lit and inhaled his cigarette, Boo continued. "The house is operated by that bitch ass nigga Black Woozie. You heard of him?"

"Thomas Fields. Yeah, I know of Black Woozie."

"Well, that was his spot. It was a little bit of everything to him—"

"Wait—do you think Woozie was in there last night?"

Boo shook his head and pulled on his cigarette. "Fuck naw. You'd never catch him ten-feet near that spot. His cousin, Yusef ran it. Money, guns, drugs, you name it—it's—well, was in there. That was Yusef and nem' that got mercked in that joint, huh?"

I wrote down everything that Boo said and ignored his question.

"Who else besides Yusef that you know hangs in that house?"

"He got a rack of niggas in his crew—Black Woozie does. Ain't no telling who else might be in there at any given time. The only other person I know for sure that probably was in there is Lil Mark."

"Lil Mark?" I repeated and wrote the name down.

"Yeah. Lil Mark Johnson. The one that own the barbershop on South Capitol Street. The ex-boxer nigga."

"Okay—Yusef, Lil Mark Johnson—any females?"

"Females what? Females that hung in the house? What?"

"Females that would've been in the house for whatever reason."

"Umm—let me see—I know that skinny ass Nina fuck with them niggas. Ladawn, Lovey, her sister Addy, Sherea, that's all I know of. Why?"

"Do you know of any reason somebody would want to kill Addy?"

"Aww—snap, dawg! Fuck me! Addy was in there, wasn't she? Addy's dead?" Boo asked animated.

I nodded. "At least she's the only one that I could I.D., but there's another female victim in the house. Any ideas who she might be?"

Boo sat all the way back in his seat and puffed the cigarette until the fire reached the butt. Then he flicked the butt out the crack in the window. "I can't believe this shit, dawg. Addy grew up with me. Any one of the bitches I just named could've been in there. Damn, dawg, that's fucked up. Find her sister Lovey. Otherwise, it might be her. Shit is about to get ugly for real, dawg. Muthafuckas loved the shit outta Addy. You know that's Wayne Perry's niece?"

"Naw, I didn't know that. You wouldn't happen to know this guy, Yusef's real name, would you? Or is Yusef his real name? You said he's some kin to Black Woozie, right?" I asked, but before Boo could answer, my cell phone vibrated in my pocket. Pulling it out, I saw that it was night dispatcher at the station. I put the phone to my ear. "Tolliver."

THE ULTIMATE SACRIFICE II
LOVE IS PAIN

I listened to the dispatcher for a few minutes and cursed under my breath. "I'm on my way there now. Roger that. I'm out." Turning to Boo, I said, "It's been fun, buddy, but I gotta go. Try to find out what the fuck went down on Canal Street for me and stay in touch." The shit eating grin that Boo gave me made me want to hurl.

"Don't I always come through for the boys in blue?"

I wanted so badly to shoot Boo right between his eyes, but I resisted that urge. "Call me."

Once Boo was out of the car, I hightailed it to the Harbor Marina not more than a quarter mile away. By the time I pulled up, the media was everywhere.

"Detective, can we have a word—"a reporter that knew me asked.

"No comment," I said simply as I got out the car and ducked under yellow police crime scene tape. One of the guys in Homicide that works with me, Carlos Joyce, approached me.

"The body is down this way, Mo," Joyce said and led me through a labyrinth of walkways past boats docked on the water. "This is one of them nights where nobody gets any sleep. First Canal Street, now this." Carlos Joyce wasn't at the Canal Street scene with me, so him mentioning it in conjunction with the body by the rail, piqued my curiosity. "Is there a connection here that I don't know about?"

"One of the cars parked outside the house on Canal Street belonged to the victim here. That's the connection."

"I take it that you've positively I.D.'d the body down here?" I asked as we walked up on a crowd of cops gathered around a body.

"Not formally, but we all know who he is. Hell, he was a hero once. He was the local kid who made history. The first black flyweight champion of the world."

At the mention of boxing, I thought about the information I had just got from Boo Haygood. And without looking I knew exactly who the man on the ground was.

"Lil Mark Johnson," I mumbled.

All Carlos Joyce did was nod his head.

Chapter Fifteen
LIL CEE

"—local news. Today's top story is a home invasion where seven people were found brutally murdered. D.C. Police received a report of multiple guns being fired in the one thousand block of Canal Street in Southwest. At 9:31, officers arrived on the scene and discovered the murders at the two-story family home. One woman was immediately identified as thirty-five-year-old Adrienne Graves, a woman wanted for questioning in an unrelated murder. The investigation into this crime is ongoing. As information is made available, we will get that information to the viewers. Our correspondent, Aniyah Fields is standing live at the SW HarborMarina where the body of a man has been found. Aniyah?"

"Good morning, Maria . . . behind me here at the SW Harbor Marina, the body of a local businessman was just discovered by the owner of one of the boats moored here. The victim was shot several times. Authorities believe the man to be thirty-nine-year-old

Marcellous "Mark" Johnson, a former professional boxer and a local business owner in this area. D.C. Police are investigating a possible link between the murder of Mr. Johnson and the brutal murder of seven people last night . . ."

As the news cut to a commercial, I focused on my breakfast of waffles, scrambled eggs, and turkey bacon. It was a little bland, but I ate it anyway. I looked at my watch and jumped up from the table. I walked my tray to the dish disposal area and dropped it in. By the time I reached the office, the midnight CO was leaving and the 8 A.M. to 4 P.M. CO was coming in. It was Ms. Ransom. After she was settled, I told her, "I'm about to sign out and go job hunting."

"Okay, Gooding, go 'head. When you suppose to be back?"

"The job coordinator told me that I have to be back in the house by 7 P.M.," I replied.

"I'll be gone by then, so I'll see you tomorrow. You be safe out there, boy."

"I will." I turned and ran out the front door. I spotted Church's truck across the street.

"Where to first?" Church asked as I put my seatbelt on.

"The Post Office on Brentwood Road."

I tried to remember everything that Ameen told me about his oldest brother as we watched the tall, dark-skinned dude dressed in a postal uniform exit the post office and walk to a waiting postal truck. He still looked the way he did years ago when Ameen first showed me all the

pictures of him. I knew his name was Thomas and he did ten years in Lorton before coming home in '99.

I remembered Ameen telling me that his brother, Buck was the shit back in the 80s before him and their cousin, Beannie came in on an attempted murder beef. "That's him, right there. Follow him."

We followed the mail truck throughout the city waiting for the right opportunity to pounce. Every stop he made on his route, Church would look at me and say, "Here?" And I'd shake my head and reply, "Naw. Not here. Wait."

Finally, after following Ameen's brother for over an hour, he turned on to the perfect street. It was made for killing. There were houses only on one side of the street and most of them were abandoned. Directly across from the row houses were all woods. When the mail truck stopped in the middle of the block and parked, I looked at Church and said, "Here."

Chapter Sixteen

DEMETRIUS CHURCH GORE

I pulled the black baseball cap low on my head. My .40 cal Smith & Wesson was in my lap with my Bible. I grabbed them both and hopped out the Expedition. I walked up the block to the mail truck and leaned on the side of it that faced the woods. Opening my Bible, I started reading. Ten minutes later, the mailman walked up on the truck. He saw me, did a double take, and approached.

"Can I help you with something?" he asked.

I looked up slowly and said, "Let your conduct be without covetousness; be content with such things as you have, for He himself has said, 'I will never leave you or forsake you.'"

A confused look spread across the man's face. "What the fuck you talkin' bout, playa?"

"So we boldly say, 'The Lord is my helper, I will not fear.' What can man do to me? Remember those—"

THE ULTIMATE SACRIFICE II
LOVE IS PAIN

"Are you retarded? You need—"

"—who rule over you. Who have spoken the word of God to you."

"Man, get the fuck off my truck, you crazy—"
I closed my Bible and raised my gun. Surprised, the man tried to back away and shield himself.

Bok!

My first shot hit him in the forehead. When he fell to the ground, I stood over him and shot him again. "Jesus Christ is the same, yesterday, today and forever."

As we left the scene of the murder, I felt good. I felt liberated. Then suddenly I was eleven years old again.

I knew that my father was gonna be drunk when I got home. He was always drunk. His life was filled with one failure after another and he couldn't accept it. Being a star in the NBA was his dream for as long as he could remember. It was almost a reality until life's cruel and twisted humor struck. He tore his ACL in a city championship game against Gonzaga in 1969. He met my mother at D.C. General Hospital as he convalesced. They dated and fell in love. I came sometime later.

He had the chance to go overseas and play ball but the foreign team wouldn't agree to foot the bill for him, a wife, and a child. His dreams were dashed. Years later when I became old enough to know the story, I often wished that my father had gone overseas and that he had stayed there. My father became a cruel, nasty, miserable beast that fell hard into a bottle of liquor and never climbed his way out. He blamed my mother and me for his diminished dream.

The verbal abuse ended and the physical abuse started. I developed a hatred for my father that was so deep it would cause me irreparable harm later.

I found solace in the God that my relatives introduced me to. As my life fell deeper and deeper into the pits of hell, I became one with the Bible. I read it every day and wondered when my God would deliver me from my father's evil.

One day my father stormed into my room and took away my Bible "Why you keep reading this shit, boy? Ain't no white man's god gonna save your black ass," he said and left the room.

I prayed and prayed and cried and cried. That night I had a vision. It was the story of David and Goliath. A voice told me that I was David and my father was Goliath. The next day I stole my father's gun from his closet and walked around with it all day. I waited for another sign from God. When I walked in the house that night, my father was beating my mother with an extension cord, a broom, and then his work boot. The look on his face was one of pure evil. It was the look of Goliath the giant slaughtering the little people who could not defend themselves. That was my sign. I went to my room to pray. My door opened suddenly and my father came in the room.

"Get your ass up off your knees, praying to the white god. Stupid ass black boy. Who taught you all that shit? Why ain't this room clean—"

That's how it started then his words raining down became his fist and feet. I was literally being pummeled. I

screamed for my mother, but as always she never came. When my father finished with me he left my room. It took everything inside me to pick myself up off the floor. I was in so much pain. But I had to get up. I had to slay Goliath.

My father was in the living room sitting in a chair, when I got there. My mother's head was in his lap, doing to him what he made her do every day before dinner.

"Let your greatness be known to all men. For the lord is at hand," I said in a loud voice. "Be anxious for nothing, but in everything by prayer and supplication, with thanksgiving, let your request be known to God—"

"Boy, if you don't get your ass back in that room while I'm getting my dick sucked, I'ma kill your black ass—"

I stood firm on my ground. I was David. "And the peace of God which surpasses all understanding—"

With one powerful hand, my father backhanded my mother's face from his lap. He stood and pulled his pants up. "Boy—you about to meet your god right now."

My father took one step before I pulled the gun from behind my back. He stopped in his tracks. Then he laughed. "What you gon' do with that, boy?"

My finger pulled the trigger and the gun exploded. The smile on his face changed to one of shock as he stared down at the crimson stain that spread across his shirt. He dropped to his knees. I fired again and watched the giant topple. I fired again into his prone body. Then again and again. My mother's screams brought me out of my trance.

I looked at her. "The fear of the lord prolongs days, Momma, but the years of the wicked will be shortened. The

hope of the righteous will be gladness, but the expectations of the wicked will perish."

"You killed him, simple boy! You killed your father! "

"No Momma, a foolish woman is clamorous; she is simple and knows nothing . . . I didn't kill my father. For the God in heaven is my father . . ." I raised the gun again and shot her . . .

"Church!"

I looked to my right and saw Cee. Then I remembered where I was. "What's up, baby boy?"

"You gotta make this turn up here and then get on Suitland Parkway. The other brother lives in Congress Park."

I parked the truck on Fourteenth Place and grabbed the picture that Cee had in his hand. "Which one is which?"

"Ameen is the brown skinned one with all the tats. His brother, Squirt is the dark-skinned dude standing up on the end, the baldhead black dude with the potbelly. Ameen gave me that picture about four years ago; I don't think the dude would've changed a whole lot. The address he gave me was 1381 Savannah Street, Southeast. That's that building over there."

As we both looked in the direction of where Cee was pointing, we saw a group of people, females included, standing in front of the building.

"You see him over there?" I asked.

"I think so. Circle the block one time so I can get a better look."

THE ULTIMATE SACRIFICE II
LOVE IS PAIN

I circled the block and we both concluded that one of the dudes in the crowd looked exactly like the picture Cee had. He was wearing a grey sweat suit and grey 993 New Balance tennis shoes. I went to open the door and step out, but Cee grabbed my arm. "Where you going?" he asked me.

"To get the other brother," I told him.

"Naw, slim. This one is mine. I'ma jump out. I want you to pull down the street and distract the crowd. I'ma walk up on 'em and crush Squirt. He ain't gon' know what hit 'im."

"I got you, baby boy. Let's go."

Cee jumped out the truck and skulked along the sidewalk in the direction of the crowd. I did a mental head count. Five dudes, two women and Squirt. I pulled down the street and stopped right in front of them, the .40 in my lap. "Aye, who got the weed out here?"

"They got that skunk in the circle, moe," one dude called out. "Go round the corner and make the first left into the circle. They out there."

In my peripheral, I saw Cee making his way up on the crowd. "What about pills? They got the X around there—"

Bok! Bok! Bok! Bok! Bok! Bok!

I saw the dude Squirt fall to the ground as everybody around him scrambled and ran.

Bok! Bok! Bok!

Cee stood over him and fired again. *Bok!*

I pulled off just as Cee took off running back the way he came. I went all the way around the block and met him

across the street from an elementary school. Sirens could be heard in the distance. Cee hopped in the truck and I peeled off.

"Dishonest scales are an abomination to the Lord, but a just weight is his delight."

"What you say, slim?" Cee asked.

"Nothing. I was talking to myself."

Chapter Seventeen
MONICA MARNIE CURRY

"This some good shit," I said as I almost choked. I passed the blunt back to Khadafi and laid down. "They don't do random drug tests were you work at now?" Khadafi asked.

"They can, but they haven't. Not in the eleven months I've been working there. Boy, Forestville Health and Rehab Center is sweet as shit. This older chick named Toi Wiseman is my boss, and girlfriend cool as shit. She'll let me know if they about to piss me. But fuck all that. You know what this mean, right?"

"Naw, what does this mean?"

"You know what you did, nigga." I laughed. "You did it on purpose."

"What?" Khadafi asked and put the blunt roach in the ashtray. "What I do?"

"You got me high 'cause you know weed makes me horny. That's what."

We both cracked up laughing.

"Stop that bullshit, Marnie. A fish tank fulla fish'll make you horny. Food make you horny. Movies make you horny. Clothes, guns—"

"A'ight, boy, I get the picture. You ready to fuck me?" I asked.

"I was born ready."

"You got some rubbers?"

"For what?"

"Fuck you mean, for what? Nigga, you ain't my man. At least not yet, anyway. You can't keep fuckin' me bare. Kemie gon' kill your ass if I get pregnant. That would fuck homegirl up for life."

"Fuck that bitch," Khadafi spat.

Then he told me what he did to Kemie a few nights ago. I cracked up laughing. "You squirted shit in her face? That's fucked up, boy."

"She some shit anyway, so what the fuck? If she fuckin' with another nigga, that's cool, but don't come up in my joint early in the morning and pop that slick shit at me. Like I'm a lame duck or something. That bitch know how I get down."

I thought about what Khadafi said and then thought about what Reesie told me yesterday. Every time I decided to say something, a voice in my head said, *you hating like shit, Mo. Hadn't I gotten my revenge on Kemie already by fucking her man? Was making her life more miserable gonna make me feel good?* I thought about that for a minute. And the answer was. *Hell yeah!* I live for Kemie's misery. I looked over at Khadafi and thought about how

much I liked him. It probably was a little more than like, but who's measuring? What can I say? I'm a sucka for them pretty boy thug niggas. Everything about him turned me on. His long cornrows that hung past his shoulders, his swagger, the way he wore clothes, the guns, the tats, especially the new ones on his arm and the scars on his chest and stomach. I love that shit. And I'm about to show him just how much I love it.

"I know how you get down, too, baby," I said and lifted my hips and slid out of my shorts and panties. Then I pulled my shirt over my head letting the twins loose. I crawled across the bed and grabbed at Khadafi's dick. I reached in his boxer briefs and pulled it out. I wrapped my lips around that muthafucka and got my Pinky on.

Later on as we lay in the bed, I decided to tell Khadafi what Reesie told me. Reesie was my girl, and I knew that I was betraying her trust, but shit, Khadafi was the one laying the pipe and in my book, he was boss.

"Look, boo." I turned over, propped up on my elbows and said, "I fucks with you and you know that. We started this shit on some lust shit. I just wanted to fuck you to get back at Kemie. I told you that already. We crossed that bridge and then the dick got good to me. You went back to jail and believe it or not I waited for you. I like being around you and I love fuckin' you. But outside of all that, I digs you as a person. That long ass scar on your stomach and that shit bag would turn most bitches off, but not me. Call me silly, but that shit shows me that you can be hurt, too. It makes Superman appear to be human, ya know? I'm

saying all that to say that I fucks with you and I got your back. So me being the real bitch that I am, I gotta keep it one hundred with you. You know me, Kemie, and Reesie used to be tight as shit. Well, even though me and Kemie don't fuck with each other no more, I still fucks with Reesie. That's my dawg right there. Well anyway, the other day she told me you kept calling her looking for Kemie. She told you that she didn't know where Kemie was. But she did."

"Oh yeah?"

"Yeah. Kemie was with the dude, Phil that she was fuckin' with before you came home the first time."

Khadafi's face contorted in anger. "Phil, huh?"

"Yeah. According to Reesie, after you went back to jail, she bumped into him somewhere and they started back fuckin' around. I know how you must feel and I hate to be the bearer of bad news, but like I said, I gotta keep it one hundred with you. She playing you, boo."

Khadafi's silence said a thousand words. He just lay on my bed and stared at the ceiling.

"I know you love her and that you're hurt, but that comes with the territory. *Love is pain.* I learned that the hard way fuckin' with your girl."

"You know this dude, Marnie? The dude, Phil?"

"I met him a few times before you came home. I know that he is from Uptown somewhere. I believe he from Ledroit Park. He gettin' some money, too. He gotta gold Benz wagon and a silver Hummer H2. He got a baby

mother that lives over by Orleans Place. That's it. That's all I know. And I got all that from Kemie."

"Is that right?"

"Yeah, that's right. I can try to pick Reesie for some information if you want me to," I offered.

"Yeah, you do that," Khadafi said and got up. "I'ma 'bout to bounce. You keep the rest of that weed and do you. I'ma call you later on before I come back through, a'ight?"

"You ain't gotta call, just come through. Better yet, I'ma give you my spare key. You can use it in case I'm sleep."

I got up, got the key for Khadafi and gave it to him. Then I lay back down. Khadafi left my bedroom and then came back. He stood in the doorway with tears in his eyes.

"I fucked up, Marnie. I fucked up bad. I let my emotions for that snake ass bitch get in the way of my good sense. When my uncle got killed, I wanted to make muthafuckas feel my pain. I couldn't find the dude I was looking for and I didn't know who actually killed Marquette at the time. So I thought about what you told me that day about Kemie fuckin' with Bean and Omar. I killed both of 'em, Marnie. That's crazy, huh? I killed two good men over a scandalous ass bitch. I was fucked up at them for fuckin' her . . . I blamed them. And all the time that bitch was the one I should've killed. Go figure."

Khadafi wiped his eyes and left the apartment.

Chapter Eighteen
AMEEN

Beaumont Pen . . .

*M*y hands were cuffed in front of me and held close to me by a belly chain. I sat at the table and leaned over until my forehead touched the table. I lifted up when I heard the door to the office open. Lieutenant Neal walked over and sat down.

"I don't know what to say about you, Felder," he said and laid a stack of papers on the table. "You are the luckiest asshole I've ever met. Either you have the best prayer group in the history of the church or you were born with a horseshoe up your ass."

"I don't believe in luck. I believe in Allah."

"Yeah, whatever, Felder. I don't care who you believe in. I know there ain't no earthly good in you. Never was. Never will be. Anyway, you're good. You successfully manipulated the system, not once, but twice." He opened a file and passed me two sheets of paper. "Even though the court acquitted you of the Barnett murder, by

preponderance of the evidence, we can still charge you at the institutional level. So here's your incident report for that. Go head and read it."

I read the incident report that charged me with a 100A and laughed in Neal's face.

"That's double jeopardy, ain't it?"

"Not at all. We can handle it at this level and there ain't no judge to throw your confession out. You'll never have another privilege in your life and this piece of paper here gets you sent to ADX. Twenty-three and one, buddy. For the rest of your time in the Feds. And if that don't hold you, this one will."

I read the second set of papers that he gave me. This was the shot that I was expecting. It was the shot charging me with a 101 serious assault on Luther Fuller. Khadafi. "This joint a little old, ain't it?"

"The FBI had it. They just released it. Without Fuller's cooperation, they couldn't get the US Attorney to prosecute. But you already knew that, huh, Felder?"

I smiled.

"Well, you've been served and given your copies of the shots. You understand your rights in the disciplinary process?"

"Yeah."

"Wish to make any statements?"

"Naw."

"What about a staff rep?"

"None."

"Alrighty then, sign both of these papers right here and then you can go back to your cell."

I signed the papers the best I could with the handcuffs limiting my movement. My curiosity got the best of me, so I leaned forward and said, "Lieutenant Neal, I was wondering. Whose idea was it to use Charles Gooding to try to get us to tell on each other? Yours or Captain Garcia?"

Lieutenant Neal calmly got on his radio and said, "SIS Lieutenant Neal to Officer Scott."

"Go for Scott."

"Would you please come and get Felder and take him back to his cell." To me he said, "Get the fuck outta my office."

I was in my cell working out the next evening when the CO came to my door with some mail. It had been so long since I received some mail that I didn't know what to do as I pulled it through the crack in my cell door. I read the return addresses on all the mail. One was from Rudy. The other two read Keisha Caldwell and Gloria Mason. Although I was happy to get some mail from the outside, I was a little disappointed that none of it was from Shawnay or my daughters.

I opened the letter from Keisha Caldwell first because I didn't know who the hell she was. There was a letter in the envelope and something else. An obituary. I unfolded the obituary and stared into the face of my smiling brother. Squirt was dead.

THE ULTIMATE SACRIFICE II
LOVE IS PAIN

In Loving Memory of Daniel Felder

I opened the obituary and read it, then stared at all the photos inside. I couldn't believe what I was seeing. How had he died? The obituary just said he died suddenly on October 2nd. I went to the letter and started reading then it dawned on me that Keisha was Squirt's girlfriend, the one with the two daughters:

> *Dear Antonio,*
> *I pray that this brief note finds you well in all aspects. I apologize for never taking the time out to write you before, but I always got on your brother because he never would. He never gave me the full story about y'alls fallout, but I always believed that y'all should've buried the hatchet and let bygones be. You of all people know how bullheaded your brother could be. I miss your brother so much that I don't know what to do. Enclosed please find his obituary. My mother and I put it together. I know your brother's death comes as a shock to you and you're probably hurting, but you are not alone. We are still walking around in a daze out here. Nobody knows why he was shot down like that. Your cousin Marco and nem' was out there. They say the dude just walked up and started shooting Squirt.*

*Your brother always told me how distant
you were and how you never reach out to
family. I just wanted to make sure you knew
about your brothers. I send my condolences
and so does my family. I wanna keep in
touch with you and hopefully we'll find a
way to heal one another.*

Sincerely,
Keisha
*P.S. I really didn't know your other
brother, either, but I heard he was a good
dude. I'm sorry for your losses.*

I read over the letter again. Why did she say losses
instead of loss? I ripped open the second letter, the one
from my stepmother, Poochie. An obituary fell out of her
card. At first, I assumed that she was sending me Squirt's
obituary. The same one that Keisha had sent until I open it
up and saw a picture of my other brother on it.

In Loving Memory of Thomas Felder

I flipped through his obituary and stared at the pictures.
I was surprised to see several photos of us as kids. He had
also died suddenly. Then something caught my attention. I
stared at it and then picked up Squirt's obituary. I knew that
I wasn't going crazy. Both of the death dates were the same.
I picked up the card from Poochie and read it:

Son,

THE ULTIMATE SACRIFICE II
LOVE IS PAIN

Hopefully, you've heard about your brothers by now. I send my sincerest condolences to you. I know that y'all didn't get along, hell, neither did we but still, I never wished such brutal deaths on them. I watched all three of y'all grow up and I am brokenhearted. I'm glad that y'all father left this world before now because if cancer wouldn't have had to kill him, this would have. The fact that Buck got shot and killed hours before Squirt has everybody baffled. They believe that both of your brothers were killed by the same people. I'll keep you posted on what develops out here. You just take care of yourself in there. Well son, I'll let you go with your thoughts. You take care and write me soon.

Always,

Poochie

The card slipped from my hand as I sat on my bunk. No tears came to my eyes, no pain came to my heart. My brothers had been dead to me for years. I was devoid of emotion for either one of their deaths. All we shared was blood and the same last name. That's it. Them niggas left a nigga in jail to rot and didn't give a fuck. They knew exactly where that rat nigga, Eric that told on me hung at, but neither of them stopped him from coming to court on me. To me, that was unforgivable. They been said, 'fuck

~ 117 ~

me', so now I say, 'fuck them.' The only thing that bothered me about the whole situation was the timing of their deaths. I was never one to believe in coincidences. And both of my brothers getting killed with both Khadafi and now Lil Cee in the streets, naw that ain't no coincidence.

Then another thought dawned on me. Khadafi was closer to me than Lil Cee had been. He knew how I felt about my brothers, but Lil Cee didn't. So the person that killed my brothers had to be Lil Cee. I wish I knew how to get in touch with him. I would laugh in his face and let him know that his plan to hurt me by killing my brothers had failed. I grabbed both obituaries, balled them up and tossed them in the corner with the rest of the trash. *Fuck them niggas.*

Rudy's letter was the last one left. I opened it and read:

Antonio,

> *How are you? Do I come through for you or don't I? I got good news, big guy. I petitioned the Court Of Appeals to rehear your motion for a new trial en banc. They ordered immediate oral arguments. I went down on the 5th and argued your issues in front of the three judge panel. I raised the issue about your previous attorney Kennedy Hicks and the conflict of interest. I was able to prove rather strongly that you received ineffective assistance from your appeal attorney. Well, today I received a fax from*

the clerk at the COA and the judges have agreed to rehear your issues en banc (with all nine judges instead of just three).

Although the fight to free you has just begun, we've won the first round. I have about five new issues that I want to raise. I think they have merit. Keep your fingers crossed on both hands and I'll see you when you get back to D.C. Your court date is November 21st. Take care.

Rudy

Rudy had gotten me back in court and I couldn't believe it. I jumped off the bunk and cleaned myself for prayer. I offered the salat. Then I thanked Allah for His mercy and blessings. I was going back to D.C. I stood in the middle of my cell and sang. I sang my favorite song just like the dude K-John who composed it . . .

"Sometimes/ I feel like, everything is passing me by/ every now and then/ it feels like/ my ship has gone and sailed away/ and I gotta be strong/ gotta hold on/ cause it won't be to long."

Before I knew what was happening, I was crying. Not because I was hurting or because pain lived in my heart. Not because I'd lost everything that I ever loved while in prison. I cried because I truly believe that my ship outta here had finally come.

Chapter Nineteen
TJ

*R*eesie came down the aisle looking beautiful as usual in dark Karen Zambos slacks and a matching blouse. Her long hair was pinned up into a tight bun and she rocked a pair of black framed Gucci personality glasses like no other. Her ability to go from "Hood Chick" to "Boardroom Executive" was one of the things I loved most about Reesie. She was one of those independent women that Ne-Yo sang about. Reesie's hazel eyes were mesmerizing and never failed to turn me on. She slid into the booth across from me. She reached over and grabbed me by my collar, pulling me to her. We kissed for a few seconds.

"Hey," she said as she slipped off her jacket. "I see you started without me."

I looked down at my half eaten plate of shrimp and broccoli penne pasta and smiled. "I was hungry as shit, boo. What's so important that I had to come all the way downtown to hear it?"

"Damn, no how you doin' baby? No how your day been, boo? Nothing. You terrible, boy." Reesie reached across the table and slid my plate of food in front of her. Then she snatched the fork out of my hand and started eating.

"Let me order you something," I offered.

"I'm cool with this right here. You know what I eat, nigga, you should've ordered me something already."

I let her eat in peace.

"Damn, I was hungry, too," Reesie said and grabbed my ice tea. After drinking almost all of it she said, "Do you know a dude from down Southwest named Black Woozie?"

"Naw. Why?" I lied and suddenly became very interested in what she had to say.

"About a week ago, somebody broke in a house on Canal Street, robbed it, and killed everybody in there."

"I heard about it."

"Well, that was Woozie's spot. His stash house. One of the dudes that got killed was his cousin, Yusef."

"And?"

"And—for some reason, Woozie thinks you had something to do with it."

"He told you that?"

"Yeah—well, let me start from the beginning. I party with a chick that works with me named Sheree. That's his baby mother. He asked her if she knew anybody from up Capers. Even though I don't hang out down there no more, Sheree knows that I grew up down there. She called me on the three-way today with him on the phone. I'm a little

fucked up at first because I hate when people do that three-way shit. Plus, I don't really know this nigga. I just know of him. He introduces himself to me and then asked me if I knew you. I told him that I did. Why? He asked me could I get in touch with you and give you a message. I told him I'd try. So he gave me the message."

"And that is?"

"He wants to sit down and talk to you."

"About what? That house that got robbed?"

"He didn't say. All he said was that he needed to sit down with you."

"You loss me. Earlier, you said something about he thinks I had something to do with the house and the murders. Did that come from him?" I asked.

"Naw, that came from her. Sheree told me that after he hung up. She was telling me about how everybody down Southwest is fucked up behind what happened on Canal Street. Especially what happened to Yusef and Addie. She said Addie's sister Lovey is on a nut ready to kill whoever."

"Did the dude give you his number?"

"Naw. He told me to call Sheree if I got in touch with you and Sheree knows how to reach him. You want me to holler at her?"

"Yeah. Call her right now and tell her to call slim. See if she can get him on the phone right now. But don't tell either one of 'em you with me. Act like I'm on your other line."

"Got you," Reesie said and pulled out her cell.

She dialed a number and waited. "Hello? Sheree? It's me, Reesie. Hey listen, I got TJ on my other line and he wants me to ask Woozie something. Can you call him?" She paused. "Good. I'll hold on." A few seconds later, she said," Yeah, I'm here. He on the phone . . . Okay, Woozie? Hey, how you doing? Likewise . . . listen, I got TJ on my other line . . . hold on . . . what do you want me to say?"

"Tell him we can meet, but he has to come to Capers, to the rec. Tell him that." I listened as Reesie relayed the message.

"He said he cool with that. When?"

"Tell him to meet me in front of the rec at eight o'clock tonight."

Reesie gave him the message and then hung up.

"He said he'll be there. Am I gonna see you after that?"

"Do you wanna see me after that?" I asked.

"Stop playing with me, nigga. You know I'm tryna see you."

"Then you gon see me then."

"You gon' kill him ain't you?"

Reesie's question caught me completely off guard. "Why you ask me that?"

"Don't even worry about it, the less I know the better. Come and see me when you leave him; I'ma be naked and waiting for you. That gangsta shit makes my pussy wet. Bring me some of that bomb ass smoke you got, too."

"I got you, boo, I got you."

Khadafi and I stood under a tree across the field from Capers rec while waiting for La La to get there. About ten minutes later, he pulled up in a silver Ford F-150.

"What's up?" he asked as we approached him.

"We gotta deal with another situation," I replied.

"What situation is that?"

Khadafi blew weed smoke out of his nose and said, "It ain't shit we can't handle, cuz."

"The dude whose spot we hit, he got at me through some bitches and said he need to holler at me. The bitch he fuckin' told my bitch that he think I had something to do with his spot getting hit."

"Fuck that nigga! What he wanna do?" La La shouted.

"I don't know, but I don't wanna sleep on these niggas. I did some homework and found out that that shit we took from that nigga ain't nothing but light shit to him, but he fucked up about his cousin. That was the nigga that Mark crushed. From what I hear he got a team of niggas that roll at his command. If this nigga think that I was involved, I'm tryna strike first. But I wanna see if the bitch got it right. Ain't no sense in killing this nigga if I don't have to. So I'ma hear 'im out. Then if he give me the impression that he want beef, I'ma cook it right there."

Khadafi threw his blunt to the ground and stepped on it. "Look, cuz, the nigga on his way here as we speak. Tee arranged a meeting with him. They gon' meet at the front of the rec. We gon' let 'im talk. I'ma be posted up on the roof out of sight. I want you to parlay in them bushes." He pointed to the bushes on the field directly in front of the

rec. "Right there. Ain't no telling how many niggas gon' be with him, but fuck it the more the merrier. TJ, walk the nigga out into the open over there by the swings and shit. That way I can see everything. They talk. If Tee don't like what he saying, he's gonna lift his sleeve and check his watch, then sneeze and cover his mouth. That's the signal to crush everything moving. Got that?"

"Lift the sleeve, sneeze, and cover the mouth. I got it," La La said and went back to his truck. He came back to us and pulled out an assault rifle. "Ain't that ironic? I get to kill these niggas with their guns. When they s'pose to get here?"

"At eight o'clock," I said and checked my watch. "He should be here in fifteen minutes."

Chapter Twenty
KHADAFI

From my position on the rooftop, I could see the whole Fifth Street. I saw two cars and one SUV coming up the block at two minutes after eight. *Here they come.*

The lead car was a dark color big body Lexus sedan. The middle car was a sleek, sporty Mercedes coupe and the SUV was a Benz truck. All three vehicles pulled in front of the rec and parallel parked beside each other. Two people stepped out of each vehicle and huddled around each other. TJ stepped out of the shadows into the light so he could be seen. One dude separated himself from the huddle and walked toward TJ. They stood close together and talked. The dude did a lot of talking with his hands and I know that made TJ nervous. I locked the Calico on fully auto spits. The 100 shot drum sat on top and waited for me to make him spin. Suddenly, TJ led the man out into the open just as we planned. With my eyes glued on TJ, I went into a heightened sense of awareness. Then as if in slow mo, it happened. TJ lifted his sleeve and checked his watch, then

he sneezed. Before he had the chance to cover his mouth, I was letting the Calico go. From that distance, I marveled at the carnage it caused as it ripped through flesh, bone, and metal. La La was all over the crowd as well with the rifle. They didn't stand a chance. Everybody was down except one. Woozie.

TJ made him kneel. Then he blew Woozie's brains out. I climbed down off the roof and became one with the wind.

"What we are experiencing now is a hike in homicides that has us all befuddled. We don't know what's going on, but we are working around the clock to get this disturbing situation under control. I have just ordered the police chief to implement the 'All Hands on Deck,' calling for all available officers to take to the streets. In hopes that that will curtail a lot of the recent homicides."

"Mr. Mayor, the 'All Hands on Deck' was criticized in recent months as being ineffective. Has anything changed with it to render it more effective? And what can the citizens of the District expect from the authorities in light of all the recent crime?"

"We are doing everything humanly possible to assure the public that the streets of D.C. are safe. The barbaric killing of six people last night in Southeast is being investigated as we speak and the animals responsible will be prosecuted to the fullest extent of the law."

"Thank you for your time, Mr. Mayor. This has been correspondent Aniyah Fields, reporting to you live from the

Arthur Capers Recreation Center in Southeast, D.C. . . . Maria, back to you."

"In other news . . . We now go live to another crime scene. CUS Fox news correspondent Michelle Lawson is standing by . . . Michelle?"

"Good evening, Maria. D.C. Police have identified the three people who were killed yesterday as they entered this Temple Courts building directly behind me here. The one man and two women were identified as a brother and two sisters. The man was identified as thirty-year-old Franklin "Diddy" Dorn. The women were identified as twenty-eight-year-old Detrice Dorn and thirty-one-year-old Arteta Dorn. A folded up piece of paper was found next to the body of Franklin Dorn. The letter read: 'You thought you couldn't be touched. All rats can be touched.'

"Authorities are looking to question a D.C. man who is incarcerated in the Bureau of Prisons. Sources close to the scene say that twenty-eight-year-old; Jihad Chase was believed to have ordered the deaths of the Dorn family from his prison cell in USP Lee, in Jonesville, Virginia. Apparently, the Dorn's all testified against Jihad Chase in his criminal trial."

The murders at the rec down Capers were all over the news and the hood was hot as shit. Detectives were all over everybody trying to figure out who killed six people in the streets. One news station said that the scene on Fifth Street resembled something from the hills of Afghanistan. I rolled around in Marnie's bed and did a few crunches. The news I had just seen was the afternoon broadcast and I thought it

was the morning edition. I sat up and looked around at all the things that belonged to Marnie and thought about home. It had been a week since I left home and camped out at Marnie's apartment.

I hadn't talked to Kemie at all, I was homesick, and I missed her. But my wounds from her betrayal were still fresh and I didn't trust myself around her. The beast inside me was still calling for her life. I knew that something was gonna have to come to a head and soon, but in the meantime, I had other shit to do.

I dressed in the hospital gown that tied up in the back and thought about how gay that shit was. *These people got a cold-blooded killer in the hospital walking around with his ass out.* The nurse said that they'd be ready for me in a few minutes. That was thirty minutes ago. *I can't wait until they take this shit bag off and reconnect my intestine so that I can take a regular shit.* The procedure would take three hours they said and then I'd have to stay in the hospital for seven to ten days until I shitted something solid. That was a long time to be out of action, but I needed the rest and the result would be worth it.

"Mr. Fuller, we're ready for you now," a male nurse said. "Just lie down on this gurney and I'll wheel you into the operating room."

The operating room was cold as shit and there were more people there than I had anticipated. A black middle-aged doctor slid on some latex gloves and said, "My name is Dr. Adam Carroll, Mr. Fuller, and I am going to perform

your reconstructive surgery today. I'm gonna place this mask of anesthesia over your face to put you to sleep. I need you to count backwards—"

I awoke early the next day, thirsty and hungry as shit. And my mouth was dry. I was in a small room with a window, a TV, and a telephone. My stomach hurt a little bit, but overall I was good. The nurse came in some time later and gave me something to drink. She said I had to be fed intravenously for the first couple of days then go to liquid foods by mouth for a day or two. She took my vitals and hit me with some pain medicine that put me to sleep.

The next time I opened my eyes, TJ was sitting in a chair in my room.

"'Bout time you woke up, slim. If I wanted to kill you, you'd be dead as shit," TJ said and smiled.

"I'm hip, cuz. That Demerol shit they giving a nigga a bad muthafucka. What day is it?"

"Today Wednesday. You been in this joint for two days already." TJ got up and came close to me. "I brought you something to make you feel better." He leaned in close and slid a gun under my pillow. "I want my four-fifth back as soon as you get outta this joint, slim. You ain't keeping that joint, so don't even think about it."

I laughed and it made my stomach hurt.

"How long you gotta be in this joint?"

"They say until I shit something solid out. That way they'll know the procedure was a success. What's up around the way?"

"Hot as shit," TJ replied and kicked his feet up on my bed. "Ain't nobody getting no money or nothing out that joint. Shop shut down like a muthafucka. So you know niggas is out there tryna find some shit to tell them peoples. But so far, the streets is talking and ain't nobody got no answers. The mayor and the police chief walked through that muthafucka yesterday."

"That's only because we so close to Capital Hill and the Marine Barracks are right there. Fuck them muthafuckas, cuz. You know what I wanted to ask you?"

"What's up?"

"What was the nigga, Woozie talking about before shit went sour?"

"Evidently, the nigga Mark ran his mouth to his wife about the plan to hit the spot. But what he didn't know was that his wife, Samantha was fuckin' one of Woozie's men named Dave. After the shit happened and Mark ended up dead, Samantha told Dave what Mark told her. She said that a dude named TJ killed Mark and so on and so forth. The nigga Dave went and told Woozie what Samantha told him. The only TJ they knew of was me.

"The nigga was talkin' a'ight at first, but then he got on some real gangsta chronicle shit. That nigga told me that I was in over my head and shit was about to get wicked if he found out that I had something to do with that Canal Street shit."

"Yeah? That nigga must've bumped his head earlier that day. Or drunk a muthafuckin' courageous cocktail," I said and laughed.

"Exactly. That nigga was horse playing like shit. That's why he ain't here now. I knew that I was gon' kill him as soon as he walked up, though. I had already made that decision. I just didn't tell you and La."

"Kill him for what?"

"For being stupid. Real street niggas don't move like that. If he thought I had something to do with his house getting hit, he should've came through and let his gun do the talking. Ask no questions and I'll tell you no lies. Those are the rules that real niggas live by. He used his tongue instead of his gun and all he got was dead. And he put a few other muthafuckas under the gun."

"Like who?"

"Samantha, Dave, and that bitch he fuckin' named Sheree. The police can't find a path when all trails lead to nowhere. All three of them'll be dead in the next seventy-two hours."

"I see you, cuz. You on one, huh?"

TJ stood up and smiled. "Nigga, don't watch me, watch TV. Preferably the news. I'm out. And I almost forgot. Kemie came through the hood looking for you earlier."

"And you told her where I was?"

"Of course, I did. You can fool everybody else with that fake go hard routine. Nigga, I'm hip to you. You love Kemie's last year dirty drawers. She came up here with me. She out in the hall waiting to see you. I'ma holla back." TJ left out and a minute later Kemie walked in.

Chapter Twenty-One
LIL CEE

Dear Comrade,

How are you doing? Sorry to hear about your brothers. Did you cry when you heard they were dead? I hope so. Does it hurt to lose two love ones at the same time? Do you feel the pain right there in the middle of your chest? I know that feeling. Trust me, I do. That's the way I felt when I found out about my family. I was fucked up—still am. But now I feel a little better. At present, I'm doing well. Still trying to locate your daughters and baby mother so that I can stop by and visit. Then I plan to visit Khadafi and his family. Please don't hurt yourself. As bad as the pain is and will be, it'll only get worse. It never stops. You'll even think about suicide. But I know you'd never do that. You too strong for that. I need you to one day make it home, slim. So I can send you to Harmony in the proper fashion. Until we meet again.

You know who.

~ 133 ~

I reread my letter to Ameen and decided that it was perfect. I wanted Ameen to know that I was the reason behind his pain. I only wished I could be there to witness it.

"Aye, Charles?"

I looked up from the bed and saw my roommate standing there. "What's up?"

"The CO want you, moe," he said.

"A'ight, slim, good lookin'."

"You wanted me?" I asked as I stepped in the office and leaned on the wall by the door.

"Yeah," Ms. Ransom said and sat back in her seat. "A Mr. Shula just called and asked me to tell you that your City Lights Program appointment is today at two o'clock, he said."

"I heard that. Good lookin'." I turned to leave, but heard my name called.

"What's up?"

"Who twisted your dreads for you?" Ms. Ransom asked.

"I did. Why?" I felt my hair. "They fucked up?"

"Naw, I like 'em. I been thinking about locking my hair up. I like the way you be rockin' them. You make 'em look sexy."

Is she flirting with me? Naw. Can't be. "Thank you. I appreciate that. Your hair already look good, you don't need to dread up."

"I been thinkin' about it."

"You got this office smelling good as shit. What you got on?"

"It's that new Mariah Carey perfume called Forever. You like it?"

"Love it. And I also like the way you rockin' your nails."

Ms. Ransom studied her nails. "They a'ight."

"They look fly to me and I love that fly shit. Are your toes as pretty as your hands?"

"Of course. I keep 'em done."

"Let me see 'em."

"Let you see what? My feet?" Ms. Ransom asked.

"Yeah. I wanna see if they proper. Make sure you ain't welling."

"I'm not showing you my feet, Gooding. I don't do no welling. They proper."

"Let me see 'em then."

I never really thought she'd do it; I was just pressed for her conversation. But to my surprise, she slid her chair back, bent over and pulled her boot off, then her sock. Ms. Ransom stuck her bare foot out around the desk and wiggled her pedicured toes. They were painted red with a glittery design on just the big toe. I nodded my head. "They proper. I respect that. Your feet pretty as shit."

"You like my toes, huh, Gooding?"

"I gotta fetish for pretty women with pretty toes, so yeah, I like 'em. They proper."

Salaciously, she said, "Everything about me proper, Gooding. My toes ain't the only thing pretty on me."

It was starting to heat up in the office. "Is that right? What else on you pretty, Ms. Ransom?"

"If I told you that you might stalk me and I don't need no more stalkers," she said and laughed.

The thought of what she was implying made my dick hard. Then it dawned on me that I hadn't had any pussy since I'd been home. I wasn't sure where the CO was trying to take our conversation, but I decided to try my hand. "I ain't tryna stalk you, so keep that to yourself. But let me ask you this: You look good. You smell good. But do you taste good?"

"You wanna taste me, Gooding?"

"Bad as a muthafucka."

Ms. Ransom's hand went under the desk. "I think I taste good. Let me see." I heard her belt unfasten and then the sound of her zipper. A second later, she put the two fingers that were just in her pants in her mouth and sucked on them. "I taste good to me. Watch that door, I'ma let you be the judge."

I leaned on the wall and watched Ms. Ransom's hand disappear under the desk again. I had to keep watching the hallway to make sure that nobody came to the office. When her lip curled up, I knew that Ms. Ransom had found what she was looking for. She was sitting in my face playing with her pussy. I couldn't believe it. I listened closely and heard her pussy talking. The look of determination and the soft moans that she made had me ready to bust in my pants. I looked, checked the hall one more time, and saw that it was clear.

"Fuck these niggas," I muttered to myself and whipped my dick out of my sweatpants. I stroked my dick slowly

and imagined myself fucking Ms. Ransom. At the sight of my dick, she went crazy fingering herself. Then our eyes locked.

"I'ma bout to cum, Gooding!" she whispered as her breathing deepened and sped up. "O-o-oh-h-h!"

Then she was up and coming toward me. Ms. Ransom reached up and put her fingers in my mouth. I sucked on her fingers and tasted her pussy juices. It turned me on so much that I came. Ms. Ransom jumped back, laughed, and said, "Why you do that?"

I was still shaking from coming so hard, so I ignored her and kept jerking cum onto the floor. "Got damn! Why *you* do that?"

"You better get that shit up before somebody come in here and—"

I took my Gucci high top and smushed all the cum into the rug on the office floor.

"You ghetto like shit," Ms. Ransom said and fixed her clothes. "You look like you did that somewhere before."

I laughed. "I think well under pressure. What else was I s'pose to do?"

"You did right, I guess. So how did I taste?"

"Good as a muthafucka, but I need to taste the real thing. The fingers were the watered down version. You gotta give me a chance to really taste you."

"I tell you what. When you get your pass this weekend, we'll hook up. Then you can taste whatever you wanna taste."

"You gon' show me all the other things that's pretty on you?" I asked.

"Of course."

"You gotta date, then."

"Your girlfriend ain't gon' mind if I borrow you for a little while?"

"No girlfriend, boo. I did that whole nine years by myself."

"You been home almost a month now, you telling me you ain't fucked nobody since you been home?"

"Nobody. That's on my mother."

"Did you ever come across my uncle or cousin in the Feds?"

"Who are they?"

"Tommy Edelin and Tony, his father?"

"Naw. I ain't hip to them," I said and looked at my watch. It was 1:38. "Let me go get ready for my appointment. I'ma see you tomorrow."

"I can't wait."

"You got money?" Church asked me as he pulled the truck up to the City Lights building.

"I'm good, slim. My mother left me a rack of money when she—. I didn't even know she had life insurance. It's enough money to last me for a long time. But thanks for asking. I'ma catch a cab back to the halfway house, so I'll see you tomorrow."

"A'ight, baby boy. Let me know when you ready to make the next move."

"No doubt, slim. That should be soon. We'll talk tomorrow. One love."

"Praise the Lord, baby boy and have a blessed day."

That nigga losing his mind. "Same to you."

As I waited to be called in the back, I sat in the lobby and thought about the house on Fifty-Sixth Street that Church and I had visited a few days ago. Ameen' baby mother's house was vacant. There was a 'for sale' sign stuck in the grass on the lawn. I felt like I had been robbed of my absolute retribution. Killing his two daughters was gonna be the highlight of my days. But it wasn't meant to be. At least not right now it wasn't. I wasn't going to stop looking for them, though. Never.

The only person left was Khadafi and his father, old man Fuller. Until I found his father, I'd have to settle with just him. Khadafi was a worthy opponent and I respected his gun game. But I had one advantage. The element of surprise. As far as I knew, Khadafi didn't know I was home. And he hadn't seen my new look. The game that I was playing was for life and death. If I win, I live. If I lose, that means I'm dead. Although I wanted to live, I'd surely die avenging my slaughtered family. My other advantage was that time was on my side. Not his. Khadafi had no clue his days were numbered. He was a walking dead man; he just hadn't lain down in his casket yet.

Chapter Twenty-Two
TJ

Reesie made the sexiest noises when she had that dick in her. I listened to her as she rode my dick and could've sworn that she was speaking a language that I had never heard. It sounded primitive, like something the cave woman said and grunted as the caveman fucked her. That shit had me feeling myself. I reached up and squeezed her nipples. Reesie threw her head back and moved on my dick like she was upset with me and was punishing me with the pussy. Then she was cumming. I always knew when she was cumming. It was the noise. They became more intense. More primal. I'd lay back, listen to the sounds she made, and allow myself to cum with her.

"Did you find out about what I asked you to find out?" I whispered in Reesie's ear.

"About what? Sheree?"

"Yeah."

"Reesie nodded her head.

"Talk to me, then."

"This is what you call pillow talk, huh?" Reesie said. "You can't just lay here and hold me, huh? That would be asking too much from you, wouldn't it?"

I moved back to the other side of the bed.

"See, I knew it. Look how you acting now. I guess you mad at me, huh?"

Without waiting for me to answer, she said, "She live over there by Eastern High School on Seventeenth and C Street. She gets up at 7 A.M. and walks her sons to school. Then she walks to the subway station by D.C. jail and catches the train to work. She gets off at the same time I do. Then she goes to the Gallery Place subway station and catches the train home. Is that enough or do you need me to find out what type of tampons she uses when she comes on her period?"

Reesie got out the bed and stomped into the bathroom. I lay in the bed, thought about how much Reesie meant to me, and instantly felt bad. Getting out the bed, I walked naked into the bathroom. The shower water was running. I pulled the curtain back and saw Reesie standing under the spray of water crying. Or was that water on her face? I stepped in the shower and stood behind her. Reaching out, I encircled her waist with my arms and held her. I moved her hair to the side and kissed her neck. Silently, we both stood under the water and let our silence speak.

The salon was filled with beautiful women when I walked in. I thought about everybody outside D.C. saying that D.C. had some beautiful women and had to agree with them. Since I was the only male in the shop, naturally all eyes were on me. I walked up to the front counter. Behind it sitting on a stool was a cafe latte complexioned woman that needed to be on TV. She reminded me of Reagan Gomez-

Preston. Since she was on the phone, I waited until she finished her call before saying, "I'm tryna get my dreads treated, washed, dried and my scalp greased."

"Let me find somebody to hook you up. Monique? You got a one o'clock? You do? Hey Crystal? You booked up? No? Can you do a dread, wash and dry for me?"

I looked into the direction of a short light skinned woman with long pretty hair and grey eyes.

"Sure, Sam. Send him back here in thirty minutes." Grey eyes responded.

"You can have a seat over there while you wait. Crystal will be with you in thirty minutes," the Reagan Preston clone said and picked up another call.

I grabbed a seat along the wall across from the counter and eyed the woman called Sam. Sam had to be short for Samantha. *At least Mark had good taste in women.* There was a stack of books on the table in front of me, I picked them up and went through them. *Hell Razor Honeys 2, Trust No Man* 1 & 2, *Alibi, Strapped, Karma With a Vengence* and *It's No Secret.* I put the books down, but kept the one by Carmen Bryan. *Nas baby mother bad as shit.*

"—girl. Kia, your crazy ass gotta get out more. You been on some nun shit ever since Quette got killed. Life goes on—yeah, but—naw. You right. I'm just saying—yeah, all of us going. We gon' shut that muthafucka down. Fuck them No Holes Barred bitches. They can't get in our business. We gotta go shopping this week—"

THE ULTIMATE SACRIFICE II
LOVE IS PAIN

Shortie is a scandalous bitch. Her husband ain't been dead but two weeks and she already planning to party. But you ain't gon' make that one, babygirl.

I looked up from my book and saw a poster on the wall behind Samantha . . .

Book Release Party of the Year

Come out and celebrate the release of the street novel that the whole world has been waiting for. *Angel Returns* is the most anticipated novel of the decade. The first 100 people in the door get a signed copy of the book. This is a grown and sexy affair. All white attire only. Guest appearance by local rap sensation Wale. Music by TCB and RE. Come to the Omni Shoreham Hotel and party with the stars.

November 22nd, huh? I filed the date and the poster in the back of my mind. I hadn't partied with RE since I'd been home and I was long overdue for a party. Even gangstas have to take a day off.

"Crystal is ready for you, boo. Walk all the way to the back. Her station is the last one to your left."

There were only three vehicles in the parking lot by the time I left out the shop, but I knew which one I wanted.

The Benz truck. I tapped it a few times just to see if there was an alarm activated. There wasn't. Getting inside the truck was child's play. I climbed into the backseat of the luxury vehicle and lay down on the floor. As pretty as Samantha was, it was a pity that I had to kill her. The day she ran her mouth to Dave and it became known. It was over for her. Dave had gotten her killed and she didn't even know it. She was a direct link between me and Mark and the murders on Canal Street, and I couldn't allow her to live. There was no telling who else she had already told the story to besides Dave. So I had to start with her. *Evaluate. Isolate. Eliminate.*

I heard the sound of heels clicking against the asphalt and a conversation. Hiding from view, I listened to Samantha chop it up with one of the women who worked for her for a few minutes and then was climbing in the truck. I waited for her to put her key in the ignition and turn the radio on before rising up on her. I put the gun in her right ear and whispered, "Don't move, Sam. If you do what I say, I swear to God, I'ma let you go. If not, I'ma kill you and leave you right here. Make your mind up. You wanna die right now?"

Samantha shook her head and said, "No, please don't!"

"You gon' help me?"

She nodded. "Yes."

"Good. Get on your phone and call Dave. Tell him that your truck fucked up—or whatever you gotta say to get him here. Do that for me and I swear to god, I'ma let you go. Call him."

Samantha picked up her cell and made the call. She told Dave where she was and that she needed him to come look at her truck.

"He says he'll be here in ten minutes, he down 203 with Meechie. Can I go now? You promised to God, I could. I swear I ain't gon' tell nobody. Please, I swear."

"I can't do that, Sam."

"Why?" she asked with panic in her voice. "You promised to God." She started crying.

"I don't believe in God."

Bok! Bok!

Sam's head hit the driver door window. I pulled her body away from the window and leaned her over into the passenger seat. I didn't want Dave to get suspicious when he rode up. Climbing out the truck, I stayed on the side that was hidden from the street. It was now dark outside and that worked in my favor. Ten minutes went by and still no Dave— headlights from a car caught my attention. I looked around the truck and saw a burgundy Lexus SC 430 stop in front of the shop. Then he pulled into the parking lot. A tall, dark skinned dude got out the car dressed in a blue sweatsuit and baseball cap. He walked up on the Benz truck. I ducked down and crept around the truck.

"Aye, Dave!" I stood up and said.

He turned around and faced me.

Bok! Bok! Bok! Bok!

I hit him twice to the head and then twice to the body and got out of there.

~ 145 ~

That night, I lay in Reesie's bed and rubbed her leg that was thrown over mine as she slept. If my heart were capable of feeling love, I would love her. But it's not. I am a man with no compassion, no conscience, and no soul. But yet she stuck beside me when I was in prison. Reesie was the only person that wrote me and sent pictures on a regular. It was Reesie who was there to comfort me seven years ago when I needed somebody most. I was twelve feet deep in the drug game back then, fucking with Manny Stone. The dude was fronting me keys of dope dirt-cheap and I was balling out of control. My bankrolls were heavy and I made sure that the whole city knew that I was the man to watch. I was one arrogant and cocky muthafucka until one night changed my whole life . . .

I had just turned eighteen and celebrated my birthday big boy style for three days straight in Atlantic City. I had two bad bitches with me at the Taj Mahal when the call came through on my cell phone . . .

"Bitch nigga, where that money at?" a voice shouted as soon as I answered.

"Who the fuck is this?" I asked, thinking it was a joke.

"This is death, nigga. You got three minutes to tell me where that money at or your peoples is dead."

I shot straight up out the bed. "What?"

"You heard me, nigga. You wasting time. I'ma start merkin shit in two and a half minutes. I'ma ask you again, where that money at?"

"Whoever you are," I hissed nice and calm, "you need to find somebody else to play with."

~ 146 ~

"Play? You think I'm playing, nigga? I got your play right here. Listen to me play. Dawg, bring that bitch over here."

I heard what sounded like a struggle going on and a female voice that I instantly recognized. "Say hello and good-bye, bitch."

"Tyrone! Help—"

Boom! Boom! Boom!

Tears stained my face immediately as the reality of the situation set in. My stepmother was gone. The gunshots that I heard had been meant to kill. Another voice screamed, "N-o-o-o-o-o!" It was my father.

"Still think I'm playing, nigga? You down to one and a half minutes. Where that muthafuckin' loot at?"

Through my tears, I said, "I swear to God, slim, when I find you—"

"Wrong answer, nigga. Bring the young nigga!"

"Don't do it—"

"Da-a-a-d-d-d-y!"

Boom! Boom! Boom!

"There's one life left. The money or you pay for three funerals instead of two. You decide. You got one minute. Fifty-nine seconds . . . fifty-eight . . . fifty-seven . . . fifty-six."

No matter what I did or said, I knew in my heart that my father was a dead man. There was no way that he was gonna be left alive to tell the story. My heart broke instantly.

" . . . forty-five . . . forty-four . . . forty-three . . ."

"You just took away everything that my father loved and there's no way that he'll ever recover from that. So go head, do him a favor, and kill him. The money ain't there anyway, so you wasted your time. And I swear that I'ma find and kill everybody you—"

"You're a stup—"

I disconnected the call and broke down crying. The two bitches in the bed with me were openly crying now. By the time I reached D.C., I knew my family would be found dead and the dudes would be long gone. So I did the next best thing and called Bean.

"Hello?"

"Slim—I need you to—"

"TJ? What's up, moe? It sound like you crying."

"Ay, slim—somebody just killed my peoples. They—"

"What the fuck you talkin' bout, slim? You still in Atlantic City, right?"

"Yeah, but I just got a call—some niggas called me and asked me where the money at—then they killed my father—"

"You serious, moe?'

"Slim, go to my father's house and see what's up—'

"I'm leaving out now. Call me back in ten minutes," Bean said and hung up.

Eight minutes later, Bean called me. "The door was left open—the house was ransacked—-they dead, moe. All of 'em. I'm sorry, moe . . . I'm sorry . . ."

I got back in town in a little under three hours and drove straight home. By the time I pulled onto my street, it

was blocked off and cops were everywhere. I ended up over Reesie mother's house. That's where I stayed for three days, and then Bean and I put our black shit on and went on a killing spree. I buried my family, my heart, my soul, and my belief in God that day. And there would be no resurrection.

Sheree was pretty, I noticed as I watched her for two straight days. She had a walk that gave off the impression that her pussy was a torch. I watched her hips sway as she got off the subway at the Stadium-Armory station. Then I darted up Massachusetts Avenue and turned left onto Bay Street. An alley ran parallel to East Capital Street. At the end of that alley is where I wanted to trap her off. Lurking in the alley with my gun already out, I waited. Five minutes later, I stepped out and saw her bending the corner. She was eight feet away . . . seven-feet away . . . six-feet away. I ran out of the alley and closed the space between us in seconds. Bringing the gun up, I shot her in the face. Then I ran back through the alley and came out across from D.C. General. Since I was already in the area, I ducked inside the hospital and went to see Khadafi.

"Aye!" a female voice called out.

Devon and I were standing on Esha's porch, when I heard the voice call out from a car. We turned in the direction of the voice and saw a red Infiniti M35 sitting in the street. The person calling out to us was a woman. "What's up, boo?"

"My girlfriend say y'all got that bombay round here. Who got it?"

"You fuck with that *blow your nose*? I asked her.

"Fuck no. I'm talkin' 'bout that skunk."

"Your girlfriend must not be from around here. They powdering their nose around here. But I might be able to help you. Park the car and get out."

We watched the Infiniti find a parking space. The driver got out and me and Devon both said, "Damn!" She was thick, bowlegged, about 5'4", about 140 pounds, pretty and fly as shit. She was the complexion of pure honey. Her beige Louis Vuitton LV printed jacket matched the high heel boots she rocked. The blue jeans she had on looked like they took thirty minutes to get into. I walked down and met her.

"What can you do for me?" the woman asked as soon as we were close.

"Huh?"

She laughed. "I didn't mean it like that. You said you might be able to do something for me."

"I got you, shortie. But how I know you ain't the police?"

"Trust me; I'm far from the police."

"Trust you? That's what all the undercovers say. You horse playing."

"Naw, nigga, you horse playing. I'm tryna smoke. And I'm tryna smoke right here in front of you. Inhaling, blowing O's and all. Police can't do that, can they?"

"You gotta point," I said and pulled out a sandwich bag full of the smoke we got from the house on Canal. "Check this out."

Pure honey put her nose in the bag and said, "Yeah, that's that. Get me?"

"What's your name, shortie?"

"Nomeka. But you can call me Meka."

Chapter Twenty-Three
DETECTIVE TOLLIVER

Captain Gregory Dunlap leaned all the way back in his seat, made a bridge with his fingers, placed them behind his head, and kicked his feet up on his desk. "And here's the best part—it's kinda funny, the Chief just congratulated everybody on a job well done. She had a report from the Federal Bureau of Investigations that reported about over-all crime dropping by fifty percent in four major cities and our nation's capitol was first on that list. D.C. only recorded 168 murders last year, that's the lowest our homicide rate has been in thirty years. The big wigs at Judiciary Square and at Municipal were toasting with champagne and passing out cigars. That was just last week. And this—

"Caps, the last coupla weeks—" Charlie Daytona started, but was cut off.

"Did I give you permission to speak in my meeting, Daytona?" the Captain sneered, then smiled.

Gregory Dunlap was affectionately dubbed "Smiley" by the entire Homicide Squad because he never smiled. The

only occasions when he did smile all hell would break loose later.

"Uh—no sir—I—" Charlie stammered.

"Well, since you are speaking without being told to speak, you're disrespecting everyone present. I hate to be disrespected. So do me a favor and get the fuck out of my meeting."

After Charlie Dayton left the room, Captain Dunlap said, "Does anybody else feel the need to interrupt me while I'm venting?"

Nobody said a word.

"Where was I? Oh—and now this—this—crime wave from hell. And I would love for somebody to show me exactly what the taxpayers' money are doing out in the streets because it's definitely not paying for police work. How do I know this? Because no reports have crossed my desk explaining to me exactly what the fuck is going on in my city.

"And nobody has been arrested. In the last eighteen days, twenty people have been killed and not one fuckin' person has been arrested. So that tells me that either criminals have gotten smarter or my officers have gotten stupider. Which one is it? Answer that to yourselves. Twenty bodies are in the city morgue stinkin' up the place and we don't know why. The influx of bodies has overwhelmed the people at the morgue. Can you believe that shit? They say they got stiffs on top of stiffs. Somebody ask me how do I know that. I know because the fuckin' Chief Medical Examiner called the Chief

personally. Go figure? The person who's paid a shitload of money to sort through the dead bodies is complaining about being inundated with bodies—'in a short period of time', were her exact words. In the next twenty-four hours, I want somebody in this room to put a report on my desk briefing me about what is causing the spike in homicides in my city. I don't care which one of you jerk-offs do it, but somebody needs to do it or I'm going to make all of your lives a living hell. Do I make myself clear?"

Collectively we all nodded.

"Everybody get the fuck outta my sight."

The On Luck Café on M Street was the perfect place to stop for a bite to eat before hitting the streets.

"Mama-san, gimme the General Tso chicken and fried rice," I called out as I approached the counter. "And a sixteen ounce Lipton's Brisk Ice Tea. Thank you."

I sat down at a booth seat and pulled out my notepad. I went over everything that I had learned since the night of the murders on Canal Street. I knew the identities of every person killed that night and even had an idea why Mark Johnson was taken to the marina and killed. I knew the identities of all the people killed at the recreation center on Seventh Street. I flipped through pages of notes, connected the dots of the Black Woozie killing, and tied it in with Canal Street. But that was as far as I could go. Everything after that was an enigma. Who killed Black Woozie and his entourage? Was it planned like that or done spontaneously? Why were they killed? What was Black Woozie doing at Capers Rec? At night? And who was he meeting and why?

And the million-dollar question is: Are the same killers who killed seven people at 1100 Canal Street, and Mark Johnson at the Harbor Marina, the same ones who killed Black Woozie and his men? Was there a drug war going on? Is the mass killing over with? Or had it just begun?

There were too many questions and too few answers. I need answers and I needed them bad. I flipped another page and stopped to look at two names I'd written down and circled. Billie Jean Fisher and Nomeka Fisher. Black Woozie's thirty-year-old sister and their mother. It was time to put pressure on everybody close to Woozie Fields and what better place to start than his mother and sister.

"Mama-san, bag that up for me, please. I'll take it to go."

Chapter Twenty-Four
LIL CEE

"*W*here are you right now?"

"I'm on Knox Place walking toward Alabama Avenue. Where you at?" I said into the cell phone.

"I just left out the door. I'm walking to my car now. You just keep walking to 7D and wait for me right there."

"I got you." Disconnecting the call, I stopped in front of the police station and waited for my ride. A few minutes later, a gold Chevy Malibu pulled up and blew the horn. I walked up to the car and got in.

Ms. Ransom looked over at me as she pulled off. I smiled. "What you cheesing for?" Then her eyes followed my gaze. "You laughing at my socks?"

She had kicked off her Nike boots and was driving in her socks. They were dark blue with little Tasmanian devils all over them.

"Don't be laughing at my socks. These my Warner Brothers socks. They have all my favorite characters."

"Them joints are hot. I fucks with them joints. They just seem a little too young for you. How old are you?" I asked.

"I'm twenty-four with an old soul, but at the same time, I'm young at heart."

"I can dig that. You grown and sexy, but at the same you ain't got no problem getting your young girl on. That's what's up," I said and smiled again.

"That's a compliment, right?"

"All day. The other day you asked me about a girlfriend, what's up with your boyfriend?"

"I'm single. I wouldn't have let you taste me if I wasn't."

"I heard that? It wouldn't be a good look for the jealous boyfriend nigga to kill me in my first thirty days on the streets."

"Nope. No jealous exes. You good."

"That's good to hear, but I got one question."

"What?"

"Where are you taking me?"

"My house. Where else? All you know is Ms. Ransom, I'm about to introduce you to Kia."

The one bedroom apartment in theWingates was small but expensively furnished with big screen plasma TVs, black leather furniture, and black lacquer everything else.

"I'm about to take a shower. You can sit out here and wait for me or you can take one with me," Ms. Ransom said and headed for the bathroom.

My decision was simple. I followed her to the bathroom. She turned the shower water on and adjusted the temperature.

"I knew you'd make the right decision."

I pulled my Hugo Boss sweatshirt over my head. "Only a homo would opt to sit out there instead of seeing you naked in here, Ms. Ransom, believe that."

"Stop calling me Ms. Ransom. Ms. Ransom is the CO at work. Since I trust you enough to have you in my bathroom, in my house, call me Kia."

She stood on her tip toes and kissed me. Then she undid my belt and unbuttoned my jeans. Kia tugged my jeans down until I could step out of them. She untied my tennis shoes and pulled each one of my shoes off. My socks came off next. I pulled my wife beater off as Kia stood up and stepped back. She slowly, methodically, unbuttoned her uniform shirt and pulled it off. Her eyes never left mine as she loosened her belt and wiggled out of her pants. Then she sat on the toilet and pulled her socks off. I stood riveted to my spot as I stared at her red lace boy shorts and matching bra. Kia stood and gave me a bird's eye view of the sexiest gap I'd ever seen on a woman. Her pussy was so phat' that it looked like she had a closed fist stuffed in her panties. Staring between her legs, I could see straight through to the tub. My dick was rock hard by then.

"My gawd—you are a sexy mutha."

Kia responded by taking off her bra and coming at me. I hugged and kissed her, and then kissed my way down to her breasts. Circling each nipple with my tongue, I grabbed each one and squeezed. Then I rubbed my face between them and smiled. I was home. Nine years in the pen and I was finally home. I reached down into Kia's shorts and felt

that pussy. It was wet and slippery. Pulling my hand out, I took it and rubbed her pussy juices all over my face.

Kia laughed. "Calm down, Wildman, it's gon' be a'ight." She tugged her boy shorts off. The sight of her shaved pussy was an aphrodisiac. I sat her down on the toilet after letting the cover down. On my knees, I put one of her legs over my shoulder. I came face-to-face with the first pussy I'd seen in years. It was beautiful just like her. First, I kissed it and then I licked it. Then I ate it like a starving refugee in a third world country. When I put my tongue inside her as far as it would go, Kia tried to get my face from between her legs, but I wasn't having it. I didn't stop until my moustache and beard was saturated with her cum.

Kia removed her leg from my shoulder, pushed me back and stood up. "Now that you know Kia it's time for me to introduce you to Kia Kitty." She leaned over and pulled my boxers off. Kia walked over me as I lay back on the bathroom floor. She grabbed my dick and rubbed the head in between her pussy lips. Then she lowered herself onto me slow. Her tightness enveloped me and sucked me in deeper. Once her walls could accommodate my girth, it was on. Straight triple X movie shit. We fucked on every vertical and horizontal surface in that bathroom until we both came several times. Then we showered. Lathering each other's bodies led to more fucking. By the time either of us realized it, a whole bottle of body wash was gone and the shower water had grown cold.

I woke up in a bed that was way too comfortable to me. I don't know how long I was asleep, but outside, I noticed that the sun had gone down. The room lights were dim, but the TV made it brighter. Kia was at the foot of the bed watching TV. I crawled to the edge and wrapped my arms around her. Kissing all over her neck and ears caused her to turn to me. That's when I felt that her face was wet.

"What's wrong with you?" I asked her.

"A friend of mine got killed. I just saw it on the news," Kia replied, her voice breaking.

"I'm sorry to hear that. Male or female?"

"Female. She was a good person, too. Always did my hair. I just talked to her—" Kia broke down sobbing.

All I could do was hug her and let her have her moment. My heart broke for her, though. I knew firsthand the pain she was feeling.

"Samantha was my buddy," Kia explained as she wiped at her tears. "I heard that somebody got killed in the parking lot next to her shop—but I never imagined that it was her and Dave."

"Dave? What Dave was that?"

"Dave Carlton. He grew up down the West. His brother, Chin went to prison on that K Street conspiracy back in the day. He was messing with Samantha—she was married. Her husband Mark got killed about a week or two ago. Somebody killed all of 'em. That shit is crazy. She invited me to a book release party at the Omni Shoreham Hotel. I picked up the tickets two days ago. We were supposed to

go shopping this weekend. I was waiting for her to call me. But now—"

"Do the police have somebody in custody?"

"Do they ever? They talkin' 'bout they still investigating and all that. But let a muthafucka go up Georgetown and kill two people, somebody gon' be locked up the same day. That's why I wanna get the hell away from D.C. This city is eating people alive. Everybody is either killing somebody or waiting to get killed. This shit ain't living."

I thought about my activities over the last few weeks and understood exactly what Kia was saying. "If you could go somewhere else, where would you go?"

"Probably down south somewhere. North Carolina, Georgia—I don't know. All I know is the cost of living is cheaper down south and life is slower. That's what I need. A slower life. That way, we'll live longer and enjoy life more. You feel me?"

"I feel you, boo."

"After Quette got killed, I almost left. I was this close." Kia put up her thumb and index finger and spaced them an inch apart.

"Quette? Who was he?" I asked.

"Marquette was a dude that I was messing with for about three years. He was my first love. He raised me. Shit—he raised a rack of bitches. I wasn't his main bun, but you know what? I didn't care. I just cared about him so much. But he loved the streets and the fast life more, and eventually it did him in. I was so fucked up behind his

death that I had to be hospitalized for about two weeks after that. I eventually got it together and decided to be single until somebody came along that I liked. And I guess that's you."

I blushed. "I feel special."

"You should. I just gave you a year and a half worth of good loving. Did you like Kia Kitty?"

"Loved her. Glad I met her. Can't wait to see her again."

"You ain't gon' have to wait that long."

"Let me ask you two questions."

"Go 'head."

"It ain't nothing major, but if your name is Kia, why does your name tag on your uniform say L Ransom and not K. Ransom?"

"The L stands for Lakia. But everybody calls me Kia or Kia the Diva." I smiled at that. "Okay, Ms. Kia the Diva, I just wanted to make sure that you ain't giving me aliases."

"Give you aliases? What for? I just gave you my body and my real name, so appreciate it. What's your second question?"

"Why me?"

"What you mean?"

"I mean, you haven't been with nobody in all that time, why did you pick me to give yourself to?"

"To be honest with you, I been horny as shit the last few months but I stuck to my guns. I got niggas that I can go to and get fucked if that's what I wanted, but it's not. It's something about you that turns me on. It all started that day

you asked me for a pass to go to church. I love a thug with morals. I get a good vibe from you, Gooding. Sometimes you can read a person and tell if he or she is a good person. I genuinely believe that you a good dude and that intrigued me." Kia laughed to herself. "And the fact that you been locked up so long without no pussy kinda worked in your favor, too. Gooding, I'ma simple girl. I don't ask for much. All I want is to be loved and to be happy. Is that too much to ask for?"

"Naw. I guess not. But I know there ain't no shortage of dudes who tryna love you."

"That's true. Niggas come at me all day, every day. But I want the best nigga, not the next nigga. There's a difference. The thing is—a man wants every woman to satisfy his one need. Sex. A woman wants one man to satisfy her every need. That's me, Gooding. That's who I need and want."

"What if I told you that I wanna leave D.C., too? When my halfway house time is up and I tie up all my loose ends?"

"You're serious?" Kia asked.

"As a heart attack. Ain't nothing to keep me here. My family is dead and all I have here are a lot of bad memories. My mother left me a stack of money when she died. We can live good for a long time. Would you leave with me?"

Kia responded by pushing me backwards and grabbing my dick. She wiped the remnants of her tears away from her eyes. Then she lowered her head and put me in her mouth. Kia sucked my dick so slow and passionately that it

was easy for me to understand that in some instances, words were not enough. Sometimes, you had to let your body speak for you. I lay back on the bed and understood exactly what Kia was saying.

Chapter Twenty-Five
LIL CEE

We walked out the front door and crossed the parking lot headed to Kia's car.

"There's a dude I need to holla at," I told Kia. "He was locked up with me and I need his help." I gave Kia directions to his neighborhood.

It took us about twenty minutes to get to Georgia Avenue and Rittenhouse Street. Kia made the left and cruised down the block. I spotted a crowd of dudes engaged in a crap game in the middle of the block. As we approached, everybody on the sidewalk looked in our direction. I was just about to tell Kia to keep going by until I spotted the dude that I came to see. He was behind the crap game leaning on a black cast iron gate.

"Stop right here," I told Kia.

Everybody in the crap game that was kneeling stood up and some dudes even started reaching in their waistbands. I threw up my hands and said, "Whoa! I come in peace. I just need to holla at Ray."

All eyes went to Raymond McCoy as he looked around them and squinted at me. "Lil Cee?" he said and came off the gate and walked into the street.

"What's up, slim?" I said and smiled.

Ray eyed me suspiciously. "Dawg, I heard some foul shit about you."

"I already know what you gon' say—"

"When you left me in Beaumont, where did you go, dawg?"

"After that shit happened, Garcia and nem' had me moved to FDC Houston—"

"For what? If you wasn't wick—"

"Slim, as long as you knew me, you knew I was a man. Cold-blooded man. And I wasn't goin' for nothing. I ain't never in my life crossed a man that didn't deserve it and I ain't never told on a nigga. Never. Them peoples used me to make Ameen and nem' tell on each other. They kept me locked away from everybody for two and a half years. I came home a month ago. But before I left, I went to court for Ameen and told them people that slim ain't do that shit. He beat that shit. Do your research, you'll see. My mother ain't raise no rat. If I was gon' tell something, I'da told on them twenty-nine co-defendants I had. Feel me?"

"I feel you, dawg, and I believe you—it was just that—"

"—so many muthafuckas was saying that shit. I'm already hip. That's why I'm tryna find Khadafi, so I can break shit down to him and hope that he'll see the games them peoples played. I know how close y'all was. I know

you seen slim since he been home or at least know how to get in touch with him."

"Yeah, that's my man. I saw him when he came home the first time—"

"The first time?"

"Yeah. Back in '08 Khadafi came home and blew up on some real gangsta shit real fast. Range Rovers and all that shit. Then he went back in on a domestic joint I heard. We hooked up a few times and went out to eat. I rapped to him on the horn a few times, but you know that shit is crazy. He way over Southeast and I'm all the way up here. Do you remember Yusuf? Joe Ebron?"

"Real quiet and sneaky. Yeah, I remember him. Why?"

"You know they gave slim the death penalty down there in Texas? Well anyway, I be talking to slim, tryna keep his head up, ya know. Well, he told me that when Khadafi came back to Beaumont on that violation, him and Ameen got into it. He said Ameen stabbed Khadafi in the rec cage and almost killed him."

"For real?"

"Yeah. Khadafi came home again about two months ago, I heard. I haven't seen him, but I know a bitch named Moet and her best friend Tosca is some kin to slim. But Tosca can't stand him. She be on some hatin' shit because she say that Khadafi don't do nothing for his little cousin, her son by his uncle Marquette. She the one that told me he was back home."

"I need you to holla at her, slim."

"Who, Moet?"

"Yeah. Tell her that I wanna holla at her friend, Tosca. Tell her to ask Tosca can I call her. It's important."

"You got that. I'ma do that right now." Ray pulled out his cell and made the call. He talked for a few minutes and then hung up. "Tosca said you can call her. I told her you just came home and she geekin'. She think she 'bout to come up. Her number is 202-429-0271."

I programmed the number into my phone. "Thanks a lot, slim. But I need one more thing from you. Well, more like two."

"What you need, dawg?" Ray asked.

"Guns. Big ones."

"You beefing with somebody? You know I'll come—"

"Naw, it ain't like that, slim. I'm straight. I just want some big shit just in case."

"How many you need?"

"Two—just in case."

"I got you, dawg." Ray called out to one of the dudes on the sidewalk. "Go get that Vietnam and bring it here." The dude walked quickly up the block. "You partied at all since you been home?"

"Naw," I replied.

"Well, look, me and my men doing this book release party in a coupla weeks. They got Essence and TCB on the ticket. It's an all white joint for the grown and sexy. You should come. The baddest bitches in the city—" He glanced at the Malibu with Kia in it and smiled. "—gon' be there. That is if you can get away."

"Slim, you the second person that done told me about that party. I'ma check it out."

A black Mazda Millennia pulled up in front of us. The dude who was just on the sidewalk was at the wheel. The trunk popped up automatically.

"C'mon, dawg," Ray said and led me to the rear of the Mazda. The trunk was full of handguns, rifles, shotguns, and machine guns.

"Damn!" I exclaimed and Ray smiled again.

"The streets'll kill you, dawg. You gotta be ready at all times when you trappin'. Get you two of them joints outta there."

I selected a Heckler and Koch ACP with a collapsible stock and reversible see through clip that held seventy rounds. A compact, fifty shot, Mac 12 sub machine gun was my next choice. "You got something to put these in?" I looked over my shoulder at my ride. "I don't want baby in my business. Feel me?"

"No doubt," Ray said and bent over the trunk. He moved some stuff over and pulled a book bag out of the corner of the trunk. He loaded the guns and some ammo into the bookbag and zipped it up. He handed the bag to me.

"What I owe you, slim?"

"Call it a welcome home gift."

"I heard that. I appreciate it, slim. No bullshit. Aye, slim, whatever happened to that broad Donnika that had you goin' crazy in Texas?"

"That bitch is my baby mother. Ain't that some shit? All that shit that bitch put a nigga through in the struggle, I came home and wifed her. What can I say? I love her, dawg. What y'all used to say all the time when we was in about love? Love is pain?"

"Yeah."

"That's a true bill. Go 'head and bounce, dawg, you ain't got no license for them hammers. Holla back another time."

"*Love is pain*, slim. That's some real shit."

I called the chick Tosca and told her that I needed to holler at her. She told me to come to her job at the All Tune and Lube on Florida Avenue in Northeast. Kia took me to see her, no questions asked. We pulled up to the shop and I hopped out. I went inside to talk, but Tosca told me she wanted to go outside. In front of the shop, I ran my spiel down about me needing to catch up with Khadafi, which was basically all lies. She hated Khadafi she told me and went on to tell me why. Then she gave me all the information I needed to launch my attack.

I pulled out a wad of money and peeled some bills off. I handed them to Tosca, thanked her for her time, and walked back to the car. When I got in the car, Kia said, "Where you know her from?"

I didn't know if what I detected in Kia's voice was jealousy or what, but I could see that she was vexed. "I don't know her. The dude that we just left Uptown sent me to talk to her about the dude I need to catch up with. Why what's up? You know her?"

Kia pulled away from the curb. All she kept saying was, "small world."

Now she had me vexed. "You know her?" I repeated.

"Yeah, I know her. That's Quette's baby mother."

"Quette?"

"My old boyfriend, Marquette. The one I told you about? That's his baby mother, Tosca. Small world."

It took me all of five seconds to put everything together. The Marquette that Kia was talking about, and Khadafi's uncle, Marquette, was the same person. I quickly decided against telling Kia what was going on in my life with Marquette's nephew. There was nothing to gain from her knowing. "Yeah, small world."

"Who is the dude you tryna catch up with?" Kia asked.

"A dude named Chris. He some kin to Tosca," I lied.

"Oh. Where to now, sir? Since you done made me your chauffeur?"

"Hold-on. Be quiet for a minute—"

"What?"

"I'm—tryna see if—yeah, I heard that."

Kia had a puzzled look on her face. "You heard what?"

"Kia Kitty. She was calling me. I had to see if it was really her. And it was."

"Oh yeah? What she say?"

"She said she need to holla at me bout something. She said it was extra important," I said.

"Well, it look like we headed back to my house, huh?"

"Yeah."

I waited until I heard Kia's light snore before I got up, grabbed my cell, and went in the bathroom. I called Church.

"What's good, baby boy?" he asked when he answered.

"Ain't shit. What time do you get out of church, tomorrow?"

"I usually go to both services and lead the choir, but if you need me, I can just go to the morning service."

"And what time is that over?" I asked.

"I should be able to leave about one o'clock. Why, what's on the agenda?"

"It's work call."

"A'ight, then. Call me tomorrow at one and I'll come and scoop you. We can go from there."

"That's a bet, slim. Love ya, big boy."

"Love you, too. Gone."

Chapter Twenty-Six
KEMIE

Buzzzzzzzzz . . .

"Who is it?"

"It's me, bitch. Let me in the building."

Click!

I made it through the lobby of Marlbury Plaza successfully without having to fend off the overly aggressive thugs that loitered there selling drugs. The Plaza is a nice place, but no matter how luxurious a building may be, niggas in Southeast never fail to bring down the property value.

Bitch, you are such a hypocrite. Both of the men you love are parasitic niggas that live off the 'hood. "Judge not, lest you be judged," I muttered to myself as I stepped on the elevator. A few seconds later, I was knocking on Reesie's door.

"Take them shoes off, whore," Reesie said at the door and then let me in.

Reesie had a serious hang up about people dirtying up her living room carpet. *Ain't nobody tell your ass to get no*

cream colored carpet put on the floor. I stepped out of my Dior heels, picked them up and entered the world according to Reesie. Reesie and I are the same age, height, and build, but she's a little thicker than me. We've always been close. I've cried on her shoulders so many times that a few of her shirts have permanent discolorations from my tears. Reesie was the only person in my life that knew all of my business. In many ways, she knew me better than I knew myself.

"Your fake wannabe Erykah Badu ass kill me. Don't you know all that candle burning shit is over with? This is the millennium of the Diva. The ladies run this muthafucka. We big pimpin' 'round here. Ain't no more 'Cater to you' we on some independent five star chick shit. You heard Trina on that Yo Gotti remix. You heard Nicki Minaj. You heard Candy Redd and nem'. Get with it, bitch."

"Whatever, whore. You the only one big pimpin' 'round here. Where Khadafi at?"

I plopped down on one of Reesie's couches and put one leg under me. "He at home. The hospital released him early, so he came home today."

"You ain't mad at him no more?" Reesie asked as she sat down across from me.

"Naw. I deserved it."

"Stupid ass hooker. You do some of the stupidest shit sometime and you be making me mad as shit, but don't ever belittle yourself enough to believe that you deserved to have a nigga throw shit in your face. You a better bitch than me. I swear to God, I'da killed that nigga as soon as he

went to sleep. Love is a bad muthafucka. The shit we put up with."

"I'm not saying that I deserved that per se, I'm just taking responsibility for what I did."

"You came clean to him?"

"Yeah. At the hospital, we had a long talk and I came clean about everything."

"You told Khadafi's crazy ass about Phil?"

"Do I look crazy for real? Of course not. I told him that I went out with a dude that I used to be friends with, and that me and the dude is real cool. He asked me why I kept the dude a secret and I gave him that look like—you know why I kept him a secret."

"And he went for that lame shit?"

"I think so. He ain't say nothing else about it after I came clean with the watered down version."

"So you gon' keep playin' with fire, huh?"

"I'm like an addict tryna wean myself off drugs. I been in rehab for the whole week Khadafi was gone. I haven't seen Phil, but—"

"I knew there was a *but* coming. But what?"

"I'm seeing him tomorrow. Football Sunday. The Redskins play Dallas tomorrow; I'm goin' over his house to watch the game. We got a big bet on the game. The loser has to pay up immediately after."

"What y'all betting? Then again—I don't even wanna know. I know how your freaked out ass get down." Reesie got up and went into the kitchen. Seconds later, I heard pots and pans clanking.

"I need you to cover for me," I said and braced myself for the tongue lashing that I knew was coming.

"Cover for you how, Kemie?" Reesie called out from the kitchen.

"I told Khadafi that me and you going out to Leesburg to the outlets. If you talk to TJ, you gotta tell TJ the same thing and then act like me and you together. That's all."

"That's all? Bitch, that's a whole lot. What if I wanted to lay in with my baby tomorrow? I gotta give that up because you wanna run around with Phil?"

"This the last time, Reesie, I swear. Do this for me and I'll never ask you to do that again."

"Damn, whore, get up off your knees begging and shit. You sound like the female Keith Sweat. I'ma do this for you one last time, but no more. Do you hear me?" Reesie said, coming out of the kitchen with two heaping plates of food. "These leftovers be tasting better days after you first cooked 'em. Here." Reesie handed me a plate and sat down. She dug into her food.

"I respect your gangsta, girl, I swear I do. And don't never get it fucked up—it's definitely gangsta because you playing with a burning inferno. You know like I know how Khadafi get down. Boyfriend cold-blooded. If he catch you and Phil together or even find out the depth of y'all relationship, he gon' kill both of y'all. He don't give a fuck."

"He ain't gon' find out. Women are the best cheaters, boo. We don't make the mental and physical mistakes that

niggas make. But you wouldn't know because you don't even cheat on TJ. That's sad."

"Don't even mention him no more please," Reesie said and exhaled.

"What he do now?"

"Nothing. That's the thing. He got me on some homie/lover/friend shit. All this time we been together, he's never told me how he feels about me. We laugh, we joke, we talk, we go out, we argue and fight, we break up, get back together and then—nothing. I've done everything I can to show him how I feel about him—everything except anal sex."

"A-a-a-ah-h! Therein lies the problem. Bitch, are you crazy or just plain dumb? That might be it, right there. You ain't givin' that black nigga that phat' ol' ass," I said and laughed.

"Fuck you, Kemie." Reesie laughed, too.

"Reesie, bitch, I'm serious as shit. We livin' in them days. These niggas out here gotta have that shit. I don't know what it is about that shit, but when you give a nigga that ass, it's a wrap. Why you think I can't get rid of the two I got?"

"Hold up—pump your brakes," Reesie said, putting her plate down on the table. "You gave Phil that ass back in the day and he still dumped your ass and went back to his baby mother."

"Okay. Fine. That mean she gave him some ass, too, and hers probably was a little better than mine. I couldn't

work my shit back then. Now, I throw this ass back like a porn star."

"So you telling me that if I give TJ some ass, he gon' miraculously commit to me?"

"That's exactly what I'm saying. That and suck his dick like you ain't got no tonsils or gag reflexes." We both laughed at that. Then we both ate in silence for a few minutes.

"Kemie?"

"Huh?"

"Do you love Khadafi?"

"With all my heart."

"Do you love Phil?"

"I think so, yeah."

"I know Khadafi loves you, that goes without saying, but does Phil love you?"

I gave Reesie's question some thought. "Honestly, I think so, but I really don't know. Why?"

"Just curious. What you doing when you leave here?"

"Picking Khadafi up and going to the movies."

"To see what?"

"That new movie called 2012."

"2012?"

"Yeah. It's a movie that everybody been talkin' bout based on the belief that the world is coming to an end December 20, 2012."

"I'm cool on all that shit. I'm still plane-shy fuckin' with that Y2K scare. All I wanna know is—if the world is on schedule to end on the 20th of December 2012, whose time

zone is it on? It's a new day overseas before it is over here. So do we die on the 19th?"

I got up and walked my plate to the kitchen. I dumped what was left on my plate in the trash and put the plate in the sink. "Let me get the fuck outta here and go pick up my husband." I grabbed my heels and walked to the door. "I gotta be on my best behavior for the rest of the evening and then fuck Khadafi real good, so he won't look for me tomorrow. Don't forget to cover for me."

Reesie followed me to the door. "I said I got your burnt out ass. Hey—do you really think if I gave TJ my tightest hole that would make him want me more?"

"I'd bet money on it. Try it and see. I love you bitch. Bye."

"Two tickets to see 2012," Khadafi said when we reached the front of the ticket counter. He paid for both tickets and led me into the theater. "You want something from over there before we go in?" he asked, pointing at the concession stand.

I looked in the direction of the stand and said, "I want some nachos with chili and cheese and a Sprite."

As Khadafi walked over to the stand and got in line, I looked behind me and saw a familiar face in line waiting to buy a ticket. And he wasn't alone. "Boo, I'm goin' to the restroom, I'll be back in a minute."

The restroom was empty except one woman that was leaving out. I walked into one of the stalls, wiped the seat off, and sat down. Reaching into my purse, I pulled out my cell phone and made a call.

"Hello? It's me, bitch . . . yeah, we at the movies. But we ain't the only ones. You better hurry up and give TJ some ass and fast, cause bitch you losing him. What? Why do I say that? Because he at the movies, too. No, he ain't alone. He with a bitch and I ain't on pussy, but if I was—do you catch my drift?"

The movie turned out to be pretty good. I enjoyed it. I told Khadafi that as we exited the movie theater and walked to the truck.

"It was a'ight. But I don't believe it," Khadafi stated.

"Why not?"

"Because Allah says that he's the only one that knows the hour and day that the end is coming. Fuck I'ma believe some Indians for? That shit contradicts Islam."

"Well, speaking of contradicting Islam, can you please do something for me tonight that you ain't supposed to?"

"And what's that?"

"I know I'ma kafir and all that, but can you please eat this pussy for me? Then I want you to fuck me in my ass until I cum about three times. Can you do that for me?"

"I think I can help you out."

"Thank you," I said and started my truck. But I didn't pull off. I couldn't, I was too horny. I pulled Khadafi's dick out of his sweatpants. "I wanted to do this in the theater, but the movie got good. Lean your seat back a little bit and enjoy this show."

THE ULTIMATE SACRIFICE II
LOVE IS PAIN

The next afternoon . . .

The Redskins were down 27-3 in the third quarter with one minute left and I was mad as shit. Donovan McNabb, the Redskins starting quarterback threw two interceptions that were returned for touchdowns. Then Clinton Portis fumbled the ball at the Redskins own seventeen yard line which led to a Cowboys' field goal. The following kick off, Brandon Banks muffed a catch that set Dallas up on the Skins thirteen yard line. Two plays later, they scored. That gave Dallas a 27-0 lead. De'Angelo Hall intercepted Tony Romo and that led to a Redskins field goal. 27-3.

"You ready to concede that this game is over?"

I scowled at Phil and wanted to fight. "Where they do that at? It's a whole quarter of football left," I answered, trying to hold on to the last little bit of my dignity.

"Kem, you know good and well that them bum ass Dead Skins ain't coming back. They can barely score. This shit over with."

"Boy, you must be crazy. Y'all ain't did shit on offense. Every point y'all got we gave y'all."

"Gave us? Hmph. Y'all ain't gave us shit, we took it. Terrence Newman picked bum ass McNabb off twice. Big Demarcus Ware hit Clinton Portis soft ass and he coughed the ball up. You know the rest. Them Cowboys like that. I won the bet."

"Whatever. I ain't lost until the game clock reads 0:00."

"A'ight, have it your way with your stubborn ass."

Twenty minutes later, the game was over and the reality of what I lost came crashing down on me. The Redskins

lost 37-6 and I was about to do something that I had never done before in my life. I wanted so badly to renege on Phil, but a bet was a bet. One that I agreed to because I really believed that the Redskins would win the game at home with the crowd, the momentum, and me behind them. But they lost and now it was time for me to pay up. *Fuck it. I'ma real bitch and real bitches do real shit. Bring that shit on.*

"When you wanna do it?" I asked. Phil couldn't stop smiling.

"Today. That's what we agreed on. What's up?"

"Well, handle your business. I'ma be in the shower. Come get me when you ready."

Undressed and standing, looking in the mirror, I thought about my life and Phil. Then something Reesie asked me yesterday came to mind: *" . . . but does Phil love you?"*

I thought about the fact that Phil never really told me what he felt about me. I thought about the fact that he was still fucking his baby mother. I knew that because I followed him one day when he went and got her. They ended up at the Ramada in Camp Springs. I thought about the fact that Phil probably had a rack of other bitches, too. Lastly, I thought about the fact that all Phil and I did was fuck. That's it. Could there be love involved? I jumped in the shower and lost myself in thought. The knock on the door broke my reverie.

"What?"

"We ready."

THE ULTIMATE SACRIFICE II
LOVE IS PAIN

Got damn! Where was that nigga at the whole time? In the parking lot? He got here fast as shit. "I'm coming out now," I said.

"... but does Phil love you?"

I walked naked into the bedroom and saw both Phil and his man standing on different sides of the room playing with their dicks. I had agreed to a ménage á trois if I lost the bet. As I walked over to Dino, the question came to mind again.

"... but does Phil love you?"

I dropped to my knees in front of Dino, grabbed his dick, and licked the length of it. That question echoed in my head over and over. Finally, I whispered to myself, "He can't love me." Then my mouth was full of a strange man.

Chapter Twenty-Seven
KHADAFI

*T*he six keys of cocaine and one brick of dope filled the bag out that I had it in. That bag sat under my seat as I waited for La La to pull up. I eyed the parking lot of the Pancake House on Branch Avenue and wondered what was taking La so long. Just as I was about to call him, I spotted La La's triple black Nissan 370ZX coming down the street. It stopped, signaled, and turned into the parking lot. La got out the car, looked around, and then walked over to my truck.

"Ay, cuz, how your big 6'2" ass fit in that little ass car is crazy as shit," I said as soon as he got in. "Reminds me of them lil' clown cars at the circus, twelve clowns getting outta that joint."

"Nigga, fuck you. Y'all little niggas love these big trucks cause y'all dicks small. Me, nigga, I'm hanging damn near to the ground, so I can ride in lil' cars."

I laughed. "Whatever, cuz." I grabbed the bag from under the seat and passed it to La La. "That's the six joints we got from that lick and a whole brick of 'Hey baby.' Where that money at, nigga?"

La La opened the bag and counted the bricks. Satisfied that there were seven in the bag, he said, "In that little ass car you keep tryna jone on, nigga. I'll be right back."

I watched La La go to the 370Z and get a grocery bag out the backseat. He walked back over to my truck, opened the door, and handed me the bag. I opened it and saw three cereal boxes. I looked at La.

"Young nigga, the money in the three boxes. That's a hundred and eighty thousand in there. Dollar for dollar. You talked to TJ?"

"Yesterday. I'm on my way down there now to meet up with him and my man, Fat Rat."

"He told you about the book release party he tryna go to?"

"Yeah. He said Rare Essence, TCB, and a rack of bitches gon' be there. I'ma go through there. I'm goin' to cop me some all white shit tomorrow."

"That's what's up. I told Taco and nem' about the joint and he said Bullock and Rico already had tickets."

"Cuz, what's up with Rico?"

"Youngin' get money, tryna get Raphael, Fice, and Jamal outta prison."

"Where that rat nigga, Pig at that told on them boys?" I asked La.

"His hot ass out Lee County."

"On the 'pound?"

"That's what we hear. But you know how that go."

"Ain't Nehemiah out there, too?"

"Yeah, but Nick laid back. He tryna give that number back; ain't no sense in him messing with them rats. If you ain't in no position to kill them rats, youngin', you gotta leave them bad luck ass niggas alone."

"I feel you, cuz. Holla back if you find somebody that want some of that tree. I still got that shit.

"That's a bet, youngin'. Be safe," La La said, closed my door and hopped back in his little ass sports car.

My paranoia was like Spiderman's spider senses. It never failed me and now it was back. As I pulled down Seventh Street, the first thing I saw was a forest green Expedition that I'd never seen in the hood before. And to make matters worse, the dude that was up under the hood of the idle truck looked up at me as I rode by. Why? If his truck was fucked up and he was trying to fix it, his concentration would be on the truck, right? I checked my rearview mirror and saw that the baldhead dude was now putting on a black baseball cap. Then the passenger door of the truck opened. I drove at a snail's pace until I reached the block where we hang out. I tried to tell myself that I was tripping, but the passenger with the dreads that was now crossing the street behind me told me otherwise. I watched my other mirror and saw the dude with the baseball cap looking in his passenger's direction and mine. Back and forth, back and forth.

So I pulled over and parked. Then I pulled the .45 from my waist and put it under the driver's seat. It was time to pull out the big shit. I reached over and grabbed the Calico from under the passenger seat, all the while watching

Dreads coming down the street on my right side. Anger rose in my gut and I decided to cook whatever beef Dreads had with me. *I ain't ducking no rec.* Hopping out the car with the Calico out, I walked around the front of the truck and opened fire on Dreads from about a half a block away.

He dived out of my line of fire and crawled behind a parked car. I never gave him a chance to pull out. He wasn't expecting to be on the defensive. His game plan backfired. He and his man thought they had a sitting duck. But I showed them otherwise.

"Let's work!" I shouted over the hum of the spinning drum of the Calico, ready for war. I hit at the car that Dreads had crawled behind. I spotted movement across the street and saw that the dude with the baseball cap was now running to the aid of his man. He randomly let off spurts from a small machine gun. I took cover behind my truck, but reached over the hood and kept firing at the place where the two dudes had to be. Then they both came out into the street firing their weapons simultaneously. I heard the metal of my truck being chewed up, sparks were flying, and I thought about taking flight. The Calico was a beast, but no match for two automatic machine guns. Behind me, I heard footsteps. *It's over. I'm boxed in. I'm about to die.* I heard new gunshots and looked up to see that the footsteps I heard belonged to my men. TJ and Fat Rat took positions on both sides of me and we all returned fire at the two dudes. Now outmatched and outgunned, my two would-be killers fled. They ran up the block to the Expedition,

jumped in and backed it all the way up Seventh Street. We ran out into the middle of the street still firing.

"Who the fuck was that?" TJ asked me once we were safely inside Esha's house.

"I don't know, cuz," I replied, trying to place the two faces I'd seen outside just now.

"Your truck out there fucked over, dawg," Fat Rat said from across the room.

"I'm hip. Fuck that shit. A nigga can get another truck. That ain't nothin'. I'm just glad that that ain't me out there fucked over."

"What happened? Tell me from the beginning," TJ said.

I ran the whole story down, starting at me turning down Seventh Street.

"I'm starting to believe that spider sense shit you be talkin' bout. That was a close call. If you had been slippin' just a little bit---"

"I'm hip." I paced the floor for a minute and got an idea. "Tee, I need you to drop me off somewhere."

"Now? You know them people out there deep. As soon as they shut down their makeshift station and leave, they got called right back out here. The police gotta be mad as a muthafucka."

"Shit, cuz, wouldn't they be madder if my brains and shit was outside all over the sidewalk?"

"Probably so, but then again probably not. Well, as soon as the coast is clear, we outta here," TJ said and walked into the kitchen.

Fat Rat looked at me as I paced the floor and laughed. "Nigga, all your trucks get killed. If I was a truck and I saw you coming on the lot, I'd say fuck it and pull off on my own."

All I could do was smile and shake my head. Then I thought about the money I'd left in the truck and the gun under the driver's seat. TJ's gun. The cops were probably towing it as I paced. *Shit!*

I patted my pocket for my cellphone. It was there. I thought I'd left it in the truck, too. Pulling it out, I dialed Kemie's number. When the voice mail picked up, I thought about the distance from D.C. to Leesburg and decided that her phone was probably out of range. So I left her a message and told her to call me as soon as she could.

Before I could finish turning the key in the lock, the door snatched open. Marnie was on the other side of the door with a look on her face that could cause instant death.

"Gimme my damn key, nigga!" she barked as I walked past her into the living room.

"Where your laptop at?" I asked, ignoring her emotional outburst.

Marnie closed her door and stood where she was with the same look on her face. "Muthafucka, are you deaf! I said gimme my got-damn key."

"Calm down, Marnie."

"Don't tell me to calm down, Redds.

"Khadafi."

"What the fuck ever! Take your ass back to whereever you been for the last eight or nine days. Gimme my key and get the fuck outta my house. Your triflin' ass couldn't even call me? I been all down Capers lookin' for you. Where you been, Redds?"

"Khadafi," I said again calmly. Then smiled.

"You think you funny, huh? This shit funny to you? I been in here worried sick about you, nigga. You walk in here today with no explanation of where you been, then you smile in my face?"

"You been cussing me out since I came through the door. You haven't given me a chance to say shit. How am I gon' say something when you won't let me?"

Marnie took about three deep breaths. "Where you been at?"

"The hospital," I said and lifted my shirt up. "They took my shit bag off."

"I—uh—why—ooh, let me see that again." Marnie walked over to me and traced the outline of my newest scar.

"I been on so much medicine that I been out of it for days. I just got out yesterday."

"Why didn't you call me? I could've—yesterday? Where did you sleep last night?"

"At home. Kemie picked me up from the hospital and took me home," I admitted, purposely leaving out the movies and sex.

Marnie looked at me and shook her head. "So y'all back together?"

"Just because I went home and slept in my own bed doesn't mean that me and Kemie are a couple again."

"Yeah, whatever, nigga. We'll see. Why did she know where you were and I didn't? What were you saying about my laptop?"

"Go get it. I need you to access the Internet and look up something for me." Marnie went in her room and came back with a sleek lightweight Mac notebook laptop.

"What do you want me to look up?" she said and sat down at the kitchen table. I stood behind her and looked at the screen over her shoulder.

"Go to the Federal Bureau of Prisons website."

"Got it. What do you want?"

"I need you to look up a dude and see if—where he is."

"That would be inmate locator. What's his name?"

"Charles Gooding." We both watched as a list of Charles Goodings came up. "This dudes last three numbers of his fed number is 007. Put that in there."

She did. "Describe him. Age, nationality?"

"Black—about twenty-five or twenty-six."

"They got one Charles Gooding that fits—hold on—it says here that he was released from FDC Houston on the 25th of September. Is that him?"

"Yeah—that's him. Ain't that a bitch? Lil Cee is home. I forgot all about him."

"Who is Charles Gooding, Khadafi?"

"The dude that just tried to kill me."

"What? Kill you? When?" Marnie asked in rapid succession.

"Today. About three hours ago, down Capers. I was getting out my truck and he tried to sneak up on me. There was a shoot out, yada, yada, yada. He tried to kill me. I didn't recognize him. He has long dreads—he looked different."

"Why is he tryna kill you?"

I told Marnie the Beaumont story, but left out the gory details. "—he switched teams."

"Switched teams? What do you mean he switched teams?"

"He became a rat. He told on us about the murder."

"And now he's home and tryin' to kill you because he told?"

"Naw," I said with a far away look in my eyes, remembering a day almost two years ago. "He tryna kill me because I killed his family. When Ameen took the murder beef so that we could come home, I promised my men that I was gonna kill Lil Cee's family. I was the first one out of three of us to go home. The same day I got home, I went to his mother's house and killed everybody in there."

I looked at Marnie and I saw the look of confusion on her face. It was almost as if she could now see the beast that lived in me. "He must've figured out that I am the one that killed his family. Now he wants revenge."

"What are you gonna do?"

"What am I gonna do? I'ma trap me a rat and kill him. That's what I'ma do."

I walked back to Marnie's living room and paced the floor again. If Lil Cee was home, then that meant he had

already testified against Ameen. The Feds wouldn't have released him until he helped them, would they? And if Lil Cee went to court and lied on Ameen, that would put Ameen on death row in Terre Haute. Or at least he'd be in ADX by now. Depending on his sentence. "Marnie, I need you to go back to that Fed site and put another name in." I gave her all of Ameen's info and waited for her reply.

"It says here that Antonio Felder is not in the BOP. He's in transit. What does that mean?"

I gave that question some thought as I paced the floor. *He's in transit. If Ameen ain't in the BOP, but he's in transit—where the hell is he?*

Chapter Twenty-Eight
DETECTIVE TOLLIVER

The P90X workout DVD turned out to be the best workout program that I had come across thus far. It was strenuous and intense and that's exactly what my body needed to try to block out everything going on in the streets. My inability to gain any ground on the case I worked on had me in a mental slump. After almost twenty-two years on the force, I was seriously starting to contemplate retirement. Tired and drenched in sweat, I clicked the big screen TV off, picked up my SOBE Lifewater, and downed it. Then I left the basement and headed upstairs to the shower.

As I walked past my bedroom's open door, I caught movement out the corner of my eye. "Ain't nobody here but me. I'm trippin'," I said to myself. But I always erred on the side of caution, so I backpedaled and peered into the bedroom.

"Hey baby. I've been waiting patiently for you." The totally naked woman lying across my bed said, "I need my medicine."

THE ULTIMATE SACRIFICE II
LOVE IS PAIN

A smile crossed my face as I stood in the bedroom door frame. Dollicia Stewart was the newest contestant on my version of the reality show *The Bachelor*. In my line of work, it was hard to find a woman who could deal with my profession and the crazy hours that it took to fight crime. But Dollicia was different. She went with the program and never complained when we hardly saw each other. I guess that was one of the reasons why I gave her a key to my home. That and the fact that the twenty-nine-year-old realtor and real estate appraiser was the spitting image of Christina Milian. And I love me some Christina Milian. Not only was Dollicia a drop dead gorgeous youngsta, she made three times what I made as a cop, yearly. She owned four properties in and around the DMV, drove a convertible CLK500 Benz, dressed impeccably, and was very intelligent. But the biggest asset about Dollicia was her desire to be a total freak in the bedroom. What more could a man ask for?

"How long have you been here waiting?" I asked.

"About forty minutes. I called your cell phone, and since I was in the area I decided to drive past and see if you were home. My libido started jumping when I saw your truck outside. I let myself in and wondered where you were. I peeped down the basement stairs and saw you working out. I knew you had to come to the shower, so I decided to surprise you. Surprise!"

My eyes were riveted to Dollicia's body. Her golden brown skin was flawless. She had a single red rose tattooed down her left leg and thorny vines inked around both

ankles. Her fingers and toes were painted a bright shade of red. Her pussy was shaved completely bald. Dollicia got off the bed and did a seductive dance over to where I stood. She ran her hand across the sweat on my chest. Then she tugged at my gym shorts and pulled them down. "I was on my way to the shower. Would you care to join me?"

"Has anybody ever told you that you look like Boris Kudjoe with hair?" Dollicia asked as she then removed my boxer briefs.

As I watched Dollicia kiss all over my dick, I couldn't believe my luck at forty years old, I was blessed to look thirty and my twice weekly intense workouts kept my body toned and muscular. My head full of unruly jet-black curls I inherited from my father. At six-foot-two, 220 pounds solid, with a Colgate smile, women always compared me to Boris Kodjoe. "I get that a lot. So how about we shower first? I am a little sweaty." Dollicia tongued my erect dick from the position on her knees. She looked up at me. "Did you know that in Thailand, the natives believe that a human body secretion, specifically sweat is a natural aphrodisiac? Sweat is made up of water, hormones, harmless bacteria and a few other things that are seen as stimulants. There they drink sweat."

"I had no idea," I responded meekly.

"Well, it's true. And I believe that we Americans should at least try it before we knock it. Plus, I need my medicine and I can't wait a minute longer." The next thing I knew Dollicia was stroking my dick while tonguing both of my sweat soaked balls.

THE ULTIMATE SACRIFICE II
LOVE IS PAIN

Closing my eyes, I surrendered and got caught up in the moment. Dollicia gave my nuts a virtual tongue bath and then put my dick in her mouth. She greedily sucked on me as if her very existence depended on the semen she was waiting to swallow. I leaned back on the door frame and again, I couldn't believe my luck. I had lived to be forty years old, avoided going to prison, lived a pretty good life, and had a woman who believed that an every day dose of semen was better than a multivitamin.

"And where exactly in the world is it that women believe that cum is the best medicine to take daily?"

Dollicia looked up at me and then pulled my dick out of her mouth. "All over the world, baby, all over the world."

"Now, tell me again, why this should interest me, Donnie? Ain't nobody dead out here, so why am I here," I asked as I got out my car and approached the man on the sidewalk.

Donnie Salsburg was a detective in the Violent Crimes Branch that I went through the academy with. He'd called me a few hours earlier and told me to come to Seventh Street in the Caper Projects area.

"There was a shootout here earlier. Multiple guns involved. We have no suspects in custody and nobody was hurt as far as we know. While investigating, I was able to coax a few reluctant witnesses into talking. I have three names. One of those names is the reason that I called you here."

As we walked down the street, Donnie pointed out possible positions of the shooters as they shot it out in

broad daylight. We passed several cars that had bullet holes. Shell casings lined the middle of the street. I silently said a prayer of thanks because no children or innocent bystanders were killed. And for some reason that only God knows, kids, women, and innocent bystanders always end up being the victims of drive by shootings and shootouts.

Donnie stopped at a government flatbed truck that a bullet-riddled midnight blue Infiniti SUV was being loaded on.

"This truck—according to one of the witnesses pulled onto the block and shortly thereafter two men approached and the man driving the truck opened fire on the two men. They all exchanged gunfire–two against one until two other men joined the gun battle. All of the men hang in the house behind us down the block. The house is owned by Ronesha Lake. We searched the truck and found a bag fulla money and a gun. The man that was driving this truck is a real piece of shit. We're investigating him for all kinds of shit. The muthafucka is a real urban terrorist and he even has the nickname to prove it. He goes by the name Khadafi—as in the Libyan dictator—"

"I know who Moammar Gadhafi is, Donnie." I wished he'd hurry up and get to the point.

"Our Khadafi's government name is Luther Fuller. I've been knowing this piece of shit and his uncle for years. Anyway, Khadafi killed a guy in his father's barbershop about thirteen years ago. He did ten years in prison and got out about two years ago. He was called Dirty Redds back then. We believe that he was involved in the murders at the

Rec a few weeks ago and that links him to your Canal Street murders. Another name that we have is Donnell Hunter, also known as Fat Rat. He was one of the shooters. And the last name is Tyrone Carter also known as TJ."

At the mention of the name TJ, Donnie suddenly had my full attention. "Last week you asked me about a TJ, but my mind was elsewhere. Today when his name came up, I decided to give you a call. You said that you have info that TJ was involved in both of your cases; I'm saying that Khadafi was involved. My Khadafi has a buddy named TJ. How much do you wanna bet that this TJ and your TJ are one and the same?"

I thought back to the day I talked to Nomeka Fisher about her brother, Woozie's murder. According to her, the word she had was that a dude named TJ from up Capers was involved in both cases—the Canal Street murders and the Recreation Center murders. "Tell me everything you know about TJ."

"I'ma do you one better, Mo. I'ma send you a file on TJ, and everybody that he hangs with. How's that?"

"That would be marvelous, Donnie. I owe you one."

"Nail these muthafuckas for me, Mo, and I'll owe you one."

Chapter Twenty-Nine
AMEEN

I opened my eyes just as the wheels of the 767 jumbo plane kissed the tarmac. The hangars on the ground off the runway read Harrisburg National Guard. I was back at the place where my federal ride started almost ten years ago. The plane pulled to a complete stop and several vans and buses converged on it.

"When I call your name, step to the front of the plane." The U.S. Marshall said over the airplane's address system. "Give me your first name and register number.... Duval . . . Benson . . . Montana . . . Ackwith . . . Johnson . . . Felder."

I stood up, scooted past the other two prisoners that were on my row, and walked up the aisle.

When I got up front, I said, "Antonio. 16945016." The marshal pointed at the door and I exited the plane. On the ground, I was led to a waiting van that read D.C. Department of Corrections. Just the sight of those words gave me goosebumps. I was on my way home to D.C. and I still couldn't believe it.

Two hours later, we were in town and all the familiar sights brought back memories. My face was glued to the

window. I stared in amazement at all the buildings and stores that weren't there when I left D.C. years ago. The Nation's Capital had changed a lot in my absence. But the one thing that hadn't changed was the reddish brown four-story behemoth building at 1901 D Street, Southeast, the D.C. jail.

"Felder, what's your D.C. number?" the CO asked me as I stripped out of my clothes in front of the black table in R and D.

"I been in the Feds ten years, I don't even remember my D.C. number."

He went through some papers, then said, "254084. Remember it. Step back . . . hands . . . lift your arms . . . nuts . . . turn around . . . a'ight. Go in the back, get your towel, and care package, then hit that shower. Next man."

The whole intake process took about four hours and I was tired as hell. I was ready to lie down. "CO, where y'all got me goin' at?"

"The same place everybody goin', the intake block," the young cop said as he led us through the halls. "Northside!" At the grill of Northwest three, the young cop said, "Northwest! One gate. Y'all got seven coming in."

A dyke looking female CO came out of the control bubble and grabbed our face cards from the young cop. She took them in the bubble and wrote on them, then came back.

"Duvall and Benson, y'all in thirty-three cell on the bottom left. Johnson and Montana, forty-one cell . . . right up there," she said and pointed. "Patterson, you in nine cell

on the top left. Felder and Ackwith, Y'all in seventy-eight cell on the bottom right."

In the cell, I turned to my celly and said, "What's your name, slim?" I needed to know who I was in a cell with. For all I knew the government might've planted the dude.

"Antoine Ackwith," he replied. "But they call me Fice."

"Oh yeah? Where you from in the city, Fice?"

"Montana Terrace, Brentwood, that whole area. You?"

"Sheridan Terrace. Where you coming from?"

"The SMU program in Lewisburg."

"Yeah? What they got you in that joint for?" I asked.

"We got into it with the Louisiana niggas down Pollock. One of them pervert niggas was jacking his dick off on this bitch and the homie walked up and seen the dick. It was work call after that."

I had heard about the situation in Pollock with D.C. and Louisiana. "Who else they sent to the SMU with you?"

"They sent about ten of us." He paused. "Let me see— me, Block, Lasmooth, Tye, Scoop, Lil Cain, Mansoo, Outta sight Mike, Lil Eric Weaver, and a Baltimore homie named Player."

Satisfied that Fice was official, I started cleaning the cell. I was on my hands and knees scrubbing the floor when the dyke CO came to the cell.

"Which one of y'all, Felder?" she asked.

"That's me," I said and stood up. "What's up?"

"Pack your bedroll back up, they coming to get you."

"Coming to get me for what and take me where?"

"They'll tell you when they get here. Ay, Sarge, pop seventy-eight cell. Come on, Felder."

"Be cool, slim," I said to my celly, wiped my hands on my jumper, grabbed my bedroll and left the cell.

In the sallyport, five minutes later, a white shirted lieutenant appeared at the grill. I recognized him instantly. "Worthy?"

He looked at me closely, smiled, and said, "Tonio, what's up, nigga?"

We shook hands and embraced. "Worthy, you a lieutenant, now, huh?"

"You know how it go. I'm just here. How you been?"

"I'm good, slim. Got back in court, so here I am. Man, what they talkin' 'bout? The broad said you coming to get me. What's up?"

"I didn't even pay the picture and shit no mind. Nigga, you know why they sent me to get you. You ain't supposed to be in population. They got on here to put you on status."

"For what?"

"Your track record, nigga. These people up here scared of you. They ain't tryna have you killing nobody in this jail. You don't wanna be out here anyway. Grab your stuff and come on, I'll tell you about it on the way to South One."

Worthy told me about all the inmates that were setting up the COs for the Feds, all the rats that ran the blocks, the dudes who smuggled a gun into the jail, shot each other and then told on one another. He told how the Feds got niggas to go through your mail while you ain't in the cell and all kinds of wicked shit.

I shook my head and said, "You right. I don't wanna be in open pop' if they doin' all that."

"Times have changed a lot, but don't worry about nothing. I takes good care of all the throw back niggas. South One is my unit. I got you. You ain't gon' want for nothing."

"I 'preciate it, Worthy."

"It's all good. Go 'head and lay back for the rest of the day and I'ma pull you out in the morning and put you on the phone."

That night I lay in my cell and thought about the letter I got a day before I left Texas. It was signed 'You know who'. And I did know who it was. I had been right all along when I told myself that Lil Cee blamed me for his mother and sister's deaths. The look that I saw in his eyes in court that day, I'd read it perfectly. But not only did he want Khadafi and me dead, Lil Cee wanted our families dead as well. *Eye for an eye.* All of my assumptions were on point. Lil Cee was behind the deaths of both of my brothers. He wanted to hurt me by killing them.

Did you cry when you heard they were dead? Does it hurt to lose two loved ones at the same time? Do you feel the pain right there in the middle of your chest?

I wanted so badly to taunt him and let him know that I felt no pain. But the letter had no return address. I wanted to write him and tell him that he was wrong about me and that I had nothing to do with his family being killed. I wanted to write him and let him know that his anger and thirst for retribution was misplaced. I wanted to let him

know that if he harmed a hair on either of my daughter's heads, I would not die until I killed everybody in his bloodline. He had to know that, to understand that . . .

Still trying to locate your daughters and baby mother so that I can stop by and visit.

All of a sudden, me sending Umar to Shawnay's house turned out to be a stroke of genius. At the time, I was hurt, angry, and emotional. I reacted rashly and somehow it cost Umar his life. But Shawnay still had her life for whatever reason and she would have it a while longer. Whatever Umar did or said to Shawnay the night he was killed a block away from her house, had spooked her. Spooked her enough to never contact me again and move from the house on Fifty-Sixth Street. By moving away when she did, she saved her life and the lives of my daughters. Without even knowing it. I was thankful for that. Had Umar not spooked her—I don't even want to think about it. I just hoped that Shawnay had moved far enough away that no one would find them. I wondered if Khadafi had seen Shawnay and had he told her what I did to him in Texas. For some reason I doubted that he had. I thought about the straight out phone calls that Worthy was going to give me tomorrow. I thought about the people that I wanted to call. It was time for me to reach out to a few folks. Shawnay included.

"Press nine and then dial straight out," Worthy said and left the office.

I called my stepmother, Poochie and talked to her for a while. She sounded excited about me being back in D.C.

and being back in court. I told her my visiting days and visiting hours and she promised to visit soon. Then I called a few other relatives and gave them my news. The last call that I had to make was the one that put the queasiness in my stomach. I didn't have a number for Shawnay and the girls, but I did have one for Shawnay's grandmother. So I called her.

She picked up on the third ring. "Hello?"

"How you doin' Mrs. Dickerson?"

"I'm fine. Who is this?" she asked.

"Antonio."

"Antonio, who?"

"Asia and Kenya's father, Mrs. Dickerson."

"Ohhh! How you doin', baby? You still in jail?"

"Yeah, I'm still in jail, Mrs. Dickerson," I said and laughed. "But I'm good. I'm tryna get in touch with my daughters. Can you give me a number for them?"

"Chile, both of them daughters of yours got cell phones. Asia ain't but eleven, but that chile is eleven goin' on twenty-one. She love them computers. Knows everything there is to know about 'em. And Kenya is grown as hell, too. She a beautiful girl and she know it, too. Got them lil' boys calling her momma house all times of the day and night. Them girls look just like you, boy. When you coming home, chile?"

"I don't know, Mrs. Dickerson."

"Well, baby, I'm praying for you. Let me get them numbers for you . . . hold on, baby."

My heart pounded in my chest. I was seconds away from being reconnected to the three people I loved with all my heart.

"—hello? Antonio?"

"I'm here, Mrs. Dickerson."

"Let me see here . . . Kenya's number is 202-280-1883. Asia's number is 202-423-6670 and Shawnay's cell number is 202-523-3780. The house number is 703-678-1962. You got all that, baby?"

"I got it. Thank you, Mrs. Dickerson and you take care of yourself, okay?" I said and wrote the numbers down.

"I will, baby. You do the same, and you keep in touch more, all right?"

"A'ight, bye."

Glancing at the clock on the wall, I saw that it was a few minutes after 11A.M. I knew that Shawnay was at work and that my daughters were in school. But since Kenya was in high school, they had to be out for lunch, right now. I held my breath and dialed Kenya's cell phone.

Ring. Ring. Ring. Ring.

"Hello?"

I exhaled and smiled all at the same time. "Kenya?"

"This me. Who is this?"

"Your father."

"Stop playing, whoever you are, and tell me who this is."

I laughed a deep laugh. My oldest child recognized it.

"Oh . . . my . . . gawd! Daddy?"

"It's me, baby."

A NOVEL BY ANTHONY FIELDS

My daughter started crying. And so did I.

Chapter Thirty
KHADAFI

I went directly to the 3900 block of S Street with a little hope that although his family was killed in the house there, Lil Cee would possibly be there. As soon as I got there, I saw that the house was boarded up. The yard was terribly unkept. The house was a stepchild that nobody wanted. Then I rode to his old stomping grounds and cruised the neighborhood. Parkland Projects was a dangerous place to come through, but what the fuck. Danger has always been my middle name. I wanted to find Lil Cee and find him fast. There would be no more Money episodes. No more cat and mouse games. Tit for tat killings. None of that. I wanted Lil Cee dead yesterday, and the fact that I couldn't find him was making me mad. And when I get mad, I kill people. Since Parkland is only five minutes from Congress Park, I decided to ride through and kill one of Ameen's brothers, just for the fuck of it. I drove through the circle on Thirteenth Place and spotted my man, Don Samuels.

Jumping out the Caddy, I walked up to Don and gave him a pound.

"Cuz, what's up with you?"

"Ain't shit, moe. What's up?"

"I'm looking for my man, Squirt that be around here. You seen him?"

"Black Squirt? Antonio and Buck brother?" Don asked.

"Yeah. He out here?"

"Squirt dead, moe. He got killed around the corner about two weeks ago. Then his brother, Buck got killed the same day."

I was taken aback by what I had just heard. Then it all made sense to me. Lil Cee. Lil Cee came straight home and killed Ameen's brothers. He was fucked up about his mother and sister and blamed Ameen and me. He went at Ameen's brothers first, then came at me. Lil Cee was more gangsta than I gave him credit for. A gangsta rat. *Like Monyay, Pappy, Lee Lee and Oscar.* "Damn, that's fucked up, cuz. I ain't even know that. That's crazy. I'ma bout to bounce, cuz. You take it easy."

"You too, moe. Stay up."

"It's a lot of strange shit goin' on, cuz," I said to TJ as we walked up and down the Cadillac car lot in Greenbelt. "It seem like it's always something with me. I keep a muthafucka gunning for my head."

"When you live the fast life that shit don't never slow down until you're dead or in prison. This what we signed up for, slim. We both lost our peoples to this shit. Your mother didn't deserve to be killed over a nigga's stash. And then they find out that she ain't even take the shit. My

father and nem' didn't deserve that shit. They weren't in the life at all. Muthafuckas killed my family over some money. Hatin' ass, jealous hearted niggas that was too lazy to get out there and get it, took my family and my soul 'bout some money. That shit changed me, slim. It made me an animal. I signed up for this gangsta shit and I'ma live it 'til I die."

"Yeah, cuz, you right. This is the life we live, huh?" I stopped at a row of Escalades and checked them out. I peered inside a black one, spotted the black leather interior, wood grain paneling, and all the features of the 2010 Cadillac Escalade, and fell in love. "This the one right here."

We left TJ's car parked at the car dealer and I drove my new truck out to Tyson's Corner Mall.

"You see them new Gucci tennis shoes that just came out?" TJ asked me as we made our way through Neiman Marcus, headed to Saks Fifth Avenue.

"That bamma ass nigga, Kanye West had them joints on in a magazine I saw. I want them joints."

"Slim, fuck all that shit. I keep it simple. I been there, done that with all that shit. Way before niggas knew who Kanye was. I'ma cop me some Kenneth Cole joints and call it a day."

"I brought you to the wrong mall, then, huh cuz?"

"Pretty much. We can hit Iverson Mall and get something for me. I can do Up Against The Wall."

"Up Against the Wall? Not me. Not at gunpoint. I been graduated from that shit. Don't nobody shop at that joint but a muthafucka that go to Howard University."

In Saks, I found some Louis Vuitton white linen slacks, a white Louis T-shirt and an all white, button up, linen shirt with gold buttons. We walked over to the shoe section.

"How you gon' cop the Gucci joints, slim and your whole fit Louis V?"

"You right, cuz. I'ma get these Louis loafers right here." "Aye, sweetheart, can I get these right here in a size nine? As a matter of fact, bring the nine and the nine and a half."

My cell phone vibrated. It was Kemie.

"What's up?" I said into the phone.

"The police, that's what's up. A detective by the name of Maurice Tolliver been calling me all day."

"For what?"

"For what? The truck. Duh? The one fulla gunshot holes right now. The one that your Aunt Mary made me cosign for. The one with all the money in it."

"They got the money." I said and shook my head. "I was hoping they didn't get it."

"As soon as I mention money, you know what I'm talkin' bout. How much money did they get out the truck?" Kemie asked.

"How much they said they had?" I replied.

"He didn't. Because I didn't talk to him. He called my mother's house and left a message. That's the number I put

~ 212 ~

on the bill of sales when I co-signed. All she said he said was something about me coming to claim the money."

"I hate to say it, but fuck that money. They tryna trick a muthafucka. I know they found that gun in there. They can keep that one-eighty."

"One-eighty? They want me to come all the way downtown to claim a hundred and eighty dollars?"

"Who said anything about—hold on—yeah, just sit them right there so I can try `em on—yeah-thanks—who said anything about a hundred and eighty dollars?"

"You did. Where you at?"

"Out Tyson's shoppin' and I was talkin' 'bout a hundred and eighty thousand. That's what the police got out the truck."

"What? Boy, I'm goin' to get that money."

"No you ain't. How you gon explain it? Your job don't pay you that type of money if you worked there for three years straight. Fuck that money. Easy come, easy go. Let me get off this phone so I can try these shoes on. I'ma call you back."

"You better. I love you."

"Love you, too."

"Sucka for love ass, nigga," TJ teased.

"Call me what you want, but don't call me for fronts, Southside got what you want—come holla at me," I rapped as I tried on the shoes and decided on the size nine.

Chapter Thirty-One
LIL CEE

I lay on my bunk at the halfway house and thought about two things—Kia and Khadafi. Some people say that our lives are defined by our wins, our losses, and how we deal with them. Over the last few days, I'd definitely won and lost. I'd lost my biggest advantage in my war with Khadafi. The element of surprise. He had to have recognized me. That was the only explanation for why he anticipated my move and turned the tables on me. I thought I had a sitting duck, but it turned out that my sitting duck became an attacking pitbull. And I had almost lost my life—bullshitting. I knew that Khadafi was a worthy adversary and still underestimated him. Killing Ameen's brothers and getting away with it had made me a little too over confident. It was time to bring it down a notch while still strategically planning my next move. The next fight I took to him couldn't be on his turf. That's something I should've learned from history. The greatest wars are lost when you fight on your opponent's home field. I would have to catch Khadafi in a neutral zone. And his vehicle would also be different since his Infiniti truck didn't survive the gun battle

on Seventh Street. And I'd also lost momentum. He'd almost certainly be searching for me now, too. I had to find a way to get out of the halfway house and soon. If Khadafi found out that I lived in Hope Village, I knew for sure that he'd bring the fight to this doorstep. No questions asked. It was time to chill for a minute until the playing field was a little more leveled. My revenge would come, I had to become wiser and not rush it. There was too much at stake. Too much to lose. Although my plan to have Khadafi in the ground by now didn't materialize, something else had. I'd won over Kia Ransom and gained a lot by doing that. I gained a friend, a lover, a companion that knew the struggle, an escape route. That's priceless to me and I didn't want to lose that for nothing in the world.

So again, people say that your life is defined by your wins, your losses, and how you deal with it. I won some things and I loss some things; the next question is—how do I deal with it? Now that, I don't know . . .

I rolled out the bunk and did ten sets of push-ups and ten sets of crunches. I went to the bathroom, undressed, and jumped in the shower. I pulled my cell phone out my pants pocket and called Kia.

Ring. Ring. "Hello?"

"What's up, baby?"

"Gooding?"

"Yeah?"

"I was just thinking about you."

"Sir, you need your birth certificate, social security card, and a proof of residency," the lady at the DMV counter told me once I reached the front of the line.

"Miss, I just told you, I just came home from prison. I did nine years straight. How can I have a proof of residency when I been locked up for nine years?"

"I don't know what to tell you, sir, but the rules are firm. You have to be able to establish that you are a resident of the District of Columbia before we can issue you any form of ID, learner's permit, driver's license, anything."

"But I just showed you the paper I got from the halfway house. That doesn't establish that I'm a resident of the District?"

"No. That just establishes that you are a resident of that halfway house. You can be from anywhere and get arrested in D.C. Then be released to a D.C. halfway house. You need some-"

I stepped away from the counter before I lost it and did some stupid shit. A security dude stepped to me as I got out of line.

"I heard a little bit of what you just went through. It happens all the time around here. That chick you ended up in front of is a bitch. She be with the bullshit, hard. I'ma tell you what you gotta do. Have you had a license in D.C. before?"

"Yeah, before I went to prison."

"Okay, cool. Go across the hall to room 1000 and tell them you need a copy of your license from whatever year

that was. They keep records of that shit that go back to the last twenty years. Get a copy of that and that establishes that you are a long time resident of the District."

"Thanks, slim. Good lookin' out."

"Don't mention it."

I did what I was told and thirty minutes later, I was leaving the DMV with a non-driver's permit. Church was outside asleep in his new car. After the fiasco down Capers, I thought it was best for him to get rid of the car. So he traded his Expedition in for a black Mercury Marauder. Hopping in the car woke Church up instantly. He looked at his watch. "Damn, baby boy, what took you so long?"

"Arguing with a bitch about a proof of residency." I relayed the whole story to Church. "That's what took me so long. I wanted to say 'fuck it', but I had to get it."

"Why?"

"Because I wouldn't have been able to get in."

"Get in where?"

"The all white book release party."

"What all white book release party?"

"At the Omni Shoreham Hotel. You ever been there?" I asked and reclined my seat.

"Never been there," Church said as he pulled out into traffic.

"Well, that's about to change, big boy."

"Why you say that?"

"Because I got two tickets that I got from Kia and I ain't tryna go by myself. So you goin' with me. You got an all white outfit that you can wear?"

"Of course. When is it?"

"This weekend. Saturday night."

Chapter Thirty-Two
MARNIE

Since it was my day off and I needed to talk to somebody, I ended up downtown meeting Reesie for lunch.

"I gotta stop and get me one of them bomb ass hot dogs from the vending stands down by the court building," Reesie said as we walked down Fifth Street in Northwest. "I gotta taste for that chili, cheese, and special sauce they be putting on them muthafuckas."

"Girl, you better be careful fuckin' with them foreigners and all that special sauce shit. You don't even know what they be puttin' in that shit."

"Ain't gon kill me. I done ate worse shit. Whatever it is can't be worse than all that pork shit we been eatin' for years. When was the last time you been in the room when somebody was cleaning chitlins? That's got to be the foulest, stinkiest, wildest shit I ever seen and smelled. What the fuck is Scrapple, anyway? Hoghead cheese? Fatback?"

"I have no clue."

"Me either, but I know one thing. We love that shit. I'll take them Africans special sauce over all that shit any day."

"I know that's right," I said while giggling. "You sound like Khadafi when you say shit like that. Speaking of him—that's what I wanna talk to you about."

"Marnie, you my girl and I fucks with you to the fullest, but boo, that shit is way anything. You my girl and Kemie is my cousin. I love y'all two dizzy bitches to death, but y'all blowing me with this Khadafi shit. Y'all act like that nigga is the only nigga in the city with some good dick. That nigga got both of y'all out here trippin'. Don't tell me you done caught feelings for this nigga."

I dropped my head in shame.

"Marnie, how could you be so dense? What the fuck is it about this nigga that got you two bitches losing y'all minds? You know that nigga love Kemie. I understood why you said you started fuckin' him before, but why did you start back fuckin' him this time? And you was totally unable to detach your heart from the dick, huh?"

"What can I say? I didn't plan it."

"If I didn't know you so well, I'd probably believe that. You are always blinded by your hatred for Kemie, Marnie. When it comes to her, you never think things through. You my girl and I gotta keep it real with you. This is some childish, anything shit y'all doin'. Is Khadafi the only nigga that you fuckin'?"

"I only do one dick at a time. You know that."

"So what you gon' do now?"

"I don't know. All I know is I can't leave him alone."

"You can't leave him and neither can Kemie. But she can find time to step out with Phil. You might as well fuck

Phil, too. That way you get all the way back at her on both ends."

"I'll think about it."

"All three of us are the real BWP."

"BWP? What the fuck is that?"

"Bitches with problems. All of us need some medication. What's wrong with us? We're three good lookin' females with good jobs, cars, apartments, and good credit. Why are we having so many men problems?"

"You got men problems, too? That's a new one on me."

"I just admitted it to myself. Sometimes I be so caught up in you and Kemie's bullshit that I forget that my love life is fucked up. I been dealing with TJ for so long, that it never dawned on me that I loved him until recently. And he don't even know it."

"How can he not know?" I asked.

"Because I never sat him down and told him. Men are like kids; you gotta take 'em by the hand and make them understand certain shit. They just don't pick up on it like we do. I almost told him the other day, though. After I did that other shit."

"What other shit?" I asked just as we reached the vending stand across from the court building.

"Let me get one of them turkey hot dogs with chili, cheese, and that special sauce," Reesie told the man at the stand. She looked at me. "You want one?"

"Naw, I'm good, boo. Just get me a soda. You do you."

Minutes later, we were walking back up Fifth Street.

"What was I saying?" Recsic asked with her mouth full of hot dog.

"I was asking you what other shit you did."

"Oh, that. I broke my cardinal rule and gave that nigga some ass."

I almost choked on the soda I was sipping. "You bullshittin'. You didn't give TJ no ass. Not you Ms. `I'd never do that nasty shit.'"

"Yep. I did it. I threw all caution to the wind and let that nigga fuck my ass. But you know the wild part?"

"What?"

"I came hard as shit. Scared me to death."

I laughed and spit soda all over my hands.

"Damn, bitch, look at your ass. You embarrassin' mc. Soda coming all out your nose and shit. I can't take you nowhere. Here take this," Reesie said, laughing.

She handed me a napkin. I wiped soda off my hands and face, but kept laughing.

"What's so funny, anyway?" she asked.

"Picturing you takin' that dick in your ass."

"I know, right? I probably made every ugly face in the book. The shit we go through for these niggas. And the fucked up part about it all is he didn't even appreciate that shit."

"How you know he didn't?"

"Because his actions said it all. He broke my virgin ass in, came deep in my butt, then rolled over, and went to sleep. Wasn't no, 'Are you okay?' no, 'Did I hurt you?' no nothing. I was hurt and mortified. All I could do was take a

long hot shower, soak my aching butt, and cry. The next morning, he left my house without his keys. I said to myself: 'How is he gonna drive his car without his keys?' So I slipped something on and ran down the stairs to catch him. By the time I reached the front door, he was getting into a red Infiniti coupe."

"So?"

"There was a bitch driving the car."

"Dayum!"

"Yeah, damn is right. I shouldn't have let Kemie talk me into doin' that shit, anyway. But fuck it, we live and we learn."

When we reached the building where Reesie worked, we hugged.

"I'ma call you when I get off."

"Okay. Aye, are you goin' to that all white party this weekend?" I asked curiously.

"Naw. My Rare Essence days are over with. You?" Reesie replied.

"I thought about it, but naw, I'ma sit this one out."

"Plus, I ain't tryna be in there with TJ anyway. I don't do no cock blocking."

"TJ goin', too? I should've known he was goin' with his boy."

"Who?"

"Khadafi."

Reesie stepped back out of the building's front door. "Khadafi goin' to the all white book release party? That's what you tellin' me?"

"Yeah," I said flippantly. "Why? What's the big deal?"

"He must didn't tell Kemie, then."

"Why you say that?"

"Because Kemie is supposed to be goin', too," Reesie answered and headed back through the front door.

"So? They'll just be there together. I don't care."

"Stupid ass heifer, this ain't about you. Kemie's goin' to the party with Phil."

"Dayum!"

Chapter Thirty-Three
TJ

"*P*retty girls/ ask 'em what do they know/ ask `em do they smoke/ ask `em can we go/ pretty girls/ sunshine in the air/ girls are everywhere . ."

"Cuz, you ain't heard nothing else about that Black Woozie shit, huh?" Khadafi asked as he pulled into the parking lot of the Omni Shoreham Hotel and turned the Wale CD down.

"Naw. I buried everybody that could link me to the house on Canal Street murders. And nobody has said a word about Woozie and nem' getting smashed up Capers. If the streets is talkin', ain't nobody we know listenin' 'cause I ain't heard shit."

"Me neither. Fuck 'em. I'ma give this joint about a hour to see what it do. If it ain't doin' shit in an hour, I'm out." I wish I knew somebody here so we could get these hammers in there.

"You, too?" I ain't feeling this, slim," I responded and pulled both of my .45's and put them under the passenger seat of the Escalade.

Khadafi parked the truck. We stood beside the truck and waited for La La to find a parking space. La La was dressed to impress in his all white outfit. His white shirt had sparkly shit on it that brought a lot of attention to the white Dolce & Gabana blazer he was rocking. The white suede D&G loafers had the same sparkly shit as his shirt. Khadafi had on his all white Louis Vuitton hook up with the white Louis V. skullcap on over his long cornrows. Me, I was outfitted in some basic Kenneth Cole Reaction from head to toe.

Standing there fully dressed, I still felt naked because my hammers were locked in Khadafi's truck. The line leading into the ballroom went kind of quick. I was thankful for that.

"Cuz, this joint reminds me of that R. Kelly video," Khadafi said to me over his shoulder as we walked through the ballroom.

"Which one?" I asked.

"That 'Step in the Name of Love' joint where everybody on that boat was dressed in all white and stepping like shit."

"I'ma 'bout to do some stepping," La La added and walked over to the booth where the dude who was releasing the book sat at a table piled with books.

We ended up on the wall not far from La La. People were everywhere mingling and waiting for the go-go bands to crank up.

"Aye, cuz?"

"What's up, slim?"

"It's a bunch of niggas in here tonight that's begging me to rob 'em. These niggas broke out all the exotic ice and everything. Look at 'em."

Khadafi was right. The hotel ballroom was filled with ballers, stunners, and wanna-bes. The whole jewelry store was on display in one room. Niggas was rocking iced out Audemars, Cartiers, and Rolexes in different hues. They had on big gold chains, platinum chains, rose gold chains, diamond rings, and link bracelets that were as thick and heavy as a motorcycle bike chain. I stared at all the blinging cuff links, iced out sunglasses, and shook my head. Fools and their money will soon part. There was a rack of dudes present on the ballroom floor that I recognized immediately. And a lot of them were predators just like us, so I already knew that they were thinking the same things as me. "Yeah, slim. You right. It's a whole lotta money in this ballroom."

"Since I believe heavily in the fact that even gangstas gotta take days off, I'ma let 'em make it. I should go up on that stage and say, 'All you niggas in here flossin' that big boy ice, thank Allah for the fact that it's my night off. Y'all got a pass.'"

I laughed at what Khadafi said.

"Cuz, I'ma 'bout to hit this bar and get me something to drink. All this money in here done made me thirsty."

"Go 'head, I'll be right here. I'ma represent the wallflowers and hold this wall up."

"You don't want nothing, cuz?"

"Naw, I'm good. Do you, slim."

Chapter Thirty-Four
LIL CEE

"What you drinkin' on?" I turned to Church and asked while sitting at the bar.

"I'ma Christian, baby boy, I don't do no drinking unless Jesus doin' the pouring."

Laughing, I turned back to the bartender. "Gimme a shot of Patron, some cranberry juice, and fruit punch for my man right here."

I quickly threw back the Patron and chased it with the cranberry juice. I was feeling good as hell and wondering if Ray and his mob made it to the party. I couldn't find that out from the bar. Turning back to Church, I said, "C'mon, slim, let's hit the ballroom."

Jumping off the barstool, I turned and bumped into somebody. "My fault, homie," I said and looked at the man. I couldn't believe my eyes. I was a foot away from the source of all my pain, the man that I had just tried to kill in broad daylight. My heart stopped beating for a minute. Our eyes locked and never wavered as we stood completely still and stared at each other. Then he smiled. A big maniacal smile that made my blood simmer. My top lip instantly curled into a sneer.

"Lil Cee. What's up, cuz? You done gained weight like a muthafucka. What they feed you in that rat joint besides cheese?"

"Cee, what's up?" I heard Church say beside me.

Khadafi looked from Church back to me with the hint of recognition in his eyes. He recognized Church from the failed attempt on his life.

"I didn't recognize you at first. You changed your whole look on a nigga. Facial hair, dreads, muscles. You almost got me. That was a smart move. That move you and your man right here pulled down Capers. That was gangsta. That was that gangsta shit that I love. See, I live this shit and I done tricked niggas like that before, so I spotted the move from a mile away. But I respect you for tryin'. Broad day, you brought that heat to a nigga, that's movie shit, cuz. Now here we are face-to-face. This shit sorta feel like that movie I saw called *Assassins* with Antonio Banderas and Sylvester Stallone. You feel it, cuz?"

"Yeah, slim, I feel it," I responded. "It does kinda feel like the movie *Face Off*, but this one gonna have a different ending."

"Oh yeah? How this one gon' end, cuz?"

I smiled a wicked smile of my own. "I ain't gon' spoil it for you, you gotta keep watchin'.

"Is that right? Tough words from a broken man. One question, though, cuz. Why you do it? Why did you give us up?"

"That's the thing, slim. All y'all was wrong. It was never me. I never gave nobody up. Them people used the cameras against us. Then they separated me from y'all to create the illusion that I was tellin'. So that y'all would fold and tell on each other."

"Well, they thought wrong and I think you fulla shit."

"Slim, I don't give a fuck what you think. Your man beat that shit in trial. I helped him out by tellin' the jury that Boo killed Keith. I did it for two reasons. One, to help Ameen beat the case and two, I wanted to take the heat off you."

"Take the heat off me for what?"

"That's obvious, ain't it? So I can kill both of y'all myself."

"Is that right?" Khadafi asked, smiling even harder. He took a step and got closer to my face. "Are you really a killer, cuz? Killing Ameen two brothers don't make you no real killer. It's too easy to kill muthafuckas that ain't tryna kill you back. What you doin' right now is the easy part. Talkin'. Everybody with lips and a tongue can do that. The hard part is actually killin' me. See, me, I'ma killer for real, cuz. I do it for bread and meat; if I don't kill I don't eat. The day I realized that it was you tryna get at me down Capers, I figured it all out. You killed Ameen's brothers to hurt him the way I did you. You figured out that I killed your peoples and you thought Ameen told me to do it. You were wrong on two fronts, cuz. One, Ameen ain't hurt about his brothers because he didn't fuck with 'em. He hated them niggas. And two, Ameen never told me to kill your family.

He never even knew I was gon' do it. That was my idea. So your beef is with me. I got off the plane and went straight to your mother's house. I shot her first—"

That was as far as he got before my fist connected with his jaw. I followed up with more punches before Khadafi could recover. The next thing I knew he was down on his knees. Church joined the fray to get a piece of Khadafi, too. By the time the security reached us, Khadafi was on the floor bloody and balled up in a knot. I started kicking him. Suddenly I was lifted off the ground and into the air, but my feet still kicked out in attempt to kick Khadafi to death. Another big bouncer type dude had Church in a bear hug and another one helped Khadafi up off the floor.

Khadafi shrugged off the dude trying to help him. "Get off me, cuz, I'm good." He looked in our direction and said, "On my mother, I'ma smash you niggas, cuz!"

Chapter Thirty-Five
KHADAFI

"*O*n my mother, I'ma smash you niggas, cuz!"

My clothes were fucked up, my ego was bruised, and murder was in my eyes. It was all that I could see as I moved through the crowd in search of my men and an exit. The taste of blood in my mouth made me hungry for food. I was in animal mode, fangs reared and in search of prey. I spotted TJ on the same wall that I left him on.

Spotting me and the way I looked he came off the wall and met me.

With his face balled up, he said, "What the fuck happened to you?"

"We gotta roll, cuz. Now!" Was all I said as we went looking for La La.

I was glad to see that he was still at the book table. People saw the way my clothes looked and the look in my eyes and got out of my way. "La, we gotta roll, cuz."

"We just got here, youngin'," La La said as he turned around. He saw me and said, "C'mon."

As we headed to the parking lot, I told TJ and La La what happened and how them bitch niggas jumped me. "I'ma burn them niggas asses up, cuz."

When we reached the hotel entrance, we jogged to our vehicles.

"Did they leave out before you?" La La asked as he came back toward us with an eight shot pistol grip pump in his hand.

"I don't know, cuz. Security still had them niggas when I left. They might've left out, they might not. I'ma lay right here and wait and see if they come out. I'm killing them niggas in front of everybody."

I glanced over at TJ, who had tied his dreads up on his head and wrapped them in the long sleeved shirt he was wearing. He was leaning on my truck with a hammer in each hand. He looked at me and shrugged his shoulders. "I'm with you, slim. You know I don't give a fuck. They violate you, they violate me."

As we watched the entrance, crowds of people were exiting the hotel. Then I saw Lil Cee. "There they go right there," I announced and acted. With my sights set on Lil Cee I made a beeline toward them. The crowd was slowly thinning out, but Lil Cee and the baldhead dude were getting closer to a row of cars and what I suspected to be their guns. I couldn't let them get that far. I lifted the Calico and fired at the crowd.

Kok! Kok! Kok! Kok! Kok! Kok! Kok!
Bloom! Bloom! Bloom!

People started falling, running, and screaming.

THE ULTIMATE SACRIFICE II
LOVE IS PAIN

Bok! Bok! Bok! Bok! Bok! Bok! Bok! Bok! Bok!

As people ran in all different directions, I stayed on Lil Cee who'd taken off in an all out sprint across the parking lot while zig-zagging. I heard sirens in the distance and stopped. I turned back around and ran back toward my truck. TJ was standing over fallen people.

"Aye, slim!" TJ shouted.

I stopped, looked, and walked over.

"Isn't he one of 'em?"

I stood over the dark skinned baldheaded dude and saw something in his eyes. To me it appeared to be relief. He was lying on the ground bleeding profusely from a wound to his chest. He was mumbling something. "What are you saying, cuz?"

"I should not be afraid of the terror by night, nor of the arrow that flies by day. For he is my Lord, he will deliver me."

I couldn't believe what I'd just heard.

"C'mon, y'all, we gotta get the fuck outta here," La La shouted.

"Yeah, that's one of 'em, cuz," I said to TJ. To the man at my feet, I said, "Don't worry about deliverance. I'm gonna deliver you, cuz." I aimed the Calico at his face and fired. Then I walked away.

"Them boys'll be here in a minute," La La told TJ and me. "Y'all go 'head and bounce. I'ma take them muthafuckas for a ride. The 370 got 500 horses under the hood, I'ma see what they do. Bounce! Now! I love y'all niggas!"

TJ and I ran to the Caddy truck and hopped inside. I tossed the Calico in the backseat and grabbed the wheel. I jumped in a long line of cars exiting the hotel parking lot. As police cars and ambulances turned into the parking lot, I was heading out onto Pennsylvania Avenue. At the light, I struggled to remain calm. I looked to my left and saw a beautiful Mercedes Benz E class wagon stalled in a line of traffic going in the direction of the hotel. My eyes became glued to the gold Benz wagon. My hand gripped the steering wheel as if it could break it. My top lip rose with my anger. As I drove through the light, I couldn't take my eyes off the Benz wagon. I couldn't take my eye off the passenger. I couldn't take my eyes off Kemie.

Chapter Thirty-Six
LA LA

I watched the Escalade make it safely out of the parking lot as cop cars rushed in. I raised the pump with one hand and fired a round in their direction. Then I ran to my 370Z and hopped in. I threw the shotgun in the back and grabbed my AR-15 off the floorboard. In seconds, I was barreling out of the parking lot with no less than 30 police cars pursuing me. I put the window down and stuck the AR out the window with one hand as I steadied the 370Z with the other. I ripped off some shots, laughed and raced through D.C. at a speed of 120 miles per hour. Turning the radio all the way up, I zoned out off the Drake mix tape.

The car vibrated a little and I looked up and saw two helicopters circling over my head. Calmly, I opened the compartment lid in the middle console in the Z. I snatched opened the zip lock bag of pure heroin. Digging my hand in, I scooped some dope out and brought it up to my nose. I snorted a generous amount into both nostrils and dropped the rest on the floor. The dope drained instantly and had me high as a kite in seconds. I nodded my head to the beat coming through the speakers.

I always imagined somebody blowing my brains out in a shootout. I never thought I would be in a high-speed chase with the police and possibly die in a fiery wreck. But I knew my death would be brutal, I had lived too rough in my life to warrant anything less. For me to die of natural causes would be like me cheating a real death. I hit the Ninth Street tunnel doing a buck sixty. Moving through the streets, with the whole D.C. police force behind me at such a high rate of speed was like nothing I'd ever experienced.

"Hey baby!" I shouted over the music over and over. The dope plus the E pill I popped at the party had me on some different shit. At first, I thought I was hallucinating when I saw the road block ahead of me. But as I raced across the Fourteenth Street Bridge, I saw that it was real. I thought about plowing through the roadblock, but quickly decided against it. I had another idea. Slowing the car down, I came to a complete stop about twenty feet from the roadblock. I opened the car door and stood up.

"FREEZE! DON'T MOVE!"

"GET DOWN MUTHAFUCKA! NOW!"

"KEEP YOUR HANDS WHERE WE CAN SEE 'EM!"

I figured that if they were gonna shoot me, they'd have done it by now. I ignored the words that I heard as I put my hands up and slowly walked to the railing of the bridge. I locked my hands behind my head and made it look even more official like I was giving up.

"STOP WHERE YOU ARE!"

"GET ON YOUR KNEES!"

When I got to the rail, I turned and face the angry mob. I was literally surrounded by cops. All different agencies. Park, DCHA, Metro, P.G. County, everybody was on hand to apprehend a murderer and person who'd shot at the cops. I looked into all the faces that stared at me. White faces, Black faces, and Hispanic faces. Some scowling, some indifferent, some afraid. From the railing that touched my back, I was able to measure the length of it. *A little over 4 feet high.*

"GET DOWN!!"

"DO IT NOW!!"

The cops were inching closer and closer to me. It was time for me to make my move. Now or never. With the practiced skill of an Olympic diver, I leapt straight up into the air, then arched my back and went over the bridge. My body was free falling through the air. Eyes closed and at peace, I prepared my body for the entry into the water. My form was perfect. It was the form that I had been taught at the Boy's Club. Back then, I was the best platform diver in the region.

A NOVEL BY ANTHONY FIELDS

Chapter Thirty-Seven
DETECTIVE TOLLIVER

"Cut the bullshit, Reynolds. You're saying that the muthafucka just up and dived off the bridge?"

"Craziest shit I'd ever seen, Bruce. He ignored our shouts to freeze. But nobody fired on him because he had both hands in the air. No visible weapon. He just backed up from the car to the railing."

"Then he jumped—dived—whatever?"

"Yup. Then he committed suicide. The under current in that water is vicious at this time of the year. Crazy Muthafucka—"

I caught bits and pieces of the conversations going on around me and they all seemed to be centered around the high speed chase of a Nissan sports car and the driver who jumped off the bridge. According to my colleagues, that man had been one of three or more now responsible for the death and mayhem that I slowly surveyed in front of me. So far, there were five confirmed dead and countless injured. White blood stained sheets covered the bodies of the five

unlucky victims. Five people that had simply come out to party and possibly have a book signed by the author, wasn't going to make it home again—ever. Death is a mysterious creature. Nobody knows exactly when it will come, but it promises to visit us all. I lifted one of the sheets and stared into the face of a young girl. She couldn't have been more than twenty years old. A single bullet had crashed into her temple and ended her life. Shaking my head, I placed the sheet back over her face. Her family would be notified. Another family crushed by senseless violence in an urban city. One leg peeked from under the sheet. I studied her white Chanel open toed heels and figured that they probably ran about four or five hundred dollars a pair. A lot of money spent to impress all for one night and yet she couldn't pay enough to cheat death.

"We gotta stop meeting like this," someone behind me said.

I stood fully erect and turned to find Detective Rio Jefferson there.

"Rio, what you been able to gather so far?"

"Been here since shortly after this thing went nuclear. The details are still sketchy, but apparently, there was a brief skirmish inside the hotel ballroom by the bar. Two guys jumped on one guy, security says. They broke it up, but didn't think anything of it. Until about five minutes later when world war three happened in this parking lot."

"And one of these guys was the one that decided to go swimming in the Potomac, huh?" I asked and wrote down what Rio had just said.

"Not exactly sure. All we know is that as officers responded to the scene, a man fired a weapon at them. Then he jumps into a car and takes them on a high-speed chase that ended with our perp taking a dive off the bridge. And from what I hear, he had Olympic style form as he went over. According to a witness, there were two other men out here shooting, but they escaped in all the pandemonium in a dark colored SUV."

I scratched my head. "Three shooters. Three people involved in the fight inside the ballroom. That means that one guy met up with two other men or the two guys who did the jumping grabbed a third accomplice. Either way, one or more of the victims here were involved in the whole situation, right?"

"I'd wager and say the answer is yes to that, but unfortunately we can't speak to the dead for information. Not unless you know Dionne Warwick and a few of her psychic friends.

"Then these victims could all be innocent bystanders."

"The hotel security should have surveillance cameras up, right?"

"I would assume so. Check it out and let me know what you find." Rio Jefferson turned and went back to work.

I had to maze my way through frantic witnesses, cops, and crime scene techs that seemed to be everywhere. Spotting a throng of men with black windbreaker jackets, that had "Hotel Security" emblazoned across the back, I changed direction and headed toward them.

Pulling out my police credentials, I interrupted their conversation. "Excuse me, gentlemen, but I'm Detective Maurice Tolliver, Homicide, I need to speak with the security personnel that witnessed the scuffle by the bar."

Of all the six security men, only one decided to acknowledge me. The others appeared afraid and mistrustful.

"My name is Donovan Bailey and I'm the chief of hotel security. Three of my staff intervened with the fight by the bar. They are all standing over there talking to—"

I glanced in the direction where the guy was looking and saw three big security guards engaged in talks with uniformed cops. "Thank you. I'll just go on over there." Being a sergeant third grade in Homicide afforded me certain privileges that regular beat cops didn't have. Top priority. Interrupting the crowd of men, I introduced myself to the three security guards. "Excuse me for a minute, fellas. I need these three gentlemen for a few minutes. Can you guys please step over here?" Once we were off to the back of the ballroom, I started my questions. Then I got my answers.

"Two guys at the bar exchanged some words and started fighting. Another dude jumps in and the two dudes punish the one dude. It happened quickly and was over quickly," The security guard with too many freckles on his face said. "I was the first one on the scene. I grabbed the dude with the dreads."

"I got there next and I grabbed the other aggressor," another security guy added. "I held him until Rick helped the guy on the ground up."

I pulled my notepad out and jotted down what I heard. "Can you give me a description of these guys?"

"They were wearing white—"

"The whole place was wearing white, jerk off," one security guard said.

"I know that, asshole. The guy that I held was about my complexion—"

"Light brown skinned?" I inquired.

"Yeah, about my height. About 6'1" and he had long dreads that hung loosely over his shoulders and back. Didn't really look at his face."

"The dude I bear hugged was tall, dark skinned and bald headed. Didn't really see his face, either."

Before the third security guy could speak, I said, "Does the ballroom and bar come equipped with security cameras?"

"Sure. There are cameras everywhere. The security room's back that way. I'll take you to it," Freckles said and headed to the rear of the ballroom.

Inside the small room, Freckles sat in a chair behind a bevy of small TV monitors. He typed in a command on a keyboard and different angles of the hotel ballroom came to view. "Here's the bar right here," he said and pointed at one of the screens. "I'ma cue it to play from 10:15 on. The fight started—well, ended about 10:32P.M. You'll be able to see everything that happened at the bar in real time."

Finding a chair on the back wall of the room, I grabbed it and sat right beside Freckles. "Before it begins, give me a heads up on who's who."

The screen was well lit and clear. I watched people walk up to the bar, order drinks, pay and leave. But a few others congregated on stools at the bar. Two men that fit the descriptions I'd been given walked up and sat down. The camera angle caught them from the back. "You can't get the front of those two guys?"

Freckles shook his head. "The cameras are mounted to face the bar. The rationale is to watch the bartenders, not the patrons."

A few minutes later, the two men, one tall and bald, and the other a little shorter with long dreads, stood up and appeared to be leaving.

The guy with the dreads bumped into a man who was approaching the bar. That man was dressed in all white with a white hat that covered his head, but I could see what appeared to be braids or dreads extending from the hat. Inching my face closer to the screen, I could see the guy with the hat, who gave up a few inches in height to the guy with the dreads. They appeared to be conversing. Then the bald headed guy stepped up beside his partner. Then the guy with the dreads swung. Then in real time, I watched the fight and security advancing on the scene to restore order. They guy with the white hat was helped up off the floor.

"Hey, I need the guy with the white hat on, I need you to freeze frame that and enlarge him."

Freckles did as I requested.

I reached into my jacket pocket and pulled two photos out. I stared at the face on the screen and down at one in my hand. "Khadafi."

"Huh?"

"Nothing, go ahead and follow that guy through the hotel ballroom. I crossed my fingers and silently prayed that Khadafi wasn't alone. Security cameras caught Luther "Khadafi" Fuller walking through crowds until he reached a wall. There was a man standing and leaning on the wall. Also dressed in all white. My heart rate quickened. "Can you get a blow up of the guy right there that the guy in the hat just approached?"

"Sure." Freckles typed frantically on the keyboard. "Voila! How's that?"

I was now staring into the face of the man that I wanted to take down at all cost. For myself, for the city, but most of all for Nomeka Fisher. I didn't have to look at the second picture in my hand to identify this man. I knew his name as well as I knew my own. Then another thought hit me. "Can you get the parking lot?"

"No. The parking lot is out of the surveillance area." My hopes were dashed, but my belief was strong. Wherever Tyrone "TJ" Carter and Luther Fuller went, murder and mayhem followed. They were responsible for all the bodies lying in the hotel parking lot.

I couldn't prove it yet, but my gut told me it was true. "I'm coming for you, TJ. And your man Khadafi, too."

Chapter Thirty-Eight
KHADAFI

"*W*hen I die, fuck it, I wanna go to hell/ cause I'ma piece of shit, it ain't hard to fuckin' tell/don't make sense goin' to heaven with the goody goodies/dressed in white, I like black Timbs and black hoodies…"

All my life I was told that real niggas never beefed over women. I remember my uncle saying, "Nephew, you never let a queen come in between two kings." I nodded my head in understanding, but that shit was good in theory only. Sayings like that only made conversations flow well. In the real world, niggas been getting killed over bitches since the beginning of time. It happened in 2008 when I killed Bean and Omar and it's about to happen again in 2010. Phillip Bowman was the next contestant on the "Price of Life." Being able to fuck Kemie was the price he paid to lose his life. And I'm the collection agency. After leaving the hotel and seeing Kemie in that Benz wagon, I remembered that Marnie said the dude Phil had a Benz wagon. Then I thought about all the lies Kemie told me at the hospital. She

never once told me that the dude she was fucking with was her old boyfriend, Phil. Even though I knew she was lying, I never let on that I knew the real deal. The fact that Lil Cee had gotten away again fueled my desire to kill this dude, Phil. Killing the dark skinned baldhead dude had been enough to temporarily feed my hunger for blood. Enough so that finding and killing Lil Cee had become secondary. Finding and killing the dude that's fucking my woman has now become primary. I never went home that night after dropping TJ off. I went to Marnie's house and fucked her for hours. We fucked in every room of her apartment, in every position imaginable. I ate her until she came. Licked her ass until she came again. Then did both all over again. And the whole while I was imagining Phil fucking Kemie at that exact moment. She asked about my bumps and bruises and I told her we were fighting at the party. If she had heard about the carnage and death that we left behind, she didn't say a word.

I left her house early yesterday morning and rode around Uptown near where Marnie said Phil hung at trying to spot that gold Benz wagon. All the while Kemie was blowing my phone up. I never answered because I wasn't ready to confront her about what I saw. And I wasn't in the mood to listen to her lies. Naw. It wasn't time to talk to Kemie. We'd talk later and when we did sparks were guaranteed to fly.

The good thing about living in small cities like D.C. is that everybody knows somebody who knows somebody. I did a little research and found out that Phil was from

Ledroit Park. His name, Phillip Bowman was known by all because his brother Chris Bowman was the biggest supplier of Ecstasy pills in the D.C., Maryland, and Virginia area. Big brother put little brother on and the two had been getting money for years. Later that evening, once I turned my brain on, I remembered that Marnie had also said that Phil had a silver Hummer H2. I had seen that Hummer on Second and V street. I went back to V Street and sure enough, it was parked outside a house on that block. I parked the Caddy and prayed that I wouldn't have to wait too long to see if it was in fact the dude that I'd seen driving the Benz wagon.

My prayers were answered when I spotted the dude from the Benz getting into the Hummer. I followed him throughout the city and then remembered something else that Marnie had said: *"He got a baby mother that lives over by Orleans Place."*

I followed Phil to an address on M Street, a block over from Orleans Place and realized that it was the baby mother's house. It was easy finding Phil after that. The next order of business was snatching him. I didn't just want to kill him. I wanted him to know why he was dying. And to do that I needed a little help.

"This nigga was with that shit from the hotel, cuz. I heard it through the grapevine. He was with them niggas the whole time," I lied as TJ followed the Hummer to Northeast. "I remember seeing him at the bar, but I didn't put two and

two together until this bitch I know named Daphne told me that Phil was with that shit."

"What you wanna snatch the nigga for, then? Just go 'head and crush him and call it a day," TJ said.

"Naw, cuz, I wanna get this nigga somewhere and talk to him before I kill him. It's a lot of shit I need to find out and I know he know. All I need you to do is help me snatch the nigga off the streets and I got it from there."

"I'm with you, slim. If that's what you wanna do, so be it. You got the cuffs and shit?"

"I got everything I need. He's going to M Street, cuz. When he turns off Florida Avenue onto Fourth Street, put the light on the roof and activate it."

I gave myself the once over and pronounced us ready. TJ and I were both dressed in black cargo fatigues, Hi-Tech police boots, black T-shirts, and black windbreaker jackets with the word POLICE emblazoned on the back of them. We looked the part of the police to me. Seven minutes later, TJ grabbed the police light off the seat and placed it on top of the roof of his Buick Roadmaster. When the Hummer turned onto Fourth Street, he activated it. The Hummer pulled over and we pulled directly behind it.

Jumping out the car, TJ and I went straight to work. TJ walked up to the driver's side and flashed a light into the Hummer.

"License and registration, big guy. You know the drill."

I stood beside TJ.

"What y'all stopping me for?" Phil asked.

"We gotta call about drugs in a silver Hummer. Something about thousands of X pills. You wouldn't know nothing about that, would you?"

"Not at all, officer."

"Yeah, I bet," TJ said as he looked over the papers Phil had just given him. "And how is it that you can afford a big pretty truck like this and your address here is listed in the Ledroit Park area?"

"I—my—mother—" Phil stammered.

"I know. I know. Get your ass out the truck. Now, big man!" TJ turned to me. "Townsend, cuff this piece of shit while I search the truck."

Phil climbed out of the truck and leaned on the back door. He was very cooperative, making it too easy to snatch his dumb ass. I placed the cuffs on him and stood there holding him. Then I told him, "Come and sit in the car, this might take a while."

I led Phil to the Roadmaster and put him in the backseat. TJ searched the truck for about two minutes and then came back to the Roadmaster. He got into the driver's seat and I hopped in the back with Phil. As the Roadmaster pulled off, Phil became panicky.

"Man, what the fuck y'all doin'? Where y'all takin' me?" He looked from me to TJ and struggled to get out the handcuffs.

I pulled the .45 out and aimed it at his side. "Move again, nigga and I'ma blow your left kidney to the right side of your body. Then I'ma put your brains on that window

over there and kick your body out the car. Think I'm bullshittin' then call my bluff."

Phil looked at me again and shook his head. "Khadafi?"

"In the flesh. You had to know I was coming to see you, right?" I said.

"Slim—" *Whack!*

I smacked him with the butt of the four-fifth and opened up a deep gash on his forehead. In seconds his face was covered in blood. "Shut the fuck up! We gone have plenty of time to talk. Tee, you know the spot where all the heads be goin' when it get real cold outside around the way?"

TJ nodded his head.

"That's where we goin'," I said and sat back in my seat.

When we reached the project tenement down Capers, I went in and ran all the crackheads and dopefiends out. Then I came back to the car and led Phil into the house. TJ and I embraced and promised to hook up later. Then he left. Somehow, the fiends had engineered a source of power and gave the house some light. I grabbed a chair out the living room and led Phil into the bathroom.

I pulled out my duct tape and told Phil, "I'm not gonna kill you, cuz. I just want you to answer some questions for me. I'ma tape you to the chair because if you feel froggy and jump bad, then I'ma have to kill you. So sit your ass down and listen closely."

Ten minutes later, I called Kemie and told her to come down Capers. I gave her the directions to where I was, went back to the bathroom and waited.

Chapter Thirty-Nine
KEMIE

When I walked up to the abandoned looking tenement, I wondered what the hell Khadafi was doing in there. I pulled out my cell and called him. Then I noticed the blood.

"I'm outside. Come to the door," I said, still looking at the blood drops that led to the door.

Khadafi appeared as the door opened a moment later. He stepped to the side and motioned for me to come inside. *Why is he dressed like a police officer?*

I walked past him and followed the trail of blood drops that stopped at a door. I looked back at Khadafi with a puzzled look on my face. Searching his eyes for some type of answer as to what was going on, I found them unreadable. A sound coming from inside the room caught my attention. As I inched closer, I heard the unmistakable sounds of muffled moans. I reached out, turned the knob, and pushed the door open. My eyes settled on the person bound to the chair. I rushed into the room. "What have you done?" I screamed as I pulled my coat off, then my shirt.

Taking my shirt and wiping at the blood on Phil's face, I turned to Khadafi.

"What did he do to you? Huh? What?" I screamed with spit flying out of my mouth. Khadafi stood in the doorway with a wounded look on his face. "Answer me! What did he do to you?"

"When I was in prison and he was fuckin' you, that was something that I couldn't control. But now that I'm home and he's still fuckin' you, he's disrespecting me."

"Disrespecting you? This is my body! I disrespected you. Are you gonna kill me, too?"

Khadafi exploded. "I should! I should split your shit and leave you and this nigga dead and stinkin' in this muthafucka. Keep running your muthafuckin' mouth and that's what I'ma do. You talkin' all this 'what did he do?' shit. Why you ain't just tell me that you wanna be with this nigga?"

"I—I—I—" I stammered.

"Don't start stutterin' and shit now. You wasn't stutterin' a few seconds ago when you ran in here, took your clothes off, and started wiping blood and shit. You in this bitch goin' off on me about this nigga. Do you love this nigga?"

I knew the answer to that question would get me and Phil killed, but I had to say it. Khadafi had a right to know the truth. "Yes," I said and the air left my body. "Are you happy now? Is that what you wanna hear?"

The pained look on Khadafi's face broke my heart into pieces.

With tears in his eyes, Khadafi asked, "Do you wanna be with this nigga?"

"I—I—yes—no—I don't know," I answered, confused.

"Does this nigga love you? Huh? Like I do?"

There was that question again. The same one that Reesie asked me that night. I couldn't bring myself to admit the truth, so I said, "Yes."

Then Khadafi laughed a deep throaty chuckle and it chilled me to the bone. "I never knew you were that gullible. This nigga got you gone off the dick and now you a hopeless romantic." Khadafi laughed again.

"What's so damn funny?" I asked, now puzzled.

"I've loved you since I was a kid and this is how you do me? I could've had any bitch—"

"Look how you do me, nigga! Loving me is throwing shit in my face, huh? Yeah right. And you have had other bitches. What? What the fuck you looking all stupid for? You think I don't know where you was all them days after we fell out? You think I don't know that you still fuckin' Marnie? C'mon, boo, give me credit for something. Or do you really believe that I'm that gullible? Remember you was laying up with that bitch—what's her name? Shawnay? You got the nerve to stand here and act like you better than me. Cheatin' is cheatin', nigga! Ain't no difference according to gender. We were both fuckin' somebody else. How y'all niggas say it? Ain't no fun if I can't get none? Don't be mad 'cause I got mine."

"Listen, if you wanna be a whore, go 'head. That's on you. I ain't gon' take no dick for you. I done told you that

before. Yeah, I fuck other bitches, but the difference is I don't love none of 'em. Never have. Never will. I have never loved nobody but you. You know why I laughed at you a few minutes ago? Because you just stood here and said that you love this nigga and guess what? He don't give a fuck about you. You think I'm lying? Ask him."

I stood in my spot stuck. I felt so stupid that it hurt. All I could do was stare at the floor. My lie had come back to haunt me. Phil had already told Khadafi what I could never accept as fact. That he didn't love me. The hurt that I felt turned to anger.

"Go 'head and ask him. What you waitin' for? Ask your boyfriend, Phil do he love you."

When I didn't speak or respond in any way, Khadafi started laughing again. I was humiliated.

"What's wrong, Kemie? Scared of what he gon' say? Well, I know the answer already. I asked Phil did he love you before you got here. You wanna know what he said? He said—naw, better yet, I'ma let him tell you."

Khadafi walked over to Phil and ripped the piece of duct tape off his mouth. Phil instantly started pleading for his life.

"Spare me out, dawg. That's your bit—I mean girl. Don't kill me 'bout tha—"

"I told you I ain't gonna kill you, cuz. I just want you to tell the truth. I want you to tell Kemie what you told me. Do you love Kemie?"

"—I—a-little—bit—don't kill me, dawg!"

"A little bit, huh? That ain't what you said earlier, but I'ma leave that alone. Do you love Kemie enough to die for her?"

Tears fell down Phil's face as he looked at me and slowly shook his head.

"What the hell does that mean, cuz? Answer the question. Do you love Kemie enough to die for her?"

"No!" Phil said quickly and started crying. "No-no—no."

Now Khadafi's tears were back. They flowed from his eyes two at a time. "Did you hear that shit? You were willing to leave me and risk your life for a nigga that don't give a fuck about you." Khadafi ejected the clip from the gun he pulled and dropped it on the floor. He walked over to Phil, reached behind him, and uncuffed his hands. He looked at me and said, "I love you more than my own life. I would willingly give mine for you."

Khadafi put the guns in Phil's hand and dropped to a knee in front of him. I looked on in shock as Khadafi put the gun in Phil's hand and placed of it to his own forehead. He kept his fingers around the gun. "Now ask me would I die for her."

Phil inched his finger to the trigger.

"No-o-o-o-o! Do—n-n't!"

I jumped as the firing pin hit an empty chamber and the gun clicked. With the alacrity of a cat, Phil leapt out of the chair and attacked Khadafi, using the gun as a weapon. They fought and wrestled around for a few minutes. They spilled out into the next room. Then I heard a gun shot and

watched Phil back up holding his stomach. In seconds, blood coated his fingers.

"Don't kill me!" Phil pleaded.

Khadafi kept the gun aimed at Phil. "Always keep a spare gun handy. Do you really think I'm dumb enough to give you a loaded gun? Kemie, get that clip over there and bring it to me."

I retrieved the clip and gave it to Khadafi. He popped the clip into the gun and now stood in the room holding two guns on Phil. Phil continued to hold his stomach and plead for his life.

Khadafi looked at me and said, "He didn't know that the gun wasn't loaded. Neither did you. If it was loaded, I'd be dead right now. Does that prove to you how much I love ya? Do you believe me now when I say that I'd rather be dead then live without you?"

I wiped tears from my eyes and nodded my head.

"Good. Now, I gotta question for you. Do you love me?"

"With all my heart," I answered truthfully.

"Do you love me enough to die for me?"

"Yes. You know I do."

"Do you love me enough to kill for me?"

Without hesitation, I answered, "Yes."

"Are you sure, cuz? Are you positively sure?"

"Yeah, I'm sure."

Khadafi handed me one of the gun. "Here, take it."

I grabbed the gun out of his hand and stared at the floor. The realization of what he was asking me hit me. Khadafi

wanted proof of my love. He wanted a declaration of love, faith, and trust. And he wanted it signed in blood.

"The fact that you love this nigga is killing me inside more and more every second. There is no way that he'll ever forgive me for what I've done to him. He's gonna want to get me back, Kemie. I can't live like that. And I can't stand to live my life knowing that there is another dude alive that you love. So prove your love to me, Kemie. Kill him."

"N-o-o-o-o! Ke-m-m-ie, no-o-o-! I do love you! I do love you!"

"You gotta kill one of us because you can't have us both. You decide."

The gun in my hand felt like it weighed a ton. I looked at both of the men in my life that I loved and made a decision. As tears fell from my eyes, I aimed the gun and fired.

Chapter Forty
MARNIE

Ever since the doctor told me the good news a couple of days ago, I'd been on some real live greedy shit. By the time I walked through my door, half of my carryout food from Ms. Debbie's was gone. I dropped my purse on the floor and kicked my shoes off. Walking into the living room, I hit the lights and damn near jumped out my skin. Khadafi was reclined in my love seat with a washcloth over his eyes.

"What the fuck are you sitting here in the dark for? You scared the shit outta me. I looked beside the chair and saw that he had a bag packed. "What's all that?"

"I'm goin' home, Marnie. For good. I wanted to tell you that face-to-face. And give you back your keys.

"You're going back home?" I repeated. "What exactly does that mean?"

"C'mon, Marnie, you know what the fuck that means."

I instantly became agitated. "Naw, I don't. Enlighten me, boo. Please."

"I'm goin' back home to Kemie."

"Oh?" I said and walked over to the table and set my food down. "You goin' home to Kemie. Okay. I get it now. So where exactly does that leave me? And us?"

"Cuz, you know how I feel about you. I—"

"Didn't I fuckin' tell you about calling me that `cuz' shit? And please don't assume I know shit. Tell me what's up. A coupla weeks ago your ass was all up in here like 'fuck Kemie this' and 'fuck Kemie's whore ass that.' Please tell me exactly how you feel about me and then tell me why you decided to go back to Kemie. I wan—"

"You just don't understand," Khadafi interjected.

My hands were shaking now and my blood pressure shot up. "Don't patronize me, you muthafucka! Talkin' 'bout I don't understand. Make me understand, then."

"We—we go thistory—it's complicated—something happened—"

"What? Speak up, nigga, you babbling. What did you just say?"

"Look, cu—Marnie, I'm sorry if I led you on. I love you, but I gotta—I still love Kemie, too. You know that."

My tears were falling by now. Khadafi's words pierced me like a tiny dagger turning in my heart. How had I allowed myself to fall for a man that didn't really love me? How had I tricked myself into believing that I could change him? Make him stop loving my enemy? Every time I sucked him and fucked him, I believed that I could sex the love he had for Kemie out of him. Suck the cum and feelings for her out of him. All the times I rode him, I tried to exorcise her demons out of him. I had actually allowed myself to believe that since Khadafi was here with me, under my roof, that he was mine. But I was wrong and he was right. I did know that he still loved Kemie. I purposely made myself forget that.

"You still love her," I repeated to myself.

Khadafi stood up and started pacing the floor. "She proved—she—she—I can't say how—but she proved—she showed me that she—she proved herself to me. History. We have history. Almost twenty years—she proved herself."

"And I haven't? Is that it? What has Kemie proved except that she can shit on you while you're in prison and you'll take her back? What has she proved other than the fact that she will fuck all your friends, cross her own friends, fall in love with the next nigga, keep fuckin' him *after* you come home and prove that she can lie good as a muthafucka? Me, I haven't proved but two things: That I will always be there for you and that I love you—"

Stopping him in his tracks, Khadafi said, "You love me for real?"

"Naw," I answered sarcastically. "I love you for play. Of course, I love you for real. I told you that before."

"I never thought you meant it."

"Well," I said feebly and wiped away my tears. "I meant every word I said. But does that change anything? Is that love enough to change your mind?"

"Marnie, do you know what you asking me? This shit is deep. You deserve a nigga that's gonna love you the way you need to be loved. I'ma outlaw, boo. I live by the gun.

Niggas out here tryna kill me as we speak. All them people that got killed at that book release party? They died because of me. Everywhere I go people die, Marnie, and I don't want that for you. You are a good woman. Me, I'ma piece of shit and I'm goin' straight to hell. Is that what you love about me? My gangsta? My lifestyle? Boo, you been reading too many of them Wahida Clark novels you got on them shelves over there. That shit ain't fact. It's all fiction. I'm livin' this shit for real and guess what? This ain't livin'. I'll never get married and never have kids—"

"I'm pregnant!" I blurted out.

"What did you say?"

"You heard me. I'm pregnant."

"By who?"

"Nigga, you can stand here and belittle me, telling me that I'm livin' in the pages of the novels I like to read. You can tell me that you thought I screamed out my love for you because your dick was the bomb. I can deal with that. I can even deal with you standing here defending the same bitch that broke your heart and betrayed you. Then listen to you call it history. I can deal with you standing in my living room implying that I ain't gangsta enough for you . . . but I WILL NOT deal with you standing here in my face—in the muthafuckin' place that I call home—and disrespect me. You know me, nigga! I'm not your girl. I never fuck more than one nigga at a time and you know that. I haven't fucked nobody but you ever since I first saw you at the beauty salon that day. My name ain't Kemie and I ain't no muthafuckin' cranker. So don't you *ever* fix your mouth to

disrespect me. You ain't the only one in this muthafucka from the streets, so don't get it fucked up. I work five days a week 'cause that's what I choose to do, not because it's all I know. Not because it's all I'm built for. If you ask me who I'm pregnant by, one more muthafuckin' time, on my mother, we gon' box in this bitch! We gon' tear all my shit up in here. Now—think I'm playin' and ask me that shit again. Go 'head! Gangsta ass nigga! Live by the gun ass nigga! Ask me that shit again! I dare you!"

"Who—"

I moved across the room and threw the coffee table that separated us out the way. I walked up on Khadafi with my fist balled up. I was furious. "What you say, nigga!"

Khadafi looked at me as if seeing me for the first time. He looked down at my fist and saw that they were ready to pounce. Then he did what I least expected. He laughed in my face. I jumped on his ass with a three piece.

Khadafi weaved my punches and grabbed my arms. "Hold on, Sugar Ray, let me talk. This shit is crazy. I don't wanna fight you. You keep actin' crazy and you gon' lose the baby."

I snatched out of his grasp. "Like you care."

"Are you gonna keep it?"

"That depends."

"On what?"

"You."

"How?"

"That depends on the decision you make in this room, right now."

"What decision?"

"Are you still leaving me and goin' back to Kemie?" I asked.

"I have—to," Khadafi responded.

"Well, go 'head then, nigga. There ain't nothin' left for us to talk about. Get the fuck out! Take your shit and get the fuck out! And don't come back when that bitch betrays your stupid ass again. Go head and leave! What the fuck you waitin' for?"

"Marnie—"

"Muthafucka, get the fuck outta my house! I don't need your ass. Fuck you! You'll hear from me and the courts after the baby is born. That's right, nigga. You ain't gettin' away like that. I'm keepin' my baby and he's gonna know exactly what kinda man his daddy is. A sucka for love ass nigga."

Khadafi's facial expression was unreadable. He picked up his bag and headed toward the door. There were so many tears in my eyes, I could hardly see.

"I'm sorry I hurt you, Marnie. But as far as you sayin' that you'll see me when the baby comes—that takes what? Nine months? I might not even live that long."

A minute later, he was gone. My lips trembled and I fell to the floor. I put my face in my hands and cried myself a river. I cried a river that would break the new levees in New Orleans. I cried a Tsunami that could drown a hundred thousand families. The pain I felt was almost human. Before my eyes, it took on a life of its own and laid

down beside me. My head and heart ached. My pain whispered to me, "You did this to yourself."

I ignored it and cried.

"You knew that he wasn't yours."

I cried even harder.

"I will always be here with you."

I shook my head. "No, you won't."

I rose up off the floor and went to my bedroom. Walking into the closet, I pulled the chain overhead that turned the light on. *Where is it?* I rummaged through all my drawers until I found what I was looking for. Reaching into the bottom of the drawer behind my sexiest lingerie, I wrapped my hand around it. The wood on the butt was smooth and the steel was cold. I lifted the gun that Khadafi had given me over a year ago out of the drawer. Without having to check the clip, I knew it was full and that there was a bullet already in the chamber just as it was the day that Khadafi gave it to me. That was the day that I first felt a connection with Khadafi. He never asked for the gun and I never gave it back. The bullet in the chamber was patiently waiting. Waiting to explode. Waiting to cause hurt, injury, and death. Waiting to inflict pain. Pain. My pain walked up on me and saw the gun in my hand.

"What are you gonna do with that?" my pain asked.

Slowly, I raised the gun to my head. "Kill myself," I replied.

"N-n-no-o-o-o-! If you do that, you won't be able to feel me or anything else again. I'll be gone—but so will you—and the baby."

My baby. I had completely forgotten about the life growing inside my belly. My baby. It needed me. I lowered the gun. My baby needed me. But my pain was still there and too much for me to bear.

"Leave me alone!" I screamed at my pain. "Just leave me alone!"

"Why should I?" my pain asked me. "I've lived inside you for years. Remember? I was with you after Black Junior left you. Remember the pain you felt then? That was me. Remember the pain you felt when your father got stabbed to death down Lorton? That was me. I have always been with you. Then and now. I am the only constant thing in your life, I will never leave you."

My pain was right. It had always been with me. Black Junior was the first dude that I ever loved and Kemie took him from me. Khadafi was the second dude that I allowed myself to love. And now Kemie is taking him from me, too. My pain wins again. Thinking about my pain, I realized that there was one common denominator. Besides my father's death, Kemie was the source of all my pain. Kemie. I looked at my pain standing there nodding and agreeing with me. A thought hit me. If Kemie were gone, then Khadafi would be with me. And my pain would go away. Again my pain nodded.

Suddenly my resolve strengthened and my tears stopped. I put the gun on top of the dresser and walked out the closet, my pain on my heels. As I undressed, I made up my mind. I knew what to do. What had to be done. There was no other way to get rid of my pain. Naked, I walked

into the bathroom and turned the shower water as hot as I could stand it. I stood under the water and put a plan together. The only way for me to be happy was for Kemie to die. *It's the only way. For me. For Khadafi. For our child. For us to be together. It's the only way.*

Chapter Forty-One
LIL CEE

*I*t was hard to believe that seven days had passed since the night of November 22nd. The day that I'd come face-to-face with the man that killed my mother and my sister and didn't kill him. Couldn't kill him. Although I tried. I tried to put my fist through his face and then my foot. But security guards and bouncers stopped me. All the while, the only other person in my life that I loved was with me. And now he's gone. I often sit back, rewind the tape in my mind, and see me and Church trying to get to his car. To the guns that we knew were there. But for some reason we never made it. We had come under fire as soon as we got out of the hotel doors. I didn't even know we had split up. All I knew was that I was getting shot at and my instincts were to run. So I ran. And kept running until I felt I was safe. Before I realized it, I was about twenty blocks from the Omni Shoreham. Twenty blocks from Church. By the time I walked back to the hotel parking lot, it was bedlam and pandemonium all over. I fought through throngs of people and counted the bodies covered by white sheets. I counted five in all. My heartbeat quickened as I looked around and spotted Church's Mercury Marauder. It was still parked in the same spot and there was no Church anywhere by it. There were several people wounded and being put into ambulances all over the parking lot. I crossed my fingers and said a prayer to a God that I didn't really believe was there. But Church believed in him and I knew that Church's god would keep him out of harm's way. I wandered around aimlessly for a while until I saw something that got my attention. I prayed that it was a coincidence as I approached one of the bodies surrounded by cops. The white sheet was covering the body, but the shoes were exposed and one of the hands. The shoes were white leather Gucci loafers with the gold links attached to each side of the shoe. Stretching across the shoe from gold link to gold link was a red and green strip of cloth. They were shoes like the ones that Church had on, that confirmed the worst for me. Tears fell from my eyes immediately as I knew that the person under the blanket was indeed Church. And he was dead because of me. I felt like a strange kind of poison. Everybody that I loved had died because of me and the bad choices that I made.

I should have never involved Church in my beef. It was my vendetta. It was my cross to carry and I had shared it with Church. And now he was gone. I don't remember how I made it to Kia's house, but I did. I don't remember telling her my whole life story all the way up to the present, but I did. I don't remember going back to the halfway house that Sunday, but I did. But I do remember the day Kia quit her

job at Hope Village and told me it was time for us to leave. It was time for us to start a new life outside D.C. And as bad as I wanted to tell her that I couldn't leave without killing Khadafi, I kept silent, thought, plotted, and planned.

I opened my eyes suddenly and saw a sign that read 'South of the Border.' There was a picture of a Mexican man with a big hat letting you know that fireworks were sold at the market there. There was a restaurant and a gas station. There was a sign that said, 'Welcome to South Carolina.'

"Stop right here, so we can gas the car up and grab something to eat," I said to Kia.

"I'm glad you said that because I gotta use the bathroom bad."

When the car was parked in the lot in front of the restaurant, we got out. I walked around the car and grabbed Kia in a warm embrace. I looked her straight in the eyes and said, "Do you have any idea what you've done? What you've given up for me?"

"I know exactly what I've done. And if I could go back and change anything, I wouldn't't."

"Good, I just wanted to hear you say that."

Chapter Forty-Two
TJ

Nomeka lifted the comforter on her bed and slid in beside me. Her body was soft as she wrapped her arms around me. She smelled like apples. I was caught up in her rapture completely. Sliding her body over mine, the wetness of Nomeka's pussy left a trail as she moved down the length of me. "Damn," I whispered to myself as her tongue became serpentine and slithered all over my face, neck and then my chest. Going lower, she found my dick standing at attention. She stroked my dick several times then positioned me between her legs. The length of my dick slid between her pussy lips and caused her to moan. I was craving penetration, but Nomeka was content at the moment with teasing herself. So I relaxed, lay back, and stared into her face as she moved all over me. Biting down on my lip, I resisted the urge to lift her up and onto my hard on. It was her show, in her bedroom, in her house, so I let her do her.

"O-o-oooh, this feel so good, TJ! I wanna feel your dick inside of me! Can I put your dick in me, baby?"

"Hell yeah!" I moaned.

Nomeka lifted and guided me into her. Slowly, she slid down my pole and I had to struggle to keep from cumming too soon. I felt her tight walls stretching to allow my whole dick.

"U—u-u-um-m-m-m! Ooooooh! Shit! Yes!"

I gave her a minute to get used to the dick and then I grabbed her waist and sat her all the way down on the dick. Nomeka built up her courage and started rocking on my dick from side to side. Up. Down. Reversing her motion. Bouncing. Bouncing. Side to side. In. Out. Up. Down. Grinding all over me, taking every inch.

"Pu-s-s-sy . . . ti-igh-t as sh-h-itt!" I groaned.

"A-i-in-n't . . . b-b-b-e-en . . . f-u-c-ckin' . . . n-n-n-o-o-b-body!" Nomeka responded.

A few minutes later, I was losing the stamina battle. I was about to explode hard and fast. "—a-ab-bou-t . . . to-to . . . c-c-u-um!"

Nomeka leapt off my dick like a gymnast dismounting the uneven bars. Her mouth found my dick and sucked a few times, then I was cumming. Nomeka pulled my dick out her mouth and jerked me off as I came. My body shivered from the powerful climax. Her fingers played in the cum now pooled on my midsection, as her head dipped low and gently nibbled at my nuts. Nomeka played with my nuts and stroked me until I rose again. Then she put me back in her mouth. This time she did things with her tongue

that scared me as I looked down at her to make sure that there was a woman on my dick and not a machine. In no time, I was ready to blow again. Nomeka sensed it and let me bust in her mouth this time. As she coaxed all the cum out of me and let it dribble out of her mouth, I closed my eyes. The tongue bath that was being applied to my dick lulled me to sleep like a song from the 'Quiet Storm.' I felt Nomeka slither up my body. Then I felt something hard pressed against my forehead. I slowly opened my eyes knowing exactly what I would find. Nomeka had a gun in her hand.

"You killed my brother!" she said with tear stained cheeks.

I looked straight into her mesmerizing eyes and said, "Who is your brother?"

"Tommy Fields."

"Never heard of him."

"The streets called him Woozie."

"Oh? Him? Don't know what you talkin' bout."

"You killed my cousin, Yusef, too. Why? That weed you gave me, it was my brother's."

When I gave the same response as before, I heard the hammer cock back on the gun.

"Last chance. Why did you kill them?" Nomeka said with a deranged look on her face, traces of cum on her chin.

"Okay . . . okay! Don't shoot!"

"Answer the fuckin' question, then!"

"I ain't gon lie to you. Yeah, I killed—" *Click! Click! Click! Click!*

"—both of them. Your bro—" *Click! Click! Click! Click! Click!*

"—ther because he was stupid. Fuck him and your cousin. Your cousin was a victim of circumstance, but your brother tried to be gangsta. He was outta his lane and didn't know it." *Click! Click!*

I saw the look of shock mixed with fear register on Nomeka's face. Her shoulders slumped and the gun slipped from her hands. Nomeka dissolved into a whimpering mess on top of me.

"I did it all. I killed your brother, your cousin, Samantha, Dave Carlton—all of 'em. You asked, so now you know," I said and started laughing. "There are two things that I love, Meka. I love good movies and good books. My favorite movie of all time is *Harlem Nights*. The joint with Eddie Murphy and Richard Pryor in it. My favorite part of the movie was when the mob put out a hit on Eddie Murphy's character. The mob used a bitch—a bad bitch—it was Jasmine Guy—to try to kill him. But he was too smart for the bullshit. The bitch failed and Eddie Murphy killed her. This situation right here with you and me kinda reminds me of that scene. Now, my favorite book of all times is a joint my man, Buck wrote and sold to Teri Woods called *Angel*.

"In the beginning of the book, the nigga Tony Bills who had all the money, connections, everything—he let the bitch Angel trick him. She put a gun under the bed earlier that day, fed him and fucked him real good. Then she killed him. I was like, "Damn!" He never even saw it coming. I

remember sayin' to myself, 'Self, that nigga should've seen that coming. She caught him slippin'. Then I vowed to myself never to get caught slippin'.

"So when you left the room and went to bathe or whatever it was you did in the bathroom, I searched this whole room. I figured that you were up to something; I just didn't know what it was. I suspected something when you came around Capers lookin' for weed. Capers ain't never sold weed, so I knew your girlfriend couldn't have never told you nothing like that. I found your gun and emptied it. I told myself that nowadays a rack of bitches carry guns and that maybe I was being too paranoid. As we started to fuck, I hoped that you were after my heart and not my life." I reached up and backhanded Nomeka off me. Her body flew off the bed and landed on the floor. Dazed, she tried to get up and run, but I was on her in seconds. I grabbed Nomeka by the hair and slung her to the floor. Dick swinging, I stood over her like an angry African warrior.

"Real killers never ask a rack of questions before they kill. They kill first and ask questions last. That was the mistake your brother made and I can tell y'all related." I stomped Nomeka repeatedly with my bare foot until blood flew out of her mouth and nose. Then I walked over to my pants and pulled my gun out.

I walked back over to Nomeka and shot her three times in the head. I wiped down everything I touched and put my clothes on. I pulled the card that I'd found on Nomeka's dresser out my pocket.

THE ULTIMATE SACRIFICE II
LOVE IS PAIN

Detective Maurice Tolliver
D.C. Police Department
First District 202-354-9643

On the back of the card, were the words: *Call me if you hear anything else about your bro.*

Nomeka had talked to the cops about her brother and cousin's death. I wondered exactly what the police could possibly have in the case and whether or not my name was ever mentioned. I wondered if Samantha, Dave, or Sheree ever talked to the cops about the murders on Canal Street. Stuffing the card back in my pocket, I wiped down every surface in Nomeka's apartment, vacuumed the rug, and snatched the sheets off her bed. Putting them in a bag, they had to go with me. I didn't want to leave behind any clue that I was ever in the apartment. Satisfied that all loose ends were now eliminated, I left the apartment. As I walked down the back stairs that led to an alley, I stopped in my tracks and realized that not all the loose ends were eliminated. There was one left. One loose end that I couldn't overlook.

"That bitch is really crazy," Reesie shouted from the bathroom.

I was fully clothed lying across Reesie's bed, still thinking about Nomeka when Reesie walked out of the bathroom. She had a towel wrapped around her head and an even larger towel wrapped around her body.

"She gon' call me and tell me all this wild shit about a big argument that her and Khadafi had. The whole time she ain't sayin' it but she implying that Kemie is the reason that she can't have Khadafi."

I was about to say, "Who you talkin' bout?" But then I remembered that she was venting about Marnie.

Reesie sat on the bed and lotioned her legs. "Don't get me wrong, Marnie is my girl, but c'mon, she knows that Kemie is my blood cousin and I can't go against her for nobody. Blood is thicker than water and all that shit, you know? I mean, ain't nobody tell her retarded ass to go against the grain and start fuckin' Khadafi. She started out fuckin' him just to get back at Kemie because Kemie fucked her boyfriend, Black Junior.

"I told her ass then, that that was a juvenile move. But nobody listens to me. When Khadafi went back to jail, I thought Marnie was gonna wise up and realize that Khadafi and Kemie gon' be together no matter what. I thought the bitch had all that shit outta her system. Then Khadafi comes back home and she starts fuckin' him again. Now she done fucked around and caught feelings for him. She all crying and shit. All fucked up because he told her that he wanna be with Kemie. Duh? Didn't I tell her stupid ass that?

"She flicking off on me talkin' bout he wrong for takin' her back when she crosses everybody and how he know that she fucked Omar and Bean and that's what got them killed. I didn't even know that crazy ass shit—"

~ 278 ~

I heard the names Omar and Bean and Reesie saying that's what got them killed that caught my attention. "Hold on, slow down—what you just say about Bean and Omar?"

"While Marnie was ranting and raving about Khadafi and how he was stupid for trusting Kemie after all she did to him, she brought up the fact that Kemie fucked Omar and Bean while Khadafi was in prison—"

"Does slim know about that?"

"According to her, yeah. She said she was the one who told him about it and that's why Khadafi killed them when he came home."

I couldn't believe what I had just heard. "You telling me Khadafi killed Bean and Omar?"

Reesie handed me the lotion. "Here, lotion my feet and back for me. Yeah. That's what Marnie said Khadafi told her. He killed Bean and Omar because they betrayed him by fuckin' Kemie while he was in." My head was fucked up. It was hard trying to comprehend the severity of what Reesie was saying.

"And you been knew about that?" I asked as I rubbed lotion on Reesie's feet.

"No, boy. I just told you Marnie just told me that shit yesterday. I never knew who killed Bean and Omar. Devon told me—"

I blocked out everything Reesie said after that. If what she said was true, then I had a problem. My loyalty to Khadafi was in jeopardy. He was my partner, ride or die, and I loved him, but if he killed Bean that was something that I couldn't forgive. Especially over some pussy. That

was absolutely inexcusable, if true. All of us had grown up together from the dirt. We had banged out together, fought, cried, lied, and beefed with the Southwest niggas together. Bean was my closest friend, just like he was to Khadafi. If Khadafi killed Bean with no regard for love, faith, and loyalty, then he wasn't to be trusted. What would stop him from killing me? On top of all that, that would make Khadafi a vicious snake because he lied and told me that he was getting a tattoo with Bean on his arm. If Khadafi killed Bean, then that meant he had no intention of getting that tat' and had lied to conceal his betrayal from me.

"—her business. Kemie was caught up on the dude, Phil, then. Phil had her ass running around like a chicke—"

Phil? Kemie was fuckin' with a dude named Phil, too? Phil? Where had I heard the name Phil? Oh shit. The other day. The dude that we snatched. His name was Phil. But Khadafi said that the dude had something to do with that shit from up the hotel . . .

"You talkin' bout black Phil from up Ledroit Park?"

"With the gold Benz wagon and the Hummer? Yeah. You know him?"

"I heard of him," I lied and then it all made sense to me. The dude, Phil, was still fucking Kemie, and Khadafi somehow—Marnie told him—that she was still fucking with Phil and Khadafi snapped. That's why he wanted to snatch the dude and question him instead of just killing him. And that's why he told me that once he got the dude down Capers, I could leave. Khadafi didn't want me to know what was really up. He didn't want me to know that

he was killing a man because of his whore ass girlfriend. And if Khadafi went through the trouble of kidnapping and killing the dude, Phil because he was fucking Kemie, then there was no doubt in my mind that he'd zap out and kill Bean for the same offense. An uncontrollable anger hit me. It grabbed and gripped my soul and wouldn't let go. I respected Khadafi. Looked up to him. Stayed loyal to him. But what about my loyalty to Bean? Together, him and Khadafi raised me, fed me gunpowder, and taught me to hunt for food. Luther Fuller and Alvin Vaughn. Khadafi and Bean. My men. My brothers. My friends. The latter killed by the former. Over a freak ass bitch. I was blindly loyal to a dude that had no loyalty. To anyone. I thought about my confrontation with Khadafi and our eventual showdown. There was no way that I could let Khadafi get away with killing Bean. He would definitely pay, but first I'ma take the one thing from him that he loves the most. Kemie. As the blinders fell from my eyes, I focused back in on what Reesie was saying.

"—why I don't even go down Capers no more. I be wanting to go down there and chill with Esha and nem', but naw, the projects take too much outta you."

I lay down on the bed and basically just let Reesie talk herself out. I sat quietly, watched her roll her hair up, and then lay out her clothes that she was wearing to work. Finally, she got under the covers and rolled over beside me. About five minutes later, Reesie was asleep. I listened to her light snore and thought about the card in my pocket with the detective's number on it. Then I thought about

what the cops might already know about the caper on Canal Street. And how they could connect me to it or any of the murders that took place afterwards. I glanced again at Reesie and thought that if I had a heart and felt love, I would love her. But I didn't have a heart. And she was the only living person besides Khadafi and La La that could connect the dots for the police. La La was still missing. Nobody had seen or heard from him after he took the police on that high-speed chase that ended with him jumping off a bridge. Nobody knew if he was dead or alive. And Khadafi already had a date with the Grim Reaper. So I really had no choice. I had to eliminate all ties. I got out the bed slowly, grabbed the pillow I was laying on and walked around the bed. I put the pillow over Reesie's face and pressed it down. Her legs kicked out as she struggled to get the pillow off her head. I lay across the pillow, pressing down on it with all my body weight. Reesie struggled for a minute more and then went limp and she was still. I raised the pillow off her face. She looked peaceful. Like she was still sleeping. I walked past the mirror on her dresser and caught sight of my reflection. What I saw shocked me. I was crying.

Chapter Forty-Three
AMEEN

—heard Mommy scream. I ran downstairs to see what was wrong and all I saw was Mommy and Asia standing in the doorway. The door was open, but there was nobody there. Mommy slammed the door and rushed us upstairs. She said that some man named Harold rang the doorbell and when she answered the door, he said that you told him to come and check on her and the kids. Mommy was crying by then and that made me and Asia cry, too. She said the man told her that he had a message from you. She asked what the message was and the man said something about betrayal, slaughter, and penalties for betrayal. Then she said he pointed a gun at her. Mommy said the man was going to kill her. She said Asia called her name and the man saw Asia—then he ran. He just left and ran, she said. I asked her what did the betrayal part mean and she said that it wasn't important. Mommy wouldn't stop crying, Daddy. We all went and stayed with Grandma Wilma. For a long time. I heard Mommy talkin' to Grandma one night. About two weeks after it happened. I was on the stairs and they didn't

know it. Mommy told Grandma that you sent the man to kill her. She said you found out about a man that she was messing with and you sent another man to kill her—Daddy?"

"I'm here, baby."

"Daddy, is that true? Daddy, did you send somebody to kill Mommy?"

Lying back in my cell, I thought about the conversation I had with my daughter a few weeks ago. What she told me had crushed me to the floor and there was no way that I could pick myself up. No matter what I did, nothing could take my mind off the revelation I got that day. Even though I wished death on Shawnay, I never thought the day would come that she would do the unthinkable.

"Did you do it, Daddy? Huh? Mommy said you did."

That day I did something I promised myself I'd never do. I lied to my child. There was no way I could tell my oldest child that her mother was fucking my friend and I was beside myself with jealousy and rage and that yes, I sent Umar to kill her. I couldn't tell Kenya that. So I lied.

"No. Never would I do something like that. I love your mother and I would never hurt her. I have no idea why she says that I sent the dude."

"That's what I said to Mommy the next day when she got off work. I told her that I had heard what she told Grandma. She said I was old enough to know the truth and told me that you felt that she betrayed you by messing with another man and that you couldn't deal with it. So you wanted her dead. I cried and cried and defended you,

Daddy, but she wouldn't listen to me. She told Asia and me that we were moving and that our phone numbers would be changed. She stopped talking about you and when Asia and I asked about you, she told us that you didn't love us and that was why you never tried to find us. She threw away all your letters and I had no way of knowing how to reach you, Daddy. Daddy, I love you and Asia loves you—

The sound of chains rattling broke my train of thought and I looked toward the bars. They were bringing a dude back on the tier. The dude had been in court all day. I knew that from his conversation with another dude on the tier. The dude was tall, brown skinned, and thick. He wore two braids in his hair that hung to his shoulders. As he passed my cell, he looked directly at me and nodded. I nodded back. "Thirty-one cell, Sarge," the CO screamed to the control bubble. A few seconds later, the cell door opened and shut. Then the CO took off the dude's belly chain and shackles.

"Ay, Walker?" the dude called out to the retreating CO.

"What's up, Shakur?"

"Y'all, got some mail up there for me?"

"I think I did see something in the bubble for you. I'll bring it to you in a few. I'm waiting on the kitchen to send your no meat/ no pork tray up here. As soon as it comes, I'ma bring your mail with it."

"A'ight, Walk."

"Big Cochise?" a voice called out from down the tier.

"What's up, moe? Who dat?"

"Randy."

"Oh, what's up, Randy Shaw?"

"Ain't shit. What happened in court?"

"The government still putting their case on. They ain't got but one witness against me. And that's the bitch that gave me the nigga's address. A hot bitch named Angie. She got on the stand, started crying, and shit. She talking about she loved the nigga and that she didn't know that I was gonna kill him. She said she just thought I wanted to talk to him. That bitch wicked as shit. She knew what the fuck it was hittin' for when I first hollered at her. They asked her hot ass why she decided to come forward. Guess what that hot bitch said?"

"What she say, slim?"

"She been having nightmares ever since she found out that whoever killed the nigga, Boo, also killed his—"

At the mention of the name Boo, I was instantly alert. I stood up in the cell and went closer to the bars.

"—daughter and grandmother. She see dead people and all that geekin' ass shit."

The dude, Randy bust out laughing. "Go 'head with that bullshit, slim. She ain't say no shit like that."

"Moe, kill my motha, she said that. She said she knew the dude's grandmother all her life."

All I kept saying to myself was, "Naw. This can't be happening. I know this ain't the dude that killed Boo, his grandmother, daughter, and Umar. Can't be."

"—and she said his baby mother, Tangie was a friend of hers—"

I couldn't believe my ears. The dude had just said Boo baby's mother name, Tangie. I had heard her name a million times as much as she and Boo stayed beefing. Tangela Primrose. That was her full name.

"—and all that. She said that she had to come and testify even though she didn't see me do it. The government grasping for straws, moe. All they got besides her is a fingerprint from a lamp they said I touched in the house."

"Slim, I can't even believe they got an indictment with that flimsy ass evidence."

"I'm hip. But it was a high profile case and since D.C. is about to be crowned the Murder Capital again, the mayor and nem' geekin' to show the world that they can handle the shit and that shit ain't outta control. I'ma beat this shit. I already know that. It's the other two cases that jive got me scared."

"What cases is that?"

"That Muslim church joint and this other joint I caught down Sursum Cordas. I was doing too much barefaced shit, moe. But you know how that shit go. I wasn't out there bullshittin' and I wasn't givin' a fuck."

I looked all around the cell. There had to be something that I could make a knife out of. Searching high and low for something—anything, I found nothing. My mind was made up halfway through dude's conversation that he was the nigga that killed my men, but when he mentioned the Muslim church, I knew that he meant Muslim Masjid. And I remembered Umar telling me that a dude opened fire on them when they were coming out the Masjid and that a lot

of the Muslims had died. Allah had to place me in this cell at this exact moment to hear what I heard. I was convinced of that. I could kill this dude, avenge the dead Muslims, and maybe Allah would grant me paradise despite my sins.

I had heard enough. I walked back to my bunk and laid back down. The combination of what my daughter had told me and what I'd just heard was enough to make a man who had never killed before, kill. I visually locked the image of the tall, muscular dude with the two braids into my brain. I knew that his last name was Shakur and that the dude on the tier called him Cochise. And that was all I needed to know. Whenever I got the opportunity, his life was mine to take. And I planned to take it. *All I gotta do is find me a knife.*

The door to my cell shook and woke me from my sleep. I knew it had to be early because we had just eaten breakfast about an hour ago. I hopped out the bed and went to the bars. I put my arm out the bars and said, "What's up?"

"Felder, you got a legal. Get ready," the CO hollered down to the tier.

After I washed my face and brushed my teeth. I stepped into my oversized orange jumpsuit that had D.C. Jail across the back and put my shoes on. Walking to the bars, I stuck my arm out and hit the top of the wall, signaling to the CO that I was ready for my visit. After I was handcuffed to a bellychain and shackled, my cell door opened. I walked to the sally port and looked at the two boards on each side of the wall. In the unit where I was housed, there was a left

side and a right side. Top and bottom. The two boards on the wall listed every cell on both sides and the name of the person in the cell. I was on the bottom left. My eyes raced down the board for the left side and settled on cell thirty-one. The name beside it read Cochise A. Shakur. *Got it.* A few minutes later, I was led through the halls of the jail to the visiting hall.

"Antonio, how are you, big guy?" Rudy said, reaching across the table and shaking my cuffed hand. "I see you made it to town safely. Glad to have you back."

"You just don't know how good it feels to be here," I responded.

"Your family been through to visit?"

"Every week somebody comes through. Old buddies, females I used to deal with. It's definitely a blessing to be back. I can catch the local news and find out what's goin' on in the city, ya know?"

"I know what you mean, big guy. I feel the same way when I'm away from D.C. too long. It's just something about this city that grows on you. All right, big guy, let's get down to business. I filed a motion in the Superior Court today."

"On what?"

"I filed a motion for a new trial. Under the 23-110 statute. The judge in your trial fucked up," Rudy said as he opened a folder and slid some papers across the desk to me.

I read the papers and couldn't believe what I was reading.

"Did you know that Eric Frazier was about to be indicted in federal court?"

Still reading the papers, I shook my head. "Naw. I had no clue."

"Well, let me tell you what happened. Your old friend, Eric was doing business with an undercover narcotics agent. They recorded thirteen controlled buys. He was recorded on camera saying all kinds of stuff that the government wanted to use against guys in the neighborhood where you two hung out. At the time of your arrest for the murder, the US Attorney's office was putting together a twenty-one count indictment that named you on two counts of possession with intent to distribute, Eric Frazier on all counts, Rondell Ball—"

"That's Eric's cousin, RB."

"Paul Thompson—"

"Fat Paul," I said, without looking up from the papers. I was reading everything that Rudy was saying. "And Jeremy Bivens."

"JB. I know all of 'em."

"Before anybody could be picked up, an investigator for Eric's attorney on another charge overheard somebody talking about the secret indictment. He passed that info on to Eric and his attorney. Eric's attorney, Renee Roberts contacted the government and cut a deal. The deal included him testifying against you and the other people on the indictment.

"Okay, here's where things went wrong. The government decided to drop you from the federal

indictment because they had Eric Frazier, who was gonna help them convict you on the murder. The government's counsel, Ann Sloan—remember her?"

"Of course. She was the prosecutor in my trial."

"Well, she went to the judge before your trial and had what's called an `Ex parte' hearing. What you're reading right now are the transcripts from that hearing that the judge placed under seal. Your last appeal attorney Ken Hicks failed to uncover the document that ordered the Ex parte proceeding sealed. I filed a motion before you got here to have it unsealed and that's what I discovered. The prosecutor was in error and so was the judge and the Appeals Court never got the chance to see this because it was still under seal. They violated your rights under the Confrontation Clause and Brady vs. Maryland. You are entitled to relief for the errors that Ken made under Strickland vs. Washington. I'm going to the COA building tomorrow and speak to the clerk of the court about getting in front of the nine judges sooner."

"Do you think you'll be able to get the date moved up?"

"It's a 50/50 chance that I'll get them to do it. If not, I can always press for an appeal bond since you have already been incarcerated for nearly ten years. Trust and believe, Antonio that I am going to do everything in my power to get you out of prison. I don't know when that might be, but I think it's gonna happen. I have a few more things that I want to discuss with you, big guy. And you are going to really love this . . ."

Chapter Forty-Four
KEMIE

For the last couple of days I could see that something was bothering Khadafi, so I gave him his space during the daylight hours, but made sure to do my thing in the bedroom at night. I think what took place down Capers with Phil really took a toll on both of us. But the funny thing was that I had taken a human life and I wasn't broken up about it. Especially given the fact that it was Phil, someone that I actually believed I loved. All the way up until he spoke that day and revealed what was really in his heart, he changed my love into hate within minutes. I didn't want to kill him, but I had to win my man back. It wasn't until real life was presented to me in that room, in that house down Capers, that I realized what I had and what I was about to lose. All over some dynamite dick. I stood in that room with the gun in my hand and thought about the day I had let Phil and his man slut me out. That day replayed in my head every day and it always made me mad at Phil. Now don't get me wrong, I have done some whorish

shit in my day. Pretty much, I've done it all sexually, with whatever dude I was with, but I never did it all with more than one dude at a time. Wasn't nobody running no trains on Rakemie Bryant. Not at all. Morally, it just seemed trifling and too freaked out to entertain the thought of sexing more than one dude at a time. And for good reason, I later learned. There is no worse feeling for a woman who loves herself than to be sandwiched between two men as they bang away at her in all different positions. Now, I'm a bitch that loves to suck dick. Absolutely love it. I'm a bitch that loves to get fucked royally in every orifice on my body. But trying to suck a dick while getting fucked is some other shit that I just couldn't get into. Double penetration on any level doesn't allow you to concentrate and enjoy one thing. So you end up enjoying nothing. That's the way I felt that day with Phil and his man, Dino. I was humiliated and degraded. The look on Dino's face as he pulled his dick out my mouth and shot cum all over my face made me feel like a two-dollar crackhead. But I never got mad at Phil for that until the day I killed him. And to be honest, I don't really feel bad about it. I realized that day that Phil never cared about me at all. He was using me the whole time. For all those years, I was too starstruck to see it because he had money, cars, and a million bitches that wanted him. It took that whole episode to happen to wake me up and see that it would be Khadafi and me forever. Just like when we were little. Peanut butter and jelly.

"Kemie?" Khadafi hollered from the living room.

I put down the skillet I was washing in the sink. "Huh?"

"Telephone."

"Who is it?" I asked.

"I don't know, but it sounds like your mother."

I dried my hands on the dishtowel and walked out into the living room. The cordless receiver was laid out on the couch. I picked it up and said, "Hello?"

"Kemie—" It was my mother.

"Ma, what's wrong?"

"Re-e-e-s-s-ie—"

Panic gripped me. "What's wrong with Reesie?" I shouted.

When my mother didn't answer, I repeated the question. "Where are you right now, Ma?"

"At—Rees—ie's house."

I threw the phone down and grabbed my coat, purse, and car keys.

"Where you going?" Khadafi asked me.

"Something's wrong with Reesie." That was all I said before rushing out the door.

I pushed the speedometer to the max as I raced to Southeast. Something was wrong and my mother wouldn't say what and that scared the shit out of me. The feeling of trepidation in my stomach wouldn't leave, and as I pulled up to Marlbury Plaza, my fears were confirmed. I saw several members of my family huddled together attempting to hold up my aunt Denise. There was an ambulance and a white van parked directly in front of the building with six police squad cars. Plain-clothes detectives were in and out of the building and talking to my family. I double parked

the truck and ran over to my relatives. The grieved look on their faces told the story. My cousin Reesie was gone.

"What happened to Reesie?" I asked Reesie's little sister, Tera, who was sitting on the curb with tears running down her face.

"They don't know yet." Tera sobbed as she wiped her eyes and slob off her chin. "We been calling her for days and she wouldn't answer the phone. She didn't show up for work for two days and Mama got worried. We called her cell phone, came over here, and banged on her door. Mama had the resident manager open her door and—and—she was in the bed—" Tera broke down crying again. "She wouldn't wake up—she wasn't breathing—"

That was all I heard before the scream came from my mouth. I dropped to the ground, twisted, and turned. There was no greater pain that I had ever felt. In seconds, I was surrounded by family.

"No-no-no-Reesie . . . N-O-O-O-O! No-no-no-no-no! Re-e-e-es-ie-e-e! No! No—gawd—please!"

Chapter Forty-Five
MARNIE

Khadafi had a thing for his trucks and me. Every time he bought a new truck, he wanted me to fuck him in it to break it in. So when he went and got the Cadillac Escalade, it was the same thing. The same day he got it he picked me up and rode me around. I gave him head as he drove, and then we pulled over in an alley off Sixtieth Street and broke that bad boy in. We crawled all the way in the back and did it, then worked our way back up to the front of the truck. Khadafi fucked me on every row of seats in the Escalade and in both front seats. He knows that when I cum, I squirt, so he made sure that I came all over each seat. That same day we rode up Montana Terrace so Khadafi could holler at one of his men named La La. When Khadafi went into the building, I got on my nosy shit and went through the compartment in the middle console of the truck. Just wanting to see what was in there. It was empty except for three envelopes. I took them out and went in them. One envelope held the bill of sale for the truck. The second one

held all the insurance information. Both were in the name of Mary Henderson. The third envelope was from Verizon and turned out to be a cell phone bill in Kemie's name. I stared at the bill and committed one thing to memory. The address on the bill. *1736 Woodlawn Drive, Tacoma Park, Maryland.*

When I looked up, Khadafi was coming, so I hurried up and put the envelopes back in the compartment and faked like I was asleep. For some reason, my instincts told me that that info would come in handy one day and my instincts were right. I went to that address the day after Khadafi left my house and sure enough, I saw his DTS and his Escalade parked outside. On the side of the house was a carport. In that carport, sat Kemie's Land Rover. I sat outside the house for a while until I chickened out and went home. I went back the next day and the same thing happened. As soon as I pulled up to the house today, I saw Kemie rush out of the house and sprint to her truck. When she backed out of the carport, I let her get a half block ahead of me before I pursued her. Something was up with her. I knew that from the way she was driving. My little Altima was almost no match for the speed of her truck, but I did a pretty good job of keeping up based on sheer will and determination. When we got to Good Hope Road, I knew exactly where she was headed. To Reesie's house. But why was she driving so fast and erratically to get there? I parked my car across from Marlbury Plaza and watched as Kemie turned into the parking lot. The police cars and emergency vehicles everywhere piqued my curiosity. I

watched Kemie jump out of her truck and run to a crowd of people. I squinted my eyes and focused on the crowd. I recognized them all. Reesie's mother was over there, and so was Kemie's mother. Kemie stopped by the curb and sat down with a young girl. It was Reesie's younger sister, Tera. What the hell was going on? And where was Reesie? Then I watched Kemie stand up and all of a sudden, she dropped to the ground. She rolled around on the ground as if she were in pain. Her family ran over to her and surrounded her. Kemie got up off the ground and pulled away from her family members. Then she ran back to her truck and hopped inside. From what I could see something must've happened to Reesie. Silently, I prayed that I was wrong, because I love Reesie so much, but something was wrong. There was no way to find out what was up without makikng my presence known. Like a bat out of hell she pulled out of the parking lot. She turned left and raced up Good Hope Road. Again, I followed her. She ran a light and took Alabama Avenue all the way down. My courage built as I maneuvered my car to keep up with her. I didn't know where she was taking me, but I stayed with her. The next thing I knew, Kemie turned into an empty lot on Southern Avenue and stopped the truck. I pulled up and rode past her. While riding past, I looked in the truck to see what she was doing. Kemie had her head down on the steering wheel.

I felt my adrenaline soar as I pulled over and parked on the Maryland side of the street. The streets were semi-deserted as I quickly walked back to the D.C. side of

Southern Avenue. Dressed in black jeans, black Reebok tennis shoes, and a black leather coat, I walked up on the Land Rover. When I got about five-feet away, I pulled out the gun. Kemie's head was still on the steering wheel when I got all the way up on the truck. I tapped gently on the window of her driver side door. Kemie looked up at me with a puzzled look on her face. I silently mouthed the words good-bye and stepped back two steps. I lifted the gun.

Chapter Forty-Six
KHADAFI

No matter what I did or tried to do, I couldn't shake all the wild shit bouncing around in my head. Where the fuck was La La? Not one body had been recovered and nobody had seen or heard from him since that night at the hotel parking lot. The news said that he leapt backwards off the bridge. Was it possible to survive a leap over a bridge that high? Was he pulled under the water by the currents, drowned and washed way down the river beyond the points where the police looked for him? Every time I think about what La La did for me and TJ that night reminds me of what Ameen did for us in Texas. *The Ultimate Sacrifice.*

That thought brought on thoughts of Lil Cee and had me on the edge a little bit. I hated not knowing anything about one of my enemies. Where he lived, slept at sometimes, hung out, what restaurants he loved. That kind of shit. I wanted to kill him so bad, it made my dick hard, but I didn't have a clue of where to start looking for him. I felt like a sitting duck waiting to be plucked off by an

overzealous duck hunter. But above all that, the situation with Marnie being pregnant had me the most vexed.

"I'm pregnant."

"What did you say?"

"You heard me, I'm pregnant."

Every word she said to me that day hit me like a punch to the sternum and knocked the wind out of me. I was about to be a father and had not one clue about how to be one. My father was never really there for me, that's why I was raised by the game, the streets, and killers. What could I teach a child? When all I knew was how to murder muthafuckas, rob, pillage, and plunder. What kind of father could I be? One who helped with homework and science projects? One who went to PTA meetings and ferried the kid to soccer practice and dance class? Never. Let the truth be told, being a father scared the shit out of me. Being responsible for another person's life was too much for me to grasp. That's why having kids was never a part of my plans. I'ma outlaw. And outlaws live for the moment. We never look past today because tomorrow is not promised to us in any way. And besides, I never wanted to ruin a kid's life the way my father did mine.

"Are you gonna keep it?"

"That depends."

"On what?"

"You."

"How?"

"That depends on the decision you make in this room, right now."

"What decision?"

"Are you still leaving me and goin' back to Kemie?"

I told Marnie that I had to go back to Kemie, and I couldn't explain all my reasons. How was I supposed to make her understand the pact that Kemie and I had just signed in blood? And when she said the decision to keep the baby depended on my decision to stay or go back to Kemie, I thought by me saying I was going back to Kemie, she'd decide to get rid of the baby. But for some reason, she did the opposite. So if I would've chosen to stay with her, did that mean that she would have aborted the baby?

"You'll hear from me and the courts after the baby is born."

If I lived to be a hundred, which I knew I wouldn't, I'd never fully understand women and why they made the decisions that they made. Marnie had to know what a terrible father I'd be. She knew firsthand the type of life I lived. Why would she want to bring a baby into the world by a dude that didn't expect to live longer than seventy-two hours? What I told her on the way out the door was from my heart and probably the realest shit I had ever said.

"You sayin' that you'll see me when the baby comes; that takes what? Nine months? I might not even live that long."

Ring. Ring. Ring. Ring.

I looked at the cordless house phone as if it was poisonous. Then I remembered Kemie had bolted out of here saying that something was wrong with her cousin,

Reesie. Reaching over and grabbing the phone, I answered it. "Yeah?"

"May I speak with Khadafi, please?"

"Who is this?"

"This is Michelle with OnStar."

"Who?"

"Sir, my name is Michelle. I am an OnStar adviser. The 2008 Land Rover Discovery in the name of a Rakemie Bryant is equipped with OnStar. We received a signal from that vehicle about five minutes ago. I conferenced into the vehicle and asked if someone needed assistance. Ms. Bryant answered and said that she was hurt—"

"Hurt how?" I asked as I stood up.

"She said she'd been shot—"

"No! No-no-no. Hell naw!"

"I immediately alerted the authorities and emergency personnel. Via GPS technology, I was able to give them the exact location of the vehicle. Ms. Bryant asked me to call you."

Tears were in my eyes and falling down my cheek. "Is she okay?"

"That I don't know, sir. Before paramedics reached the scene, Ms. Bryant became unresponsive. The 9-1-1 operator told me that paramedics did arrive minutes later and Ms. Bryant was taken to Prince George's County Hospital—"

Dropping the phone, I ran upstairs and got my keys, my hammer, and my cell phone. *She said she'd been shot.*

A NOVEL BY ANTHONY FIELDS

Somebody had shot Kemie. But why? Was it something I did? I asked myself as I hit the Capital Beltway en route to PG Hospital. Was it somebody connected to Phil? His brother and relatives had to know he was dead by now because his body was found down Capers a couple of days ago. Was Kemie shot in retaliation for his murder? Had Phil told somebody about Kemie and her boyfriend, the killer? The one from Capers projects? Then they put two and two together and came up with four? I could barely see the road with all the tears in my eyes. I had to keep wiping my eyes every minute. I started praying to Allah to save Kemie. *Because if she died; no one would be safe around me.*

About eight minutes later, I was pulling up to the emergency entrance at PG. Hopping out the truck with my hammer in my waist; I walked frantically in search of somebody who could tell me something. I ran into a nurse.

"About twenty minutes ago, an ambulance brought a woman in here."

"Sir, ambulances have been coming in all night with people," the annoyed nurse answered.

"She was shot. Her name is Bryant."

"Gunshot victim? Female? She's in OR three. I almost—"

I looked at the signs on the walls and doors and followed them to OR three. Medical staff was coming and going quickly in and out of the room.

"May I help you, sir?" a security guard appeared from nowhere and asked me.

"Yeah, cuz, I'm lookin' for my woman—" My voice faded and it took me a minute to get myself back together. ". . . they said she got shot."

"Rakemie Bryant?"

"Yeah—"

"She just got here about fifteen minutes ago. She's in there, man, and I ain't gon' lie to you; they say she's in bad shape."

I moved past the security guard and was about to enter the O.R., but was grabbed from behind.

"Hold on, main man, you can't go in there. It's for medical personnel only. I know how you feel, but trying to go in there ain't gonna help your woman. We got some of the best surgeons on the East Coast at PG; let them do what they do. When they finish, they'll come out and I'll have them speak with you." Then he led me to a waiting area and left. I sat down in one of the chairs, put my face in my hands, and cried. And waited to hear something. *If my baby dies . . .*

"Main man."

I looked up and saw the security guard standing over me. I must've nodded off for a while. "What's up, cuz?"

"They just came out of the O.R. The surgeon who operated on your girl is right over there at the counter."

I rose quickly and walked over to the surgeon. He was standing at the counter writing something in a folder. "Doc, how is she?"

"Excuse me?"

"Rakemie Bryant. The woman you just operated on. How is she?"

"And you are?"

"Her fiance."

"She's stable right now. But she's still not out of the woods. Ms. Bryant was shot three times from a close proximity. She has a bullet in her head that we can't go near out of fear that it may do irreparable damage if removed. She was shot once in the face. The bullet entered her cheek, broke the cheekbone, ricocheted off that bone, and exited below her right ear lobe. The third bullet is the one that did the most damage. It entered her neck and went straight through shattering the second and third vertebra in her spinal column. We stabilized her head and put a metal splint in where the vertebrae were shattered. She had tiny pieces of glass embedded in her face. Given the report, we have from the police and the EMT's, that would be the window that shattered as the bullets passed through on the way to Ms. Bryant. I would venture to say that the window being up is what changed the trajectory of those bullets. Had it not been there, she would have likely been killed instantly. We also had to abort the child she was carrying. She was in her first tri-mester. The fetus would not have survived the trauma—"

Kemie was pregnant?

"—the bullet in her head concerns me a great deal, but we've done all we can do at the moment. The next twenty-four hours is critical to her recovery. The next twenty-four hours will determine if she survives. We have to monitor

her response to the medications we gave her. See if her body rejects it or responds to it. So in a nutshell, only God knows how this will turn out. If I were you, I'd pray for her a lot. It's all anybody can do at this point."

I stood there in that spot stuck. I willed my legs to move, but they wouldn't. My mind was too busy trying to comprehend what the doctor had just said. Kemie was pregnant. Why didn't she tell me that? *Unless she knew that the baby wasn't mine.* There was a possibility that Kemie was going to die. The thought of it alone fucked my head and heart up. I couldn't believe the turn of events. A few days ago, Kemie killed a man to prove her love to me and now somebody had tried to kill her. Somebody had shot the love of my life three times. Three bullets. Three instruments of death. It didn't take that many to kill one woman. And a child.

As I walked back to the waiting area, I decided that Kemie's mother needed to be here, too. So I called her.

By the time the whole Bryant clan showed up at the hospital, it was too much for me to handle. Mentally. One thing that I learned from them nagged at my mind. They had found Reesie, Kemie's cousin, in her bed dead. No one knew how she died, but the fact remained she was dead. I wondered if TJ knew that. If he did, why hadn't he called me and told me. That must've been the reason—hold on. Another thought hit me. I walked back over to Kemie's mother.

"Ms. Bryant. When you called the house and spoke to Kemie. She rushed out of the house. Did she ever make it to where you were?"

"Yeah. She was at Reesie's building with us. She took the news real hard, which was expected and she flicked off. Everybody tried to console her and talk to her, but she wasn't having it. Then suddenly she just got up, ran to her truck, and pulled off."

Reesie was dead and somebody had followed Kemie from Reesie's building and shot her. I scrambled and unscrambled my brain trying to put the pieces together. But still no answers came to mind.

I camped out at PG Hospital for the next two days. Kemie's condition hadn't worsened and it hadn't gotten better. The doctors were optimistic that she would pull through and that was all I needed to hear. I decided to go home and bathe, shave, and change clothes. But I was so hungry that I couldn't walk five feet without my stomach reminding me that I hadn't eaten. So I walked to the hospital's cafeteria in search of something edible.

The cafeteria ended up having some pretty good food. It was set up like a buffet. I picked out the barbecue chicken, potato salad, and rice pilaf. Coming through the check out line, I turned around and almost knocked over my food and somebody else's.

I steadied my tray and myself and looked into the face of the woman that I'd nearly toppled and the air left my lungs. She was still one of the prettiest women in any room.

I stared her up and down. Shawnay was wearing grey pinstriped slacks that hugged her every curve, a black long sleeve blouse that accented her ample breasts and black open toed high heels. A pink and white french manicure decorated her toes. Her fingernails bore the same design.

"Are you gonna say hello, or just stand here and stare at me after you almost knocked me down?" Shawnay said and smiled.

"You look beautiful."

"Thank you. How have you been?"

"I'm good. Is everybody okay? What are you doing here?"

"I work here. And everybody I love is okay. What are you doing here?"

"My-my-my cousin got shot. I been up here two days waiting to see if she gon' be a'ight."

"Sorry to hear it. Is she gonna be okay?" Shawnay asked with a concerned look on her face.

"We still don't know. You look beautiful."

Shawnay smiled again. "You just said that."

"I did? My bad. I mean it though. You look good as shit. I called you—"

"I know. I was going through some stuff and I needed some time off from you. From us. Then I found out you were back in prison. I looked you up on the computer and saw that you were back in Beaumont. I started writing you a letter, but never finished it. After awhile, I just decided to let sleeping dogs lie. But it's good seeing you and you look

good, too, despite the wear and tear of the last two days you been here. We need—"

"Mommy, Kashon, keep crying—oh! Excuse me for interrupting."

I looked at Ameen's oldest daughter with a baby in her arms and realized how big and grown she was. She had to be at least sixteen years old and she looked exactly like her father. She cradled a small child in her arms that looked to be about five or six months old. Ameen had to be sick that his daughter had a baby.

"Give him to me. Here, take this stuff, pay for it and go over to the table with your sister. I'll be over there in a minute."

We both watched her daughter leave. When she was out of earshot, Shawnay turned to me and said, "I was saying that we need to sit down and talk."

"Cool. That would be good. When did your daughter have a baby? Does Ameen know?" I asked.

"No, Ameen doesn't know his daughter has a baby and that's because she doesn't have a baby. This cute little guy here is mine. Ours. Khadafi, say hello to your son, Kashon."

Chapter Forty-Seven
SHAWNAY

"*I* got trouble with my friends/ trouble in my life/ problems when you don't come home/ at night/ but when you do/ you always start a fight/ but I can't be alone/ I need you to come back home/ I know you're messing around/ but who the hell else is gonna hold me down . . ."

I walked around my living room singing Melanie Fiona's hit song "It kills me" as I picked up after the kids. Running into Khadafi yesterday at the hospital while I had Kashon with me, to me was a sign from God that my son needed to know his father. Laughing to myself, I thought about the look on Khadafi's face when I told him that Kashon was his son. I thought about what he said.

"Say hello to your son, Kashon."

"My son? Kashon?"

"Yeah. Look at him. He looks just like you and me. That's why I named him Kashon. I took the 'Ka' sound in your name and put it with mine. Just spelled differently.

He's eight months old and he's the best little boy in the whole world."

"My son? I don't know what to say. Can I hold him?"

"Sure. He's your son."

"My son?" Khadafi repeated as he reached out and took Kashon in his arms.

"If you say my son one more time, I'ma think you losing your mind."

The conversation that Khadafi and I had after that was good but not sufficient to say everything that needed to be said. So I did what I thought was best and invited Khadafi to my house. I told him that we could sit down and talk comfortably, just him and me. The looks that I was getting from my girls at the table in the cafeteria were a bit much and I didn't feel like explaining myself to my children just yet. But in time, I would. They had a right to know who Kashon's father was and how everything came to be. Being an old-fashioned woman, I knew that it wasn't a good idea to have any man around my daughters. That was the reason I requested that Khadafi and I talk alone. And alone meant just that. So after school, my daughters went to my grandmother's house, where Kashon already was and would be, until I picked them up. I looked at my watch and saw that I still had an hour before Khadafi was scheduled to show up. In that hour, I could shower and make myself a little more presentable, a little sexier. I wanted to impress him. Don't ask me why. I just knew that something inside me still called out for his body, his touch, his tongue, his dick. The thought alone made me shiver. It had been about

seventeen months since we'd last been together and I missed him with a passion. That last hour or so, we were together, I had no idea that it would be our last time together. I had no idea that I was already pregnant with his child. I had no idea that a man with a beard would try to kill me: ..

Somebody had rung the doorbell. I stopped what I was doing and went to the door. "Who is it?" I called out as I approached the front door.

"Harold," a voice on the other side of the door said. "Ameen told me to come by and check on you and the kids. He says—"

I didn't think anything suspicious because Antonio had all kind of friends that were loyal to him. "When did you speak to Antonio?" I asked as I took the top lock off the door and opened it. I stood face-to-face with one of the men that I recognized from the pictures Antonio sent home from Beaumont. "Yesterday," the caramel complexioned man with the long beard, low haircut and pointed nose said. "He sent you a message."

"He did? What's that?"

The next words I heard chilled me to the bone. They were the same words that Antonio had told me he said to his childhood friend, Eric, who had testified against him in court.

"He said to tell you that betrayal is worse than slaughter. And the penalty for betrayal is death." The next thing I saw was the gun. The man with the beard brought it from behind his back and aimed it right in my face. I froze

in terror, riveted to the spot where I stood waiting to die. Expecting an explosion from the gun, what I heard next was, "Mommy, I need you to-"

My daughter had walked up on the scene and I saw the man with the gun look at her. I screamed then. The man turned and ran. My other daughter rushed to the door. "Mommy, what's wrong?"

I took my girls upstairs after that and we all cried together. But it wasn't until they were tucked safely in their beds that night that I allowed myself to face the reality of what happened. I felt hurt, angry, scared, and betrayed. I thought again about what the man with the gun had said, "The penalty for betrayal is death." How could Antonio have done something like that to me? Even though I had given myself to another man physically, didn't he know that I would always love him? Never in my wildest dreams had I imagined that Antonio would send someone to kill me because I slept with Khadafi. And how in the hell had Antonio found out about me and Khadafi anyway? That was the question that never left my mind as I cried myself to sleep that night. The next day I decided that it was time to leave Fifty-Sixth Street. I took my daughters to my grandmother's house and hired movers to pack up all our property and put it into storage. Leaving the house that I'd lived in for thirteen years; I jumped in my car and never looked back. We stayed with my grandmother until I found another house in Virginia. I hated uprooting my daughters and forcing them to change schools in the middle of the year, but I had no other choice. By the time we moved into

our new house, got situated and relaxed, I noticed the lump in my stomach. I ended up keeping my pregnancy a secret until I could no longer hide it. Khadafi was back in prison then and I saw no sense in telling him about my pregnancy. I looked at my watch again. It was 6:10 P.M. Fifty minutes before Khadafi arrived. A pain in my back forced me to sit down for a minute. The leather La-z-boy recliner that I sat in was so comfortable to me. I had been running around so much in anticipation of my meeting with Khadafi that I never realized how exhausted I really was. I allowed myself to close my eyes briefly. I needed to get up and finish cleaning up and then shower. A knock on my door caused me to glance at my watch. It was only 6:24P.M. Then I smiled. I wasn't expecting anyone but Khadafi and he was early. All kinds of carnal thoughts crossed my mind as I walked to the front door. Even though Khadafi was early, he was right on time. I knew that I needed a shower and if he played his cards right, he could take one with me and after that, who knows. As I reached the door, I said, "You're early, aren't you?"

Snatching the door open, I went to say something else, but my words got caught in my throat. My lungs constricted and I felt like I had asthma. The man standing on my porch smiled. It was a smile that I hadn't seen in years. That smile belonged to the man that believed I betrayed him. The one who sent someone to kill me.

"Antonio!"

TO BE CONTINUED ...

*A*fter being sentenced to fifteen years in prison for attempted murder, Anthony Fields discovered his love for the written word. Born and raised in Washington, D.C., a desire to rise above his conditions caused him to pen his first novel, *Angel* presented by Teri Woods. Having watched that book receive critical acclaim and staying on the Essence Magazine Bestsellers list for months, Anthony was inspired to pen and publish his debut novel Ghostface Killaz. He also co-wrote Bossy with Crystal Perkins-Stell. Now signed to Wahida Clark Presents Publishing, Anthony hopes to broaden his fan base and give the

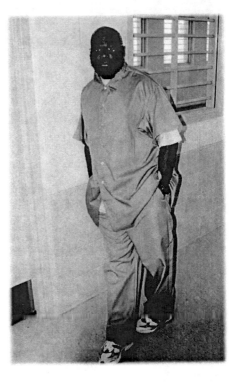

people great street tales to read. When he's not writing, he spends his time mentoring younger inmates and helping them to attain their dreams of becoming published authors.

Anthony Fields currently resides in a federal penitentiary in Pollock, Louisiana. You can contact him at:
Anthony Fields #16945-016
USP CANAAN
P.O. Box 300
Waymart, PA 18472

WAHIDA CLARK
PRESENTS
BEST SELLING TITLES

Trust No Man
Trust No Man II
Thirsty
Cheetah
Karma With A Vengeance
The Ultimate Sacrifice
The Game of Deception
Karma 2: For The Love of Money
Thirsty *2*
Lickin' License
Feenin'
Bonded by Blood
Uncle Yah Yah: 21st Century Man of Wisdom
The Ultimate Sacrifice II
Under Pressure (YA)
The Boy Is Mines! (YA)
A Life For A Life
The Pussy Trap
99 Problems (YA)
Country Boys

NUDE
Awakening
A NOVEL

VICTOR L. MARTIN

WAHIDA CLARK PRESENTS

COMING SOON!

STILL FEENIN

A NOVEL BY
SERENITI HALL

UNCLE YAH YAH

21St. Century Man of Wisdom

VOL 2

COMING SOON!

AL DICKENS

WAHIDA CLARK PRESENTS
COMING SOON!
LICKIN' LICENSE II
A NOVEL BY
INTELLIGENT ALLAH

UNCLE YAH YAH

21ST. Century Man of Wisdom

VOL 2

COMING SOON!

AL DICKENS

WAHIDA CLARK PRESENTS
COMING SOON!
LICKIN' LICENSE II
A NOVEL BY
INTELLIGENT ALLAH